GOODNIGHT BEAUTIFUL

Also by Aimee Molloy

The Perfect Mother

GOODNIGHT BEAUTIFUL

a novel

AIMEE MOLLOY

HARPER

An Imprint of HarperCollins*Publishers*

GOODNIGHT BEAUTIFUL. Copyright © 2020 by Aimee Molloy. All rights reserved. Printed in the United States of America. No part of this book may be used or reproduced in any manner whatsoever without written permission except in the case of brief quotations embodied in critical articles and reviews. For information, address HarperCollins Publishers, 195 Broadway, New York, NY 10007.

Designed by Bonni Leon-Berman

ISBN 978-0-06-288192-2

To my mom and dad

GOODNIGHT BEAUTIFUL

prologue

I LOOK UP AS a man with ruddy cheeks and a crew cut walks into the restaurant, shaking rain from his baseball cap. "Hey, sweetheart," he calls to the pink-haired girl mixing drinks behind the bar. "Any chance you can hang this in the window?"

"Sure thing," she says, nodding toward the piece of paper in his hand. "Another fundraiser for the fire department?"

"No, someone's gone missing," he says.

"Missing? What happened to her?"

"Not her. Him."

"*Him?* Well, that's not something you hear every day."

"Disappeared the night of the storm. Trying to get the word out."

The door closes behind him as she walks to the end of the bar and picks up the flyer, reading aloud to the woman eating lunch at the corner seat. "Dr. Sam Statler, a local therapist, is six foot one, with black hair and green eyes. He's believed to be driving a 2019 Lexus RX 350." Whistling, she holds up the piece of paper. "Whoever he's gone *missing* with is a lucky lady." I steal a glance at Sam's photograph—those eyes, that dimple, the word MISSING in seventy-two-point font above his head.

"I saw the story in the paper this morning," the woman at the bar says. "He went to work and never came home. His wife reported him missing."

The pink-haired girl goes to the window. "Wife, huh? Sure hope she has a good alibi. You know the old saying: 'When a man goes missing, it's always the wife.'"

The two of them laugh as she presses the photograph of Sam's face against the rain-blurred glass and I dip my spoon into my soup, taking small, careful sips, my eyes on the bowl, a sick feeling in my stomach.

chapter

1

Three Months Earlier

THAT ASS.

It's incredible.

An ass so perfect there's no way Sam can pull his eyes away as he walks half a block behind her up the hill, past the cheese shop, the bookstore, the lauded new wine place with the bright red door. He pretends to browse the table of American flags, half off at Hoyts Hardware, as she approaches the Parlor, the upscale small-plate restaurant that opened three months ago. A man on his way out behind his wife holds the door open for her, lingers to catch a glimpse of her from the back, no doubt praying his wife doesn't see.

Like Sam said: that ass.

The restaurant took over the space once occupied by two generations of Finnerty dentists, the brick facade replaced by a sleek glass wall. Sam pauses in front of it, watching her cross the room and sit at the bar.

Linen blazer off.

Drink ordered.

She takes a book from her bag, her shoulder blades rising like the wings of a bird under a thin white tank top as he passes, stopping to look at the listings in the window of the realtor's office next door. Exactly nine minutes he waits, long enough for her to be nearing the end of her drink, feeling the familiar rush of adrenaline as he loosens his tie an inch and turns around.

Game on.

The door to the Parlor opens as Sam approaches, releasing an air-conditioned gust into the humid evening air. "Dr. Statler." A patient is standing in front of him, and he has to hunt for her name. Started two weeks ago. Carolyn. Caroline.

"Catherine," Sam says. *Fuck.* What absolutely never happened to him back in New York happens all the time here— running into patients on the street, in the grocery store, yesterday at the gym, where he ran three miles on the treadmill while Alicia Chao, the newly divorced humanities professor with a history of anxiety, worked the elliptical—and it makes him feel off-balance every time. "How are you?"

"I'm good," Catherine says. Catherine Walker. She's a well-known painter in New York, bought a million-dollar home overlooking the river. "This is Brian." Sam shakes his hand. Brian: the restaurateur who doesn't satisfy her in bed. "I'll see you tomorrow," Catherine says as Sam steps inside.

"Will you be dining with us tonight?" the girl at the podium asks. She's young and blond. Tattoos. Very pretty. An art student is his guess, with a piercing hidden somewhere under her clothing, the type he once would have assuredly had in bed by ten tonight.

"No," Sam says. "Just a quick drink."

The bar is crowded with recent transplants from the city,

sharing plates of roasted brussels sprouts and nine-dollar pickles. Sam makes his way toward the woman, allowing his elbow to graze her arm as he passes.

Her purse is resting on the stool between them, and Sam bumps one of its legs as he sits, hard enough to knock it to the floor. "Sorry," he says, reaching down for it.

She smiles as she takes it from him, hooks it under the bar, and returns to her book.

"What'll it be?" the bartender asks. He's got slicked-back hair and shockingly white teeth.

"Johnnie Walker Blue," Sam says. "Neat."

"A man with expensive taste," the bartender says, as Sam pulls a credit card from his wallet. "My favorite kind."

"And I'd like to buy this woman a drink. For inconveniencing her purse like that."

She smiles tersely. "That's nice of you. But my purse is fine."

"No, I insist. What are you drinking?"

She hesitates, takes stock of him. "Okay, fine," she says. "Gin martini. Five olives."

"A martini? Would have pegged you more as a rosé drinker."

"How gendered of you," she says. "But you know what they say about martinis."

He's learned to observe people unobtrusively, a professional necessity that allows him to see that underneath the white tank top she's wearing a pale pink bra with lace trim, that the skin on her shoulders glistens. "No, what do they say about martinis?" Sam asks her.

"'The proper union of gin and vermouth is a great and sudden glory; it is one of the happiest marriages on earth and one of the shortest-lived.'" The bartender sets her drink in front of her. "Bernard DeVoto."

Sam nods down at her book. "Is that who you're reading?"

She flashes the cover, revealing an image of a woman in silhouette. "No, this is that thriller everyone's talking about."

"Any good?"

"Good enough. Another unreliable female narrator. I'm getting a little tired of the way women are being depicted in fiction right now, to be honest."

"And how's that?" Sam asks.

"Oh, you know," she says. "That we're prone to neurosis and/or hysteria and our judgment shouldn't be trusted, thus legitimizing the hegemonic idea of masculinity and men's dominant position in society and justifying the subordination of women." She picks up her glass and returns to her book. "Anyway, thanks for the drink."

Sam allows her to read one more page before leaning in. "Hey, smarty pants. You visiting for the weekend?"

"No," she says, turning the page. "I live here."

"You're kidding. Chestnut Hill is a small town. I think I would have remembered seeing you."

"I'm new." She looks up at him. "Moved here last month from New York. A 'cidiot,' I believe we're called by the locals?" She slides an olive from the plastic stirrer with her teeth, and he's imagining how salty her lips must taste when he feels a hand on his shoulder. It's Reggie Mayer, the pharmacist. His wife, Natalie, is a patient; she thinks Reggie smells like salami. "Natalie's not feeling well," Reggie says, holding up a plastic to-go bag. "Bringing home some soup."

"Tell her I hope she feels better," Sam says, leaning in a few inches, detecting no smell.

"I will, Dr. Statler. Thanks."

"Doctor?" the woman says after Reggie has left.

"Psychologist."

She laughs. "*You're* a psychologist."

"What? You don't believe me?" Sam reaches for his wallet again and pulls out a business card, which he slides next to her drink.

"Weird," she says, reading the card. "Would have sworn you were a podiatrist. So, you want to analyze me?"

"What makes you think I haven't already?"

She closes her book and turns to face him. "And?"

"You're smart," he says. "Confident. An only child is my guess."

"Very good, Doctor."

"Two devoted parents. Private school. At least one graduate degree, probably two." Sam pauses. "You've also had to become adept at shouldering the burdens of being an exceptionally beautiful woman in the world."

She rolls her eyes. "Wow, that was *bad*."

"Perhaps. But I'm serious," he says. "I'd bet if you were to survey every man in this place as to who they'd want to take home tonight, one hundred percent of them would say you."

"Ninety-nine percent," she corrects him. "The bartender would say you."

"Constantly being on the receiving end of the male gaze can have an effect," Sam continues. "We refer to it as objectification theory."

Her face softens. "So, it's like a *thing*."

"For some people, yes."

"Do you think I should get a therapy dog?"

"Are you kidding? A hot girl with a dog? That'll make matters worse."

She smiles. "Did you come up with all of this while you

were walking behind me up the hill, staring at my ass? Or was it while you were standing outside, watching me through the window?"

"I was on a phone call," Sam says. "Existential crisis that needed immediate attention."

"That's too bad. I was hoping you were out there building up the courage to come hit on me." She keeps her eyes on his as she lifts another olive to her lips and sucks the pimento out of the center, and there it is, the feeling he's been chasing like a drug since he was fifteen years old, the thrill of knowing he's about to plant his stake into a beautiful woman.

"You do have an exceptional ass," Sam says.

"Yes, I know." She looks down at his Johnnie Walker Blue. "Speaking of exceptional, I've heard good things about this drink of yours. May I?" She holds it up to the light and studies the color before lifting it to her lips and draining the glass. "You're right. That's a good drink." She leans in close, the scent of his whisky on her breath. "If you weren't a married local therapist, I'd invite you inside my mouth for a taste."

"How do you know I'm married?" he asks, the heat rising on the back of his neck.

"You're wearing a wedding band," she says.

He slips his hand in his pocket. "Says who?"

"Does your wife know you're out tonight, analyzing the confident only children of Chestnut Hill, New York?"

"My wife's out of town," Sam says. "What do you say? You want to join me for dinner?"

She laughs. "You don't even know my name."

"It's not your name I'm interested in."

"Is that right?" She puts the glass down, turns to face him, and reaches under the bar. "Well, in that case . . ."

"You guys doing okay?" It's the bartender. He's back, scratching an itch over one eye, as she slowly slides her hands up Sam's thighs.

"Yes," she says. "We're doing great."

The bartender walks away as her right hand arrives between his legs, where it remains for another minute at least, her eyes locked with his. "My goodness, Doctor," she says. "From what I can tell, the poor sucker who married you is a lucky woman." She returns her hands to the bar. "Be sure to tell her I said so."

"I will." Sam leans forward and softly cups her cheek, his breath hot on her ear. "Hey, Annie Potter, guess what? You're a lucky woman." She smells like Pantene shampoo and is wearing the earrings he gave her last night. "Now put your hand back on my dick."

"I'm sorry, Dr. Statler," she says, pulling away from him. "But that was just part of your anniversary gift. You'll have to wait until we get home for the rest."

"Well, in *that* case." Sam raises his hand and signals for the check as Annie picks up the stirrer and bites into the last olive.

"How was your day, dear husband?" she asks, smiling at him.

"Not as good as my night's going to be."

"You see your mom?"

"I did," he says.

She brushes a hair off his shoulder. "How was she?"

"She was fine."

Annie sighs. "Everyone over there seemed so grumpy yesterday. They hate the new management."

"It's *fine*, Annie," Sam says, not ready to replace the feeling of his wife's hand between his legs with thoughts of his mother sitting alone and unhappy at the five-thousand-dollar-a-month nursing home he moved her into six months before.

"Okay, fine, we won't talk about it," Annie says. She raises her glass. "To another successful week of marriage. These past six weeks have been so good, I give us at least six more."

Sam adjusts Annie's tank top to cover the bit of bra strap on display at her shoulder. "You sure you don't resent me for all this?"

"All what?"

"Giving up New York. Moving to this shithole town. Marrying me."

"I happen to love this shithole town." She intercepts the check from the bartender and quickly signs his name. "And if nothing else, you're very rich. Now come on, Doctor, take me home and pleasure me."

She stands up, slowly slips her jacket back on. Sam follows her toward the door, so content at the sight of his wife walking in front of him through the restaurant that he barely registers the seductive smile from the pretty blonde at the podium as he passes. He has no need to notice things like that anymore. He's a changed man.

No, really.

chapter
2

I WAKE UP HOT, the sun glaring at me through the window, a warm square of light aiming right for my eyes. There are footsteps coming up the driveway, and I sit up, seeing a woman in a flimsy blue sundress and two-inch sandals walk decisively past the porch, down the stone path lined with zinnias I planted, to the door to Sam's office on the garden level. It takes me a minute to reorient myself and remember I'm not in my one-bedroom apartment in the city but here, waking up bleary-eyed from a nap in Chestnut Hill, New York, Sam at work downstairs.

I check my watch—4:16 p.m.—and ease off the couch, staying low as I approach the window and study her, Sam's last patient of the day. Late forties. Bag is genuine leather. Blowout is recent.

And now it's time for everyone's favorite game: Guess the patient's problems!

Two tween daughters, contemplating a divorce and a real estate license.

Wrong! A pediatrician, staring down menopause, still trying to figure out her own mother.

A steady buzz unlocks the door from the inside. She enters, and I wait for the slam of the outside door, imagining her stepping into his waiting room. I can picture it perfectly: Sam's in his office with the door closed. She'll take a seat on one of the four white leather chairs, place her bag on the glass coffee table next to the two neat stacks of *In Touch* and the *New Yorker*. ("I'll know everything I need by which one they pick," Sam joked when the first issues arrived in the mailbox.) There's a Nespresso machine on a side table; small glass jars hold tea bags and both brown and white sugar. She'll be wondering if she has time to make a cup of Earl Grey when Sam opens his office door, four thirty on the dot.

I asked him once what he and his patients talk about downstairs—them on the soft beige couch, him on the expensive leather chair he special-ordered from some Scandinavian company with a weird name. "Come on, just one," I teased. It was happy hour, and I'd mixed us some drinks. "What sort of problems are the rich ladies of Chestnut Hill grappling with?"

He laughed. "I'm sorry to disappoint you, but that's confidential."

I linger at the window, taking in the front yard and manicured row of hedges, shielding the house from the street. *My* house, the Lawrence House, the noble Victorian three miles from the center of town, with a steeply pitched roof and wraparound porch. It's one of just two houses here on Cherry Lane, accessible via a narrow wooden bridge that crosses the wide creek running along the side of the house, no official name assigned to it on any map I've seen.

It was built in 1854 by the town's founding family—five generations of millionaires hatched right here in this house, with its grand living room, its formal dining room, its library behind a pair of pocket doors—perhaps my favorite spot in the house. It has custom-built mahogany bookshelves that reach the ceiling, the highest accessible via a wooden ladder on a rail. Such a far cry from the last place I lived: a one-bedroom apartment above the Happy Chinese takeout restaurant on Broadway, the pink neon sign blinking on and off outside my window every night.

I head toward the stairs, trailing my fingers along the original oak banister, counting my steps—twelve to the top, eight down the hall, past three spare bedrooms to the master. In the adjoining bathroom, I step into the shower and turn on the water, jolting the old pipes awake, my spirits rising. Forty-five minutes until happy hour, the highlight of my day. One stiff drink on the porch when Sam's done with work—tonight it's vodka and lemonade, freshly squeezed from eight of the best lemons I could dig out of the sticky bin at Farrell's, Chestnut Hill's Most Pitiful Grocery Store.

Sam will ask what I did all day, coaxing out the details, forcing me to lie (a homemade bisque for lunch and a bike ride into town!), too self-conscious to admit the truth (an hour shopping at Amazon and another three leaving product reviews!). It's not like I have a lot of other choices. I am a list person, and I've been keeping a running inventory.

Ways to spend my days in Chestnut Hill: A List

1. Improve my Amazon rank. I am the twenty-ninth-ranked reviewer on Amazon, thankyouverymuch. (I'm not bragging, that's my user name.) Neck and neck with Lola from Pensacola, a woman I'm convinced is actually midwestern.
2. Volunteer, so Sam stops wondering what I do up here all day.
3. Fix the door to Sam's office. He keeps complaining about it. It slams loudly every time someone comes or goes, disrupting the sessions. He's said he'll call the contractor himself, but I've assured him I'll take care of it, that it's the next thing on my list.

But I have no intention of taking care of it, and it's never made it to any list. The truth is, I like the reminder that he's downstairs, that I'm not completely alone here, roaming a house with a storied past. Because that's another thing about this place. The last owner, an unmarried sixty-seven-year-old woman named Agatha Lawrence, died here, lying blue-lipped on the floor of her study for five days before her body was discovered by the housekeeper. The story has become part of the town's folklore: the wealthy spinster dying alone, every woman's worst nightmare. All that's missing are the nine cats.

It's no wonder I struggled with the idea of being alone here all day, and while Sam was originally intent on finding an office somewhere (air quotes) "downtown," I convinced him to consider an office here, at the garden level of the house, in the large airy space once used for storage.

"You could knock out the wall in the back and make it all windows," I suggested, showing him the rough sketch I'd drawn. "Right here would be the waiting room."

"You're right," he said, having gotten a sense of the other options in town. "I think this is it."

And as it turns out, I *was* right; everything has worked out spectacularly. I found a contractor who (for a hefty price) agreed to a rush job, transforming the once sterile space into a gorgeous office with radiant floor heating, top-of-the-line light fixtures, and a floor-to-ceiling window offering a view of the rolling backyard and the woods beyond.

I dress quickly and rush down the stairs, hearing the slam of Sam's office door. In the kitchen I mix the drinks, and as I'm about to open the front door and step onto the porch, I see the patient through the pane of glass, Ms. Flimsy Sundress, loiter-ing at the top of the driveway, absorbed in whatever's happening on her phone. I step away from the door and silently will her to leave—*Scram, lady! It's my turn with him*—and then Sam's office door slams shut again.

"You're still here," I hear Sam say.

"Sorry, got distracted by some work thing." I walk to the living room for a peek out the picture window that overlooks the porch and the driveway beyond, catching sight of Sam and Flimsy Sundress, noticing the dreamy look on her face. I'm accustomed to the way women respond to Sam and his square-jawed good looks, his face straight out of an Abercrombie & Fitch catalog. "It's certainly nice to see this place become a home again, after the sad story of the last owner," she says. "And thanks again for today, Sam. I don't know what I'd do without you."

I hear the tinny beeps of her car door unlocking and wait until the sound of her engine disappears down the hill before opening the front door. Sam's at the mailbox, sorting through the stack.

"Hey there, heartbreaker," I say. "How was your day?"

He smiles at me, awakening that dimple. "Long," he says. "I'm exhausted."

He mounts the porch steps and hands me the mail addressed to me as I give him his glass. "What shall we toast to tonight?"

He looks up at the house. "How about to a new life for the Lawrence House?"

"Yes, that's perfect."

I clink my glass against his and then tip back my head to take a long sip, wondering if he can sense it, too. The wrongness of this place.

chapter

3

SAM TURNS UP THE radio, a can of Brooklyn Lager gripped in his
hand. "Bottom of the eighth, two outs," the announcer known
as Teddy from Freddy murmurs from the speaker, with that
slow-rolling delivery that has made him famous across Maryland. "Bo Tucker takes the plate. Fast pitch. High pop up to
right field. And . . . it's an out."

"*Damn* it," Sam yells, squeezing the can so hard he sloshes
lukewarm lager all over his lap. The game goes to a commercial as the phone buzzes on the passenger's seat. A text message
from Annie.

Hello dear husband.

He checks the stopwatch on his phone—forty-six minutes—
and opens another beer as a woman appears suddenly, walking
toward Sam's car. He slides the beer can, his third in the last
forty-six minutes, between his knees, and she startles when
she sees him, clutches her purse. He can't blame her. He's a
dude drinking beer and listening to minor league baseball in
the parking lot of a long-term elderly care facility. He understands the optics.

She side-eyes him as she passes, and Sam smiles, a weak
attempt to convince her he's not as creepy as he looks. It's the
woman who runs the dining hall, Gloria something, whipping

up soft foods three times a day, fettuccine Alfredo every Monday night for the residents of Rushing Waters Elderly Care Center, population sixty-six or so, depending on who died overnight.

The commercial break ends, bringing listeners home to the bottom of the ninth. "What do you think, Keys fans?" Teddy from Freddy asks. "We gonna pull this one out?"

"Of course we're not," Sam says. "We've won exactly fifty-eight games in three years. You know that, Dad." Teddy from Freddy, a name that makes zero sense—nobody refers to the city of Frederick, Maryland, as Freddy—but it's stuck. Twelve years now his father, Theodore Samuel Statler, has been sitting in the booth at Harry Grove Stadium, calling home games for the Frederick Keys, the worst farm team in baseball history.

Of course, before Theodore Statler was known as Teddy from Freddy, he was known as Mr. S, the charming and handsome math teacher at Brookside High School who left his wife for the hot model on page twenty-four of the June 1982 Talbots catalog. Her name was Phaedra, the only name dumber than Teddy from Freddy. Someone on the baseball team got a hold of the catalog, where Sam's father's new girlfriend could be seen sitting on a beach in a bikini, her thighs covered with sand. It got passed around the locker room for weeks, everyone admitting that while the girls inside weren't *Sports Illustrated*-level hot, they still did the trick.

Ted met her at Camden Yards on September 6, 1995, the day Cal Ripken Jr. surpassed Lou Gehrig's record for consecutive games played. Sam's grandfather grew up in Baltimore, and like every Statler man since 1954, Sam was a die-hard Orioles fan. He idolized Cal Ripken, and the tickets to the game were an early birthday present from Sam's mother, Margaret—his dream gift, in fact—paid for with the money Margaret had been setting aside for months from her paltry secretary's paycheck.

Phaedra had the seat directly in front of Sam, and she kept banging into his knees, turning around to laugh at his father's jokes, her ugly hat with the orange-and-black pom-pom blocking his view. Sam hated that his dad was barely paying attention to the game, and hated it even more when he suggested Sam and Phaedra change seats.

Turns out that on top of the white teeth and long legs, she was also a Tupperware heiress with whom Ted Statler had a truly uncanny connection, something he chose to share with Sam and Margaret two weeks later, on Sam's *actual* birthday. He stood up as Margaret cut into a Pepperidge Farm coconut cake, acting like he was about to make a speech at a wedding. Said he had no choice but to be honest with himself. He'd met his soul mate and could no longer live without her.

It was 1995, the year of the first flip phone, the year before the minimum wage was raised to $4.25, which is what his mother earned after Ted Statler packed his bags and left for Baltimore. To a harbor penthouse built out of Tupperware, a little time to figure out what he wanted to do next, until landing his ideal job: sitting up high in a glass booth, providing the color for the Keys, managing to stay upbeat despite a three-year losing streak, including this game, which ends 9 to 3 with an out in right field as Ted invites his listeners to join him tomorrow night, when the team takes on the Salem Red Sox. Sam clicks off the radio and picks up his phone.

Hello dear wife, he writes back to Annie.

Typing bubbles appear right away, and Sam imagines her at home, flour-faced, the ties of the floral apron pinching her waist as she studies the Rachael Ray recipe she printed out last night. You at your mom's? she writes.

He glimpses the entrance to the nursing home. A woman is leading a man with a walker through the sliding doors. He can imagine the scene inside. A crowd of old people sitting on couches in the lobby, no purpose whatsoever, the furniture marinating in the scent of urine. He pictures his mom, the same place she was the last time he saw her: sitting at the small dining table in the corner of her private room, looking nothing like herself.

Yes, I'm at my mom's, Sam writes to Annie. (Technically.)

How is she?

Good.

Much longer?

Sam checks the stopwatch. Fifty-nine minutes. Not too much.

Tell her I'll see her tomorrow.

Tomorrow, Annie's day to visit. They take turns. Every month Annie clips a calendar into the back of his appointment book, one she draws herself at the kitchen table, guiding a black Sharpie along the edge of an envelope, a grid of shaded boxes. The blue ones are her days, the pink ones Sam's. (Annie likes to subvert gender norms. It's a thing.)

"You think we need to go every day?" Sam asked when she showed him the first schedule.

"Visiting your mother is the main reason we moved here," she said. "Of course we need to go every day. She needs us, Sam. She's got dementia."

Behavior variant frontotemporal dementia, or bvFTD, if you'd like to get technical, which Sam often does. The condition is characterized by prominent changes in behavioral disinhibition (trying to lick the waiter) and interpersonal relationships and conduct (repeatedly telling the cashier she's an asshole), and is "an important cause of younger onset dementia" (in her case, sixty-four). That's how the doctor explained it to Sam last year, as he sat beside his mother in a cold office on the fifth floor of St. Luke's Hospital, an ache in his chest.

It came on quickly. Spells of confusion, and then outbursts at work. They were minor at first, but the day came when she marched into the office of Principal Wadwhack (the sad sack) and told him that if he didn't immediately adopt a dog with her, she was going to burn the school down. That was the day that his mom, Mrs. S, the sweetest secretary Brookside High had ever known—*way* too good for that loser of a math teacher who left her for a model (Talbots, but still)—lost her job, and Sam began the research, eventually landing on this place. *Rushing Waters Elderly Care Center: Insured. Trusted.* Sixty-six private rooms on eight shaded acres up a windy mountain road outside Chestnut Hill, his middling hometown in the middle of the state, the major employer a so-so private university with five thousand students. "Chestnut Hill: Keep It in Mind." That's the town slogan, printed on a signpost at the city limits. *Keep It in Mind.* That's the best they could do.

And yet here he is, local boy moving home after twenty years away. There's even an article about it in the local newspaper, "Twenty Questions with Dr. Sam Statler." His realtor, Joanne Reedy, suggested the idea. Her niece wrote the column for the local paper, and Joanne thought it would be good for business. Sam's been spending the last few years trying hard to be a nice guy, so he agreed. Turns out the niece was a girl he'd slept with in high school, and she kept him on the phone for an hour, reminiscing about the old days before asking him a long list of inane questions about his interests. His favorite television show? (*West Wing*!) Favorite drink on a special occasion? (Johnnie Walker Blue!)

Given a dearth of both art and entertainment, the article appeared on the front page of the *Arts and Entertainment* insert, including a color photograph of him, legs crossed, hands folded across his lap. *Former resident (and renowned heartbreaker!) Sam Statler, is moving home. But don't get too excited, ladies! He's married!*

Annie hung the article on their refrigerator, Sam's big, dumb smiling face on display every time he reached for the milk, the charming only son moving home to take care of his beloved and ailing mother.

That's the great irony of this whole thing. He supposedly moved back home to this shitty river town to take care of the mother who spent a lifetime doting on him, and now he can't do it. In fact, he hasn't set foot inside Rushing Waters in three weeks.

He takes a long swig of beer, trying his best to avoid thinking about it, but like all mechanisms of defense, repression isn't always reliable, and the memory of their last visit abruptly returns. He could see his mother's confusion when he opened the door to her room, the few moments she needed to put together who he was. Her good days were becoming less frequent; she was angry most of the time, yelling at the staff. He'd brought her favorite lunch—ziti with meatballs from Santisiero's on Main, the local joint still hanging on after thirty-two years. She ate her portion sloppily, asking him the same two questions again and again. What time is bingo, and where is Ribsy? He explained that bingo was every Wednesday and Friday at four in the recreation hall, and Ribsy, the family spaniel, dropped dead in 1999—the same week, the little fucker, that Sam left for college, leaving her completely alone.

"You're exactly like him, you know," Margaret said out of nowhere.

"Like who?" Sam asked, ripping the hard end off a piece of Italian bread.

"Who do you think? Your father." She put down her fork. "I've spent my whole life keeping this in, and I can't anymore."

The bread lodged in his throat. "What are you talking about, Mom?"

"You know exactly what I'm talking about, Sam. You're selfish. Self-centered. And you treat women like shit."

He reminded himself it wasn't her speaking, it was her disease. And yet even now, the beer has trouble going down as he remembers the look of disgust on her face. "And you want in on a little secret?" She lowered her voice conspiratorially. "You're going to leave her, too. That nice new wife of yours. You're going to end up just like him."

He pushed back his chair and walked out of the room, out of the building, to the parking lot. When he got home, he told Annie he wasn't feeling well and went straight to bed. Sally French, the center's director, stopped him in the hallway on his next visit, two days later, and asked him to come with her to her office.

"Your mother has stopped speaking," she explained from the other side of the desk, assuring him it was probably a temporary symptom of her condition. But it wasn't temporary. In fact, Margaret Statler never spoke a word again. None of her doctors had seen a case of mutism ("the inability to generate oral-verbal expression," as explained in her medical report) come on so fast. Over the next week, Sam begged her to talk—to just say *something*, so those wouldn't be her last words.

But she'd give him an empty stare, the weight of her accusation hanging between them. *You're going to end up just like him.* And so he did what he always did when life didn't unfold the way he wanted: he walked away.

He knows it's cowardly, but he hasn't been inside to face her since—a small detail he's been hiding from Annie—choosing instead to avoid the heartbreak by sitting in his car, drinking beer, wondering how long he has to stay.

He looks down at his phone—sixty-six minutes—and turns the key in the ignition.

Good enough.

chapter
4

IT'S OFFICIAL. I'M BORED out of my gourd.

It's not that I'm not trying, because I am. The other day, after Sam went downstairs to work, I put on an actual outfit and drove to the bakery, where I found the coffee burnt and the "lifestyle boutique" next door selling a scented candle called "Bookmobile" for thirty-eight dollars, and that was all I needed to see. Chestnut Hill, New York: zero stars.

I'd never tell Sam that, of course. He's settling in nicely, and business is thriving. A little over two months since he opened for business, and his days are filling, former New Yorkers lining up, desperate for one of their own to complain to. (His looks don't hurt. I was roaming the aisles of the CVS the other day and overheard a woman in the diaper aisle, talking about him on her phone. "He's so cute I'm considering developing a personality disorder just to get an appointment.") That aside, I'm happy for him. He told me the first time we met that he'd been dreaming of this for a while—a quiet life, a private practice outside the city. He'd earned it. Since getting a PhD in psychology ten years ago, he'd been working in the children's psychiatric unit of Bellevue Hospital, a very trying and difficult job.

Meanwhile, I feel like a loser, hanging around this house

all day, nothing to do except water the plants. Which is why I have resolved to be more productive, starting today, the day I tackle the project I've been avoiding for weeks: Agatha Lawrence's study, the room where she died of a heart attack, which is filled with her personal papers.

It was the deal on this house. It came as is, and as the attorney representing the estate of Agatha Lawrence explained, this included "all furnishings and any other items left behind by the previous owner at Eleven Cherry Lane." I didn't know this was going to mean six file cabinets encompassing a complete history of the Lawrence family, going as far back as 1812, when Edward Lawrence established Chestnut Hill. I poked my head into the room a few times, wishing I was the type of person who could throw a dead woman's papers away without even a look. But I'm not, and so each time I shut the door, and put it off for another day.

This day.

I finish watering the plants in the kitchen and take my tea down the hall, steeling myself before opening the door. The room is small and simple, with a window overlooking the garden, largely obstructed by a boxwood that needs a good trim. I peek inside the empty closet and trail my fingers along the yellow wallpaper. It's an interesting color—chartreuse yellow, with a repeating pattern of shapes that seem to feed into themselves. Agatha Lawrence favored bright colors, and I've surprised myself by liking them so much I've hardly made any changes to the decor. Apple-green walls in the kitchen, bright blue in the living room.

I hear a buzzing noise and notice a dozen or so tiny moths fluttering against the window, trying to get out. I cross the room and nudge it open, careful to avoid a crack running down the middle of the glass, yet another thing to take care of. As I shoo the moths outside, I see that Sam's car is gone. He's probably off to the Y, where he goes during lunch sometimes, returning with a mop of wet hair.

Looking around, I consider my options. I could turn the study into a guest bedroom, but what's the point? There are three spare bedrooms upstairs already, and who's going to visit me here? Linda? I highly doubt anyone from the city would be enticed by a tour of the strip mall and the additions to the dollar menu at the Wendy's on Route 9.

I decide to table the question and start with the papers, quickly realizing that this was a family that did not throw things away. Original drawings of the Lawrence House, designed by one of the most renowned architects of the time. Newspaper clippings from as far back as 1936, when Charles Lawrence was a confidante of FDR. Dozens of scrapbooks— stoic Europeans, posing straight-backed on the porch. I become so caught up in the family history—they made millions in oil and, later on, plastic—that it takes a few minutes before I register the noise coming from one of the boxes I've moved to the corner of the room.

A voice.

I stop reading. I'm not imagining it. Someone is talking.

I set down the folder I've been paging through and walk toward the window. Maybe it's that neighbor from the brown house on the other side of the narrow bridge, the only other house on the street, coming to say hello. The one with swingy blond hair and that strange-looking dog, always peering over the hedges, trying to get a look at the house. Sidney Pigeon— that's really her name. I got a piece of her mail once, some bogus car insurance offer, and looked her up. Three boys, their

photos all over Facebook. From the window of one of the upstairs bedrooms I can see her front lawn, and I've watched her
out there with her husband, the way she follows him around
the yard, pointing out chores like he's two weeks into a job at
Home Depot and she's the brand-new assistant manager. *And
when you're done here in lawn care, Drew, I'll have something for
you in the plumbing department.*

But there's nobody on the street when I look outside, and I
tell myself I must have imagined it. As soon as I return to the
papers, though, it starts up again. I inch forward, closer to the
boxes in the corner, the voice getting louder as I kneel down
and rest my ear against the cardboard. "It's time for the delivery of the day," a man is saying. "When our friends at UPS
surprise one lucky fan with a special delivery."

I laugh out loud in relief. A radio inside one of these boxes
must have gotten turned on somehow. I strip off the rigid tape
and open the flaps, rooting through the contents. There's no
radio here, or in the second box I search, and yet I can still hear
a faint voice. I move the boxes aside, and that's when I see it, in
the floor where the boxes were: a shiny flash of metal. A vent.

I lean forward.

"Jose Muñez up to bat, Silas James on deck." Sports radio? I
sit back on my heels and clasp my hand to my mouth, putting
it together. I can hear downstairs, directly into Sam's office. I
rise slowly and look out the window. Sam's car is in the driveway, parked behind mine.

I'm frozen, unsure what to do, when a red BMW appears at
the top of the hill and turns into the driveway. A woman steps
out. It's Catherine Walker, a patient. I heard her answer her
phone two weeks ago on the way out of her appointment—
the type of woman who says her name rather than hello when

she answers the phone. If Google can be trusted, she's a rising painter from New York, Andy Warhol Lite, and lives in a house fancy enough to get her a feature in *Architectural Digest* (who knew acrylic paintings of lipstick tubes could sell so well?).

Catherine's dressed casually today: black leggings and a white button-down shirt, ankle boots with a heel on them. I step away and press my back against the wall. I know what I should do. I should cover the vent, return to the business of cleaning, and tell Sam what happened later, at happy hour. *I thought I was going crazy, hearing voices, but it turns out the thing I was hearing was you, downstairs in your office. We have to get that fixed.*

I push up my sleeves and return to the folder I was paging through—financial documents from the family business—when I hear the faint buzz of Sam's bell. A moment later, the outside door slams shut.

I hesitate. I should leave, find something else to do. But instead I put the folder down, walk quietly to the vent, and kneel down beside it.

"Hello, Catherine," Sam says, his voice clear as day. "Come on in. Sit wherever you like."

I slide onto my stomach and press my ear to the vent.

Just for a few seconds. Just this once.

chapter
5

"IT SOUNDS LIKE YOU'RE feeling better, creatively at least," Sam says. He crosses his legs and glances at the clock on the floor next to the couch, where patients can't see it. Six more minutes.

"Yeah. That place has got good energy," Christopher says. "Something about it unlocks me." Christopher Zucker. Early thirties. Creative director at a new design firm colonizing the former paper mill along the river. Sam started seeing him after Christopher's doctor recommended he talk to someone about his anxiety. He's spent the last twelve minutes of the session telling Sam how he's been working in the coffee shop on the ground floor of his office building, trying hard to overcome a creative block. "Great views, too," Christopher says.

Sam nods. "Has a patio overlooking the river, right?"

"Yeah, but I mean the girls. Yoga studio on the second floor. If you time it right . . ." He winks—*patient attempting to normalize habit of objectifying women through alignment with therapist*—and then changes the subject to Sofie, the twenty-one-year-old Czech model he met online. Sam nods, forcing himself to acknowledge a sudden pang of irritation, tracing it back to the idea of Christopher and Annie being at that coffee shop at the same time. Annie mentioned this place to him the other day, telling him she stopped there for lunch after a run along the river, and Sam imagines the way Christopher would have checked her out, the look of disdain she would have given him in return. (She'd *hate* the guy—his comments about women, his adult scooter.)

Sam has to be careful not to let his mind wander—Christopher can be hard to follow, and staying engaged takes focus—but before he can stop himself, he's back in Brooks Brothers in lower Manhattan at four in the afternoon on a cold afternoon last fall, where he saw Annie for the first time, standing at the tie rack in tight jeans and a tweed blazer.

"Let me guess," she said when he approached to ask if she knew what "cocktail attire" meant. "You're a bad boy turned cool/approachable academic who favors band shirts, but only if they're ironic. You play basketball on your lunch hour with your nonacademic bros and then tapas and whisky with your colleagues. You've been invited to a wedding—his second—somewhere south of Fourteenth Street, and now you need a jacket." She pointed toward the back of the store. "Wait for me in the dressing room."

She brought him five different suit and shirt combinations, eight choices of ties, a classic navy blazer. Waited outside the room while he changed, stood beside him in front of the large mirror, swiping away lint and pressing wrinkles from his sleeves.

He bought everything she suggested. "That was more than I've ever spent on clothing in my life," he said, finding her back at the tie display after he'd paid. "You should get a raise."

"Oh, I don't work here," she said. "My boyfriend's birthday's coming up. Came in to buy him a tie." That boyfriend was gone an hour later, about the time Sam and Annie finished their second drink at the bar across the street, where

Sam probed her about her life, learned about her childhood in Maine, growing up in a house her father—long deceased—built himself.

She was his date to the wedding the next week, his wife within the year, marrying him in the backyard of their new home the day they closed on the house. Annie Potter, a woman like no other. Brilliant, funny, exciting as hell. He still has trouble believing he convinced her to follow him to Chestnut Hill, New York. *Charming*, that's the word she used, the first time she came, ninety-nine minutes on the train from New York. "Did you know petroleum was discovered right here in Chestnut Hill?" she said, tugging him by the arm to point out the historical marker he'd never noticed outside the ice cream shop.

And she still thinks it's charming. She even likes going to see his mother at Rushing Waters, where she's made a list of every resident's birthday, stopping at Mrs. Fields in the strip mall to buy them a cookie the size of a dinner plate, coming home to tell him that this was the right thing to do, moving here to help Margaret.

His mom was wrong. He'd never hurt her.

The thought is interrupted by the sound of a phone, and he feels his body tense, realizing it's *his* phone, ringing from the inside pocket of his sports jacket. Christopher stops what he was saying—*What the hell was he saying?*—and Sam reaches into his pocket, embarrassed. "I'm sorry," Sam says. "I usually remember to turn this thing off." He sees the 1–800 number, another credit card company, before silencing the phone and returning it to his pocket. He allows Christopher a few moments to finish what he was saying and then shifts a little in his chair. "Looks like we're out of time," he says.

"Already?" Christopher says, making no move to stand.

Something changes in his expression. "Because there was something else I wanted to mention."

"Oh?" Sam says.

"A girl at work accused me of sexually harassing her."

Sam has to restrain himself from laughing out loud. Classic doorknob revelation. A client spends the session talking about something mind-numbingly innocuous like the pros and cons of pour-over versus drip coffee and then right before time's up—bam!—he drops a bomb, walks out. He needs to say whatever it is out loud, inside the room, but doesn't want to hear the therapist's response. "Well, that certainly sounds like something you and I should talk about," Sam says. "Next Wednesday?"

"Sounds good." Christopher slaps his knees and they stand up. "See you next week," he says. "Same bat time, same bat channel."

Sam flatters Christopher with the same chuckle he forces every time Christopher says this. The outside door slams loudly behind him. *That fucking door.* Sam takes out his phone, the sinking sensation growing in his gut as he plays the message. He was wrong. It wasn't a credit card company, it was the bank that holds their mortgage. He deletes the voice mail without listening to it. It's all going to be fine. The phone calls he's avoiding. The bank. The credit card companies. He needs to avoid them for another week or so, just until he gets access to his father's money.

Sam came across the letter from his father in his mother's kitchen cupboard while preparing to sell the house. She'd been living at Rushing Waters for a few months when he found it, typed on the expensive stationery that his father used for the letters he sent Sam a few times a year, with his name embossed on the top. Other than a phone call every year or so, this was the extent of their relationship. Each was typewritten, and Sam imagined his father speaking a few sentences into a Dictaphone and handing it to a secretary. "Get that thing off for me, okay, sweetheart?"

He sat down at the kitchen table, the same table where he once choked down the world's worst piece of Pepperidge Farm coconut cake, and tried to make sense of what he was reading. It was addressed to his mother. *I have some things I need to say, Maggie.*

Three pages long, the letter explained the regret his father had felt for the last twenty years—how hard it was for Ted, living with what he did to the family. *I understand why you wouldn't talk to me when I tried, but I want you to know that not knowing my son has been the most painful part of my life.*

And then Sam got to the last page, with the big reveal. Ted and Phaedra had divorced, and he'd been given a sizable amount of money in the settlement. He wanted Margaret to have half of it. *Two million dollars*, Ted wrote, explaining he had already deposited the money in an account in Margaret's name at NorthStar Bank. *Please don't be stubborn about this. Use the money as you'd like, for you and Sam. You've worked hard raising our son, and truly I can never repay you for that.*

Margaret was watching television when Sam went to see her the next day. He could tell by the look on her face that her mood was stable. "Mom, what is this?" he asked her.

Her face reddened when she saw the letter, embarrassed, like the time she found Sam in the garage with a copy of *Hustler* magazine. He said he found it at school, too ashamed to tell her that his father had given it to him; that Ted had been giving Sam his copies since Sam turned twelve.

"Sit down," Margaret said, taking the letter from him. "Let's talk." And just like that he was a kid again, that look on her face as she tried so hard to connect with him, the only guy she had left. But this time he was actually interested in what Margaret was saying. The whole thing made her so mad, she confided. Ted Statler, thinking he could make up for everything he'd done simply by throwing money at her—money he did nothing to earn. Her jaw was clenched with anger as she spoke, which Sam found utterly thrilling. His mother was angry at Ted Statler, the world's biggest shitbag. *Finally.* "Which is why I'm giving all the money to you," she said at the end of her diatribe.

He couldn't believe this was his mother, the same woman who had been such a doormat all his life. "What?"

"I've started the process of giving you power of attorney," she said. "You're getting everything I have, including your father's money."

He must have read the letter two hundred times on the train ride back to New York the next day. The whole thing infuriated him at first. His mom was right, it was exactly as hypocritical and manipulative as one would expect from Ted Statler, a man who'd deigned to call his son no more than a handful of times in the last several years, thinking all could be forgiven with the sweep of a pen.

But then Sam started to think what his father's money could afford him—a simpler life, a little bit of luxury. He'd been ready for a change after nearly a decade working in the children's psych ward at Bellevue Hospital, teaching grad students and treating irrevocably damaged children. And suddenly he felt better about the whole thing. On their second date he told the story to Annie, who wisely suggested he wait until his mother signed power of attorney over to him before spending the money, but it was complicated. Sam couldn't say no to the money, nor could he stand the idea of having it. So he spent it, compulsively, every purchase aimed to wipe that smirk off Ted Statler's face. Once he got started, he couldn't stop himself—and on the stupidest shit. A nearly $5,000 Eames executive chair made of polished die-cast aluminum and locking casters? Thanks, Dad! A Lexus 350 with leather interior and automatic ignition? Thanks, Dad! Living large on credit, all of it to be immediately paid off as soon as his mother signs the money over to him, which is literally any day now, according to Sally French, the director of Rushing Waters.

But that was three months ago, and his mother still hasn't signed the documents. "We're working on it, Sam," Mrs. French keeps assuring him. (She's also been telling him to call her Sally, but she was their next-door neighbor growing up and he finds it impossible to reimagine her as a peer.) Margaret has deteriorated more quickly than anyone expected and, as legally required, has to endure a series of tests to prove she's signing the papers in sound mind. She keeps failing.

He's trying not to worry. It will all be fine. She'll pass the tests, and he'll get power of attorney. The money will transfer into his account, and he'll wipe away the pile of debt he's accrued, dozens of bills he's been hiding here in his desk drawer, keeping them from Annie. (No need to worry her. It's all going to be fine!)

The doorbell rings, and he slips the bills back into the drawer. With a deep breath, he presses the button to unlock the door.

"Hello," Sam says, greeting the patient standing by the couch. "Come on in, sit wherever you'd like."

chapter
6

"A TYPICAL FEMALE CAN lay between 500 and 600 eggs," I read on the website, repulsed. "Brown and yellow, with a skull shape on its thorax, it's known as the death's-head hawkmoth." I take a closer look at the illustration, wondering if these could be the annoying things that came out of Agatha Lawrence's boxes, eating their way through the linens. "In many cultures, they are thought to be a bad omen, and—"

Someone's outside. I peer out the window. It's Sam, sitting on the bottom step of the porch, reading. By the time I open the front door to join him, he's on his feet, the book tucked under his arm.

"Shoot," I say. "Was about to join you for a cup of coffee. Am I too late?"

"Yeah, I have to get downstairs. Was trying to get in some reading."

"What's the book?" I ask.

He holds it up. "*Misery*, by Stephen King. It's totally deranged." He lowers his voice. "Speaking of deranged, back to work."

I shoot him a playful look and watch him retreat down the path. Back inside, I click the dead bolt into place and head to the study. He's right: back to work.

. . . .

I know his routine by heart:

He makes a cup of coffee in the waiting room.

Walks to his desk and flips on the radio, depressing himself with politics on *Morning Edition* while waiting for his first patient to arrive.

The bell rings, and he goes to the closet, where he keeps his blue Brooks Brothers sports jacket.

Jacket goes on, radio goes off, door opens.

"Good morning," Sam says.

"Hi, Sam." It's Numb Nancy, right on time for her ten a.m. She's the head of development at Meadow Hills, a private boarding school twenty-three miles north, recently lost her lust for life.

"Come in, have a seat where you'd like," Sam says. He says this a lot. Allowing patients to choose where to sit is all part of the work (I've been reading up on therapy techniques in my spare time, and people in the biz would see this as diagnostic). Nancy takes a seat on the far side of the sofa, the farthest point from Sam's chair (and directly under the vent). It's the spot chosen by a majority of patients. Only the Pharmacist's Wife chooses the opposite end.

Nancy unzips a bag. "Give me a minute to set up," she says.

She has a health condition. Tarsal tunnel syndrome. It causes numbness in both heels and treatment includes rolling the soles of the feet along two hard, spiky balls at least three times a day. What better time to do this than the next forty-five minutes, which, if last week was any indication, Nancy will spend grousing to Sam about Angela, her seventeen-year-old daughter.

"Angela asked me this morning if she can invite that boy on vacation with us," she begins. Bingo. "That boy" is what she calls her daughter's boyfriend, despite the fact that he's twenty-two.

Nancy knows about the relationship only because a few weeks ago, she set her alarm for four in the morning and snuck into Angela's room to snoop through her phone. She discovered their texts, as well as her daughter's secret Instagram account, which, to be honest, is pretty damning. I've looked. The account is private, and I had to create a fake account, pretending to be the brooding but attractive seventeen-year-old girl whose photo I copied from the Facebook account of someone in Brisbane, Australia. It worked: Angela accepted my request the next morning, allowing me access to all two hundred and six photos, which prove that she and "that boy" seem to like each other *very* much.

To be clear, I know it's wrong what I'm doing (i.e., binging on Sam's therapy sessions, five days a week for the last month), but who wouldn't? The things I've heard. The Lipstick Painter's impotent boyfriend! The Pharmacist's Wife's waning interest in the Pharmacist! The Somber Superintendent of Schools, who I often see at the grocery store, and her existential anxiety. How am I supposed to stop?

And it's not only them I'm interested in, it's him, too, Dr. Statler. Hearing the way he speaks to his patients—the comfort with their vulnerability, the *sympathy*—I can't turn away. And just because something isn't right doesn't mean it's *wrong*. It's not like I'm putting children in cages. In fact, I think what I'm doing is good for Sam's patients, another dose of positive energy, as I am genuinely rooting for every one of them.

Well, everyone except Christopher Zucker, VP of Idiots at

a new widget company where he earns enough to spend a half hour blabbing to Sam about his blind adoration of David Foster Wallace. Skinny Jeans, that's my pet name for him, after I saw him sauntering out of Sam's office in those ludicrous three-hundred-dollar Diesels. He's Sam's only male client, and just the kind of guy I've always hated. Pretty boy with a model girlfriend. His is named Sofie with an *f*. She's Czech and, according to Skinny Jeans, crazy in bed. Eastern European girls are known to be this way, he explained, assigning it to "all that Communist oppression," and it took every ounce of restraint not to shout at him through the vent, reminding him that the Czech Republic returned to a liberal democracy in 1989.

Sam and Numb Nancy talk for a while—her husband says she's being too strict with Angela, but he's not in touch with what today's world is like—when the room goes suddenly quiet.

"Something happened the other night," Nancy says. "I was making dinner, and out of nowhere, this memory pops into my head. My mom, going out at night and leaving me and Jill alone."

"How old were you?" Sam asks.

"Six, probably. Which would mean Jill was three. I can see it so clearly. Getting out of bed, finding the house empty, her bed made. I was terrified."

"Where do you think she was?"

"I have no idea."

Sam waits a moment. "How often would this happen?"

"Definitely more than once." Her voice is strained. "I called Jill the other day, asked her if she had any recollection of this. She didn't."

"Have you asked your mom?"

"No. I'm afraid I'm making it up."

"Why would you make it up?" Sam asks.

"You're the doctor. You tell me."

"Okay. You're not making it up. Rather, it's an experience you've had to suppress, even in the moment, dealing with the fear of knowing you and your sister were in the house alone. As the oldest, you were in charge, which heightened the anxiety. It's natural for the brain to shut down in some ways during traumatic moments like these, suppress the memory so that it can't be easily accessed."

"Traumatic?" Her voice is strained. "Isn't that a little much?"

"No, I don't think so." Sam pauses, and his tone takes on a more gentle quality when he speaks. "I've been working in the field of childhood trauma for most of my professional career, and trust me, trauma comes in many forms."

I imagine what he looks like right now. At ease in his chair, his legs crossed, his fingers tented in front of his mouth.

"Let's talk a little bit more about your childhood," he quietly suggests. "What was it like in your house?"

I close my eyes. *My house?* I ask. *It was a disaster. I left as soon as I could.* I do this sometimes, I pretend it's me down there, sitting across from Sam on the couch, admitting to things I've never told him.

I hate to say this, Dr. Statler, but I haven't been completely forthcoming with you, I would say.

For instance?

For instance, I'm not the self-assured person I portray, the one with the sunny background and two devoted parents. In fact, my parents hated each other, and neither had any idea what to do with me.

I want to believe that he wouldn't be mad. Instead, he'd suggest we explore why I felt the need to lie to him. After a good forty-five minutes discussing it, we'd agree that I wanted to believe the lies I've told him. In fact, there's nothing I've ever wanted more than to be part of a happy family, so I devised an alternative reality.

It wasn't my intention to lie to him. After all, if there's anyone equipped to handle the truth of a messy childhood, it's the man who coauthored "Stored Childhood Trauma and Symptom Complexity: A Sample of 1,653 Elementary Students," appearing in the January 2014 issue of the *Journal of Personality and Psychology*. But then I met him, and he was so accomplished and impressive—a PhD, a teaching position at Bellevue Hospital—and what was I going to do, tell him the truth?

"This was useful," Sam says. "Let's be sure to come back to this next week."

Startled, I open my eyes and look at the clock on the floor beside me. It's 10:46. We're one minute over the end time of Numb Nancy's session. I'd lost myself daydreaming.

"It's crazy," Nancy says with a laugh, sounding a little less numb. "I came in here today thinking I had nothing to say."

"Always my favorite kind of session," Sam says. "I know it's not easy, but it's good to delve into this."

As I hear Sam lead her into the waiting room, I wonder if I'll ever be brave enough to tell him the truth and finally show someone who I am.

Because if not Sam, who?

chapter
7

SAM PARKS, FLUSTERED, FORTY minutes late to meet Annie. She's
coming from visiting his mother, and he texted her a half hour
ago that a patient had run late and he was on his way, but in
reality he was at home, waiting to intercept the mail. Still no
paperwork from Rushing Waters, granting him power of attorney over his mother's accounts. He dashes across the street
into the restaurant. A four-piece jazz ensemble is playing in
the corner, doing nothing for the headache he's been fighting since lunch, and he notices the fireplace in the back, the
French doors open to a stone terrace lit with clear lights and
scattered with the leaves that have begun to fall.

Sam can't believe this is the same place that was once the
Howard Family Restaurant, the shabby diner at the edge of
town where everyone gathered after school, where the girls
would chain-smoke Salem Slim Lights and dip their french
fries into a shallow bowl of ranch dressing as he looked on, deciding which among them to pursue next. It was now Chestnut, owned and operated by some guy from California, on his
way to his first Michelin star, chicken on the menu for $31.

Sam scans the room for Annie, praying to God none of his
patients are here. A woman in a navy suit with a baby strapped
to her chest is surrounded by a crowd in the dining room.

That must be her: the mayoral candidate hosting this meet-and-greet. A thirty-three-year-old mother of newborn twins, vying to become the first woman elected mayor of Chestnut Hill. Annie suggested they come.

Sam feels on edge and makes his way to the bar for a double whisky, noticing a blond woman with wiry arms in a black sleeveless dress eyeing him from the corner seat, a coy smile on her face. Sam nods and looks away, knowing nothing good ever comes from a woman flashing that kind of smile, and spots Annie talking to an elderly couple near a table set with coffee. She's wearing a baggy linen dress that still somehow shows off her curves, and he feels a flash of heat, remembering last night. He went to the gym to work off the stress—two phone calls from credit companies and a letter from a debt collector—and the house was dark when he got home. Five minutes later the doorbell rang, and he opened the door to find Annie standing on the porch, wearing bright red lipstick. "I'm sorry to bother you," she said, that look in her eyes. "But my car broke down nearby, and my phone is dead. Can I use yours to call my husband?"

She stepped inside and looked around, complimented him on the lovely decor.

"I can't take the credit," he said. "My wife's the one with taste."

She nodded, trailed her fingers along the leather sofa, and examined the painting above the fireplace, which she'd bought herself from an artist in Bushwick before leaving New York. "What a shitty day I've had," she said. "Any chance you want to pour me a drink?"

She was naked a half hour later, didn't even make it to the bed.

"The chase," that's what she calls it, introduced him to it

early on in their relationship, at the wedding he'd been shopping for at Brooks Brothers. She approached him at the dessert table as the evening drew to a close, introduced herself as if they'd never met. Her name was Lily, she said. She was a distant cousin of the groom's, visiting from Boise, where she raised sheep and sold hats she knitted herself. He played along, offered to share a cab with her. She chatted with the driver, telling him she'd never been to the city before, never seen so many people in one place, Sam's hand up her skirt the whole time.

It quickly became a regular thing. The hot waitress. The accountant with a dark side. She was astonishingly good at it: surprising him, imagining different characters, role-playing them to perfection, leading Sam in a slow dance toward the inevitable finale: mind-blowing sex with a stranger of sorts.

Annie Potter, his gloriously sexy, brilliant wife.

He waits until the older couple walks away before crossing the room and approaching her. "Sorry I'm late," he says, kissing her.

"Are you late?" she asks, avoiding eye contact. "I hadn't noticed."

"You okay?"

"I'm fine."

"What's wrong?"

"Nothing." She snatches a canapé from a passing tray. "Just wishing I wasn't married to a cheater."

He shoots her a look of disbelief. "Don't tell me you're still mad about last night."

"I'm not mad," she says. "But I *am* a native English speaker, so I'm aware that *geocache* is a made-up word."

"Annie." Sam takes her gently by the shoulders and turns

her to face him. "Look it up. *Official Scrabble Player's Dictionary.* Fifth edition."

She squints at him, skeptical. "How do you even know that?"

"I read it somewhere. They picked it as the word of 2014, from a contest. It beat out *zen*."

"A contest? *That's* how we're adding words to the language now?" She takes a bite of the canapé, leaving a smudge of melted brie on her lip. "Reality television. Is there anything it hasn't destroyed?"

"Well, if you'd like . . . ," Sam whispers into her ear. "I'm happy to declare you the winner. We can find a broom closet somewhere, let you claim your prize."

"Sorry, buddy," Annie murmurs, softening. "But I'm here to meet my candidate."

"You talk to her yet?" he asks, thumbing the cheese off Annie's lip.

"I want to, but I can't figure out what to do first," Annie says. "Do I meet her, or do I greet her?"

"You greet her," he says.

"No. That would be a greet-and-meet, and the invitation clearly said 'Meet and Greet.'" There's commotion around them, and Sam turns to see the candidate making her way into the bar area, pausing to shake hands. "I guess this is it," Annie says, finishing her wine and handing Sam the glass. "Wish me luck."

Sam rests an elbow on the bar as Annie walks to the back of the room and takes her place in line.

"Well, howdy neighbor." It's her, the blond woman he noticed when he walked in. She looks vaguely familiar, and he's able to put it together. She's the neighbor from Cherry Lane, with the brown house and small dog. She's waved at him a few times from her front yard, raking leaves in that bright red coat with the logo of the university. The Big Reds. ("Like the gum?" Annie asked on the afternoon of the first home game, insisting she and Sam show their hometown pride and attend.)

"Sam Statler," he says to the woman, extending his hand.

Her eyes grow big, and she laughs. "You're kidding, right?" She can tell by his face that he's not. "It's *me*," she huffs. "*Sidney*."

Sidney? "Sidney Martin!" There it is. Summer, 1999. Her basement, the couch with scratchy plaid upholstery, praying like hell her father, the beefy guy with the lawn service, didn't come downstairs for one of the beers he kept in the fridge.

"I'm Sidney Pigeon now," she says, flashing a diamond. "Married Drew, class of '93? Anyway, I read that profile of you in the paper. Nice photos."

"It was the realtor's idea," he says, self-conscious. "She thought it would be good for business."

"Well, it seems to be working, if the number of cars pulling in and out of that driveway are any indication. Couldn't believe when I realized it was you across the street, in that big mansion—" Sidney's interrupted by a peal of laughter from behind her, and she turns, noticing Annie and the candidate, leaning in close like old friends. "Looks like someone's pinned you down," she says. "How long you been married?"

"Thirteen weeks."

"Thirteen *weeks*?" she says. "That's awfully precise."

"It's a thing," he says. "We celebrate every week."

"Well, isn't that adorable. Thought you'd still be single and breaking hearts."

"Not anymore," he says. "I'm a changed man."

"Sure you are," she says, in a tone he doesn't love. "Speaking of which, do you remember . . ." Sidney nods her head toward the far wall, where the bathrooms are, and yes, he does remember. The women's bathroom at three in the morning the night of senior prom. She wasn't even his date. "Jody still won't talk to me," Sidney says, referring to the girl who *was* his date, the one who walked in on them. "Twenty-two years, still gives me dirty looks every time I see her at the grocery store. She *really* hates you."

"Who hates you?" A woman appears next to them. She's their age, pretty, holds two glasses of wine.

"This is Sam Statler," Sidney says, taking one of the glasses.

"Sam Statler," the woman says, nodding. "Of course." She extends her free hand. "Becky. We went to high school together, but you never spoke to me."

Sam shifts uncomfortably, praying for Annie to hurry back and save him. "I've been hearing good things about you," Sidney says. "It must be crazy, listening to people's secrets all day." She leans in. "Tell us the truth. What's the juiciest thing someone's ever talked about in therapy?"

"Juiciest thing someone's talked about," Sam says contemplatively. "Probably an orange."

They both stare at him a moment, silent, and then burst into laughter. Sidney slaps his arm. "You're still as charming as ever, Sam."

"Isn't he though?" Annie's back by his side. Sam slips an arm around her, relieved.

"Congratulations on nailing down Mr. Least Likely to Commit," Sidney says.

"No, that wasn't Sam," Becky corrects her. "That was Mike Hammill. Sam was voted Class Heartbreaker. Right, Sam?"

"That's right," he says, aware of Annie's gaze. "And don't forget prom king, two years in a row."

"Oh please," Annie says under her breath.

"What's it like being married to a therapist?" Sidney asks, addressing Annie. "He must read you like a book."

"Yes, he does," Annie says. "But one of those books where the woman is crazy and you can't trust a thing she says."

They're interrupted by the sound of someone clinking a glass, and the crowd begins to disperse, moving toward the front of the room, where the candidate is poised to speak. "Listen, there's a bunch of us who get together sometimes," Sidney says, in a hushed tone. "Dinner Club, we call it. Mandy, Ash. You remember them, Sam."

Sam nods, though he hasn't the faintest idea who she means.

"You should join us."

"That'd be fun," Annie says. "Sam will bake cookies."

The women smile and walk away, toward the candidate, who is calling for people's attention. Sam reaches for his drink, seeing the expression on Annie's face. "What?" he whispers.

"'Probably an orange'?"

"You heard that?" he asks, smirking.

"Yes, I heard that."

"It was funny."

She rolls her eyes again and walks past him, toward a guy with a tray of champagne. "Okay, heartbreaker. Whatever you say."

chapter

8

SAM IS AT WORK, and I am in a five-star mood.

The Mumble Twins had a major breakthrough during their session this morning, and I couldn't be happier. Mumbly Wife wanted to spend the summer in Spain, but Mumbly Husband took a job without telling her. A freelance design gig for Apple (at least I think that's what he said; the two of them talk like they've got marbles in their mouths). He couldn't turn it down, and it led to a big fight, which led them to an appointment with Sam at ten o'clock this morning and the realization of a harmful and long-standing dynamic between them. It's related to how critical Mumbly Husband's mother was, and it's too much to get into, but between their good news and the crisp scent of autumn in the air, I am in a fabulous mood.

I can hardly remember the early days anymore, those first weeks after moving here, when I wondered if I'd made a terrible mistake, agreeing to this whole situation. Moving into a money pit of a house. Giving up the city for this place. *Chestnut Hill, NY, where every day feels like Wednesday.*

But if Wednesday is going to be anything like this past Wednesday, I am all for it. That's the day I pulled out of Farrell's at 1:00 p.m. with a trunk full of groceries and spotted Sam through the window of the Parlor. I parked at the bank, snuck up behind him at the bar, where he was doing the crossword puzzle and nursing a seltzer with lime. We enjoyed a quiet lunch, the fish sandwich for him, a Mediterranean sampler for me. The whole thing was so marvelously relaxed, nothing like the stress of the city, where I would *never* think of ordering a twenty-dollar lunch entree, not worrying about a thing in the world. Until I lied to Sam again.

Not for the first time, he asked if I had given any more thought to my long-term plans, and while he did his best to keep any judgment from his voice, I could sense the underlying message. *Are you ever going to do something useful with your days?* I hate feeling stupid, and so I lied. "Funny you should ask," I said. "I just so happened to accept a volunteer position today. I was planning on telling you at happy hour."

Tour guide at the Chestnut Hill Historical Society, I said, all smiles. I'd been thinking about volunteering for some time (somewhat true), and, on a whim, went to the organization's website (less true, but not out of the question). I saw the volunteer posting and decided to apply (patently false).

Sam was polite enough not to point out what we both know is true: I am *exceedingly* overqualified for this (fake) volunteer opportunity. But we agreed it was something to do, and to be honest, I've been enjoying the image of myself leading a busload of old biddies from Boston up and down Main Street, pointing out all the shops under new management, necessary amenities for the recent settlers from the city. Mid-century floor lamps. Farmhouse dining tables. Eighteen-dollar hamburgers that don't have the decency to come with a side of fries.

And while lying to Sam is a terrible habit, there are worse things for me than getting into the shower and out of the house two hours a day, three times a week (that's my schedule, subject to change). I've made a list of the cultural destinations I plan to visit on the hours I need to be out of the house, making the most of this lie, starting right now, at three o'clock on a lovely Wednesday afternoon, my first day on the "job": the Chestnut Hill Historical Society. It is, after all, only fitting that I start here, and my spirits are high when I pull into the parking lot in front of the little white house. Built in 1798, it houses a collection of pieces from when Chestnut Hill was a thriving center of brick manufacturing, a display of artifacts from the Civil War, and a permanent exhibit on the Lawrences, the town's founding family.

I park beside the only other car in the lot, a dark-brown Buick, and climb the three rickety steps. The bald man behind the desk looks genuinely surprised to see me. "Help you?"

"Yes, I'm here to view the permanent exhibit." I hold up the paper I'd printed from the website. "The Lawrences: Chestnut Hill's Founding Family." I can't resist leaning forward to offer a bit of advice. "This title? You might want to suggest something a little more inspired."

"Second floor," he says, blank-faced. "Elevator's broken, use the stairs."

"Thank you." I take the stairs two at a time, excited to learn more about this family whose house I occupy—chemical magnates, building a fortune off polluting the earth, their efforts memorialized here on the second floor: thirty-two foam-core panels that could use a good dusting.

I start at the beginning. James Michael Lawrence, made his money in oil before turning to chemicals.

Philip, big patron of the arts.

Martin, invested in newspapers, and his wife Celeste.

I feel like I know them all intimately, having worked my way through most of Agatha Lawrence's papers. James's bout with scarlet fever. Martin's nagging colitis. Philip's work to bring prohibition to Green County.

Of course, it's Agatha who intrigues me the most.

People here think they knew her: the single sixty-seven-year-old woman who died alone; the poor spinster up on the hill. But that wasn't her at all. In fact, she may be the most interesting woman I've ever come across. Yesterday, in between patients, I found her journals, and the portrait that is emerging is truly fascinating. She was brazenly independent and smart, part of the first class of women admitted to Princeton in 1969. After leaving for college, she rarely spoke to the others in her family, all of them staunch conservatives. A textile designer, she traveled the world, most of the time alone. Her work was exhibited in galleries in New York and London, and she was living with a woman in San Francisco when she got news her father had died. She knew this day was coming, that she'd become the sole heir of the Lawrence estate, and she returned to Chestnut Hill, to the family house, where she surprised everyone by selling the company and using most of the proceeds to buy large swaths of land that she put into a trust, making amends for her family's role as the worst polluter in New York State for several decades.

"Spitfire," that's what my dad called women like her, and it was not meant as a compliment. Too ambitious and brash. But I'm enamored. There's a photograph at the end of the exhibit of her in front of an easel set up in the living room of the house, along with a caption: "Agatha Lawrence died in the Lawrence House at the age of sixty-seven. She was the last surviving member of the family." I stand in front of it for a long time, transfixed by the curious expression on her face, the bright red hair; wondering if she felt afraid the day she died, alone in her study.

The alarm on my watch chimes loudly, my reminder that happy hour with Sam starts in forty-five minutes. I head for the door, eager to go home and see him. He'll want to hear all about my day.

chapter

9

SAM TAKES A STEP forward in line, giddy, the paperwork signed by his mother on Rushing Waters letterhead tucked under his arm. There's one bank teller—a girl in her twenties with auburn curls and a face full of freckles. She chews her bottom lip as she waits for the woman at the counter to fish her ATM card out of her wallet. Sam shifts back and forth, impatient. The bell rings. He steps forward and clears his throat.

"I'm here to close an account and place it in my name. I have this document—" He slides the letter toward her.

"I can help you with that," she says, shooting him a bright smile. He keeps his eyes on her face, away from her blouse, where the buttons are battling it out in a magnificent tug-of-war across her breasts. *Don't do it, Sam. Don't look down.* She scans the paperwork, turns to her keyboard. "You got your Halloween costume ready?" she asks, her long pink fingernails click-clacking across her keyboard.

Sam smiles, the response he would have once offered on the tip of his tongue. *No, but I like yours. Hot bank teller. Very clever.*

"Not yet," he says instead. In his mind he's already on his way to the Parlor, where he's scheduled to meet Annie in twenty minutes. She doesn't know that the letter arrived. She wasn't home when the mail came, and he opened the letter standing at the mailbox, feeling the weight lifting. Finally. A letter was included from a physician on staff, saying he had deemed Margaret of sound mind. Relieved, Sam went inside and wrote checks to the credit card companies before calling the Parlor to reserve the table in the back and a bottle of the 2009 Château Palmer Margaux with notes of graphite and licorice and a $150 price tag.

Sam reaches for a mini Snickers from the bowl next to the cup of pens as a piece of paper shoots out of the printer. The girl sets it down in front of him. He feels obscenely awkward; surely she's not accustomed to people walking in here worth $2 million. But her expression is immobile, and he has to hand it to her. She's a real pro.

"Okay," she says with a wink when he finishes signing. "You want this in cash?"

He laughs. "Definitely. Maybe you can dump it all into a few large trash bags?"

She laughs along and then hesitates, unsure. "You serious? You want cash?"

"No," he says. "Cashier's check is fine."

She taps the keyboard again as he feels a rise of excitement.

"All set," the girl says, sliding a check toward him.

$274.18.

"This isn't right." He looks up at her, panic surging through his body like a jolt of adrenaline. "It's um . . . more."

She returns to the screen. "Let me see." She traces a finger down the screen, checking the tally. "Sorry, you're right." He exhales, relieved. "I should have explained that we recently started charging four dollars to close an account. Wish there was something I could do, but it's programmed in here automatically." She leans forward and lowers her voice. "Banks, man. They sure do know how to screw the little guy. Anyway, that explains the discrepancy." She shoots him a bright smile. "Anything else we can help you with today? We're offering a pretty good deal on a new Visa."

"No, I think that's it," he says, his voice wobbly.

"Well, thank you for banking at NorthStar, and oh—here." She pulls a Tootsie Pop from a drawer and slides it to him. "It's my birthday. I'm giving these out."

"Thank you." He takes the lollipop and turns around, barely making it to a chair in the waiting area. He's having a hard time breathing and his palms are tingly and he has to remind himself that the impending sense of death isn't real. He's experiencing the symptoms of a panic attack. Which is unnecessary, because there's an explanation for this. There *has* to be. Another account with a different number, maybe. Something in his father's name.

"Tell me that isn't Sam Statler." It's a man's voice, coming from behind him. *Not now.* He turns around.

Crush Andersen. Class of 1993. All-star linebacker, known for taking Joey Amblin's dare and downing six liters of Orange Crush at a field party after they lost the state finals. "How you doing, man?" Crush says, slapping Sam's hand and pulling him in for an awkward hug.

"I'm good, Crush, I'm good." Except for a serious concern that he's about to vomit.

"Yeah, man?" Crush says. "What's happening?"

"Oh, you know," he says. "Same old same old." Sam doesn't know why he says this, other than it's what he expects a guy like Crush is used to hearing when he asks this question, and then Crush is telling him how the other day Jesse Alter came in, and what is this, some sort of class reunion at NorthStar

Community Bank? Sam tries his best to feign attention—three years as assistant branch manager, six as a volunteer EMT for the fire department—but he needs to focus on keeping his lunch down. "What about you?" Crush lowers his voice and curls his lip. "Your dad still with the *Sports Illustrated* model?"

"It was Talbots," Sam says. "And no, that didn't last. Listen, Crush." Sam takes Crush by the elbow. "Any chance you can check and see if there's an account here under his name? Ted Statler."

"Sorry, buddy, not authorized to share that information," Crush says, then leans in close and winks. "But why don't we go discuss it in my corner suite?" He leads Sam to a small glass cubicle and sits down behind the desk, gesturing for him to take a seat on a hard plastic chair. Crush pecks at the keyboard as Sam tells himself it's going to be okay. His mother made a mistake. The account is not in her name, it's in his father's. It's—

"Nope," Crush says. "No account for any Statler except your mom."

"All right then." Sam smacks his thighs. "Thanks for the help."

"Nice to see you, man. And listen, dude. A bunch of us might go watch the game this weekend. You should come. You're not too good for us, are you, Stats?"

His legs feel weak as he stands. "No, Crush. No way, man. Of course I'm not."

chapter
10

I'M IN THE BATH, a chorus of bubbles popping at my neck, a chill in my bones. Everything is cold. The air, the water, Sam.

Three days now he's been in a state. Grouchy, short, showing exactly zero interest in my (fake) volunteer position. I thought he'd be at least a *little* curious to hear about the interesting pieces of trivia I picked up as the town's newly anointed resident expert, but I got barely a half-hearted grunt the other morning when I asked him if he knew that in 1797, Chestnut Hill came within one vote of being named the state capital. And then the incident with the Post-it note. It was stuck to the front door, neon-green paper and fat Sharpie letters so I'd be sure to see it on my way out. *Can you move your car up. Patients need room.*

That's it. Not even the common decency of proper punctuation. It wouldn't have been that big a deal if that note hadn't basically been our only communication all day, as apparently he also wasn't in the mood for happy hour. (A headache, he claimed. I recommended two glasses of water and a good night's sleep, choosing to stay silent on the fact that his headache probably had something to do with the two cans of beer I heard him open downstairs, where he stayed for an hour after the Somber Superintendent of Schools left, forlorn as usual, at five thirty.) It pains me to say it, but it's a side of him I haven't seen before, and which I don't particularly like: trudging around, all Eeyore-eyed.

But too bad. I've decided I'm not going to allow Sam's crankiness to get me down.

Reasons to Remain Happy Despite Sam's Mood: A List in Descending Order

3. It's true what they say: hard work pays off, because as of yesterday morning, I am the *fifteenth*-ranked reviewer on Amazon (suck it, Lola from Pensacola!).
2. It's been raining all morning, and surely no fake tour takers are going to show up at my fake job, allowing me a well-earned afternoon of self-care, leading me to the top item on my list, the best reason of all to stay on the bright side:
1. President Josiah Edward Bartlet, the essence of humility.

The West Wing, my god. It's Sam's all-time favorite show, and now I can see why. I have never seen it, and I decided to turn it on this morning after he went to work, take a look at the pilot. Three hours later I couldn't be any more invested in the conflict between Jed Bartlet the president and Jed Bartlet the man. I'm going to cheer Sam up with the news at happy hour tonight. *I did it, I watched season 1. You're right, it's genius.*

I pull the plug in the bathtub and stand up, my skin prickling in the cold air as I reach for the towel, reminding myself that whatever is going on with Sam probably has nothing to do with me. After all, it's not only me he's being weird around, it's them, too: our patients. Distracted, unfocused. Yesterday's one o'clock was a new woman named Pamela—a therapist herself from twenty miles east, thinking of sending her troubled son to boarding school. Twice he called her Marlene before she corrected him, and I could feel all three of us cringing through the remaining thirty-two minutes of the session.

I brush my hair in the mirror, noticing the gray, reminding myself to take care of that. It's a fear of mine: coming here and letting myself go, just like a local. I should try something bold—bright red, maybe, like Agatha Lawrence. I found four boxes of her hair color—Nice'n Easy in Flaming Red—in the bathroom closet, and I'm thinking I'd look good as a redhead as I go to the window and thumb away a circle of mist, checking in on Sidney, the friendly neighbor. The Pigeon, as I've come to call her, like those annoying birds that can't take a hint. She's everywhere: *Hi neighbor!*-ing from behind the potato chip display in the middle of the produce section; strolling across the bridge with that weird-looking dog two days ago, as Sam happened to be on his way out of work, stopping to say hello, all doe-eyed.

My instinct was right: the two of them dated in high school. I found out during stop number two on my cultural scavenger hunt, the Free Library, where I discovered the shelf of Brookside High yearbooks, every issue since the school was built on a cornfield in 1968. (I googled it, by the way, and the closest brook is a good three miles away.) I almost missed noticing them above the magazines, the high school name printed on the spine in the year's most popular font. I couldn't resist taking an armful of yearbooks to a square wooden table, cramming myself onto a chair meant for a child, discovering photos of Sam's dad, the ruggedly handsome math teacher; Margaret, the beloved secretary with the pretty smile; and then Sam himself, his first appearance on page fourteen of the 1995 edition, all chisel-cheeked and red-lipped.

Stats. That's what they called him, and it doesn't take being voted Most Likely to Be in the CIA like Becky Westworth, class of '95, to figure out that this refers to the number of girls Sam slept with—including, it appears, Sidney Pigeon née Martin. She was very much his type: short legs, mousy brown hair, a little chunky. (I'm kidding, of course. She was adorable and thin.)

There's smoke coming from her chimney, and a light's on upstairs. I imagine her in the living room, watching the morning shows, folding laundry. I'm about to turn away when I notice the car in the driveway, parked behind Sam's. A dark green Mini Cooper with a white racing stripe, which I've never seen here before.

I hang up the towel and pull on the robe I found in Agatha Lawrence's closet when I moved in (what can I say? It's from the Neiman Marcus cashmere collection), knowing I should forget I ever saw that green Mini Cooper and keep with the plan: fresh sheets on my bed, *West Wing* episode six, two Oreos waiting patiently for me on the bedside table. But before I know it I'm dashing to the stairs, toward the study, moist footprints trailing behind me on the wood floors. Exactly what everyone around here needs.

A new patient.

····

The cold air from the cracked window strikes me as soon as I open the door and head through the boxes toward the happy-face rug I ordered from Urban Outfitters. It was probably unnecessary, as Sam has no interest in what happens to this room, but then I read the description—*Happy vibes all through your space with this plush smiley face area rug*—and how could I not buy it to cover the vent?

"What kind of things did it make you aware of?" Sam is asking.

"How powerful I am." Female with an accent. French. Possibly Italian. "You would think it'd be the opposite, right?"

"What do you mean?" Sam asks.

"I was seventeen years old, sleeping with the forty-year-old father I babysat for. *He's* the one expected to wield the power in that dynamic, but I could have made him do anything." Strong cheekbones, short brown hair. A French Natalie Portman. I do this sometimes, imagine what they look like and who'd play them in the movie based only on their voice. It usually takes me at least three sessions (I'm still deciding between Emma Thompson and Frances McDormand for Numb Nancy), but with this one it's immediate. Dark Natalie Portman, *Black Swan.* "And now it's second nature to me."

"What is, exactly?" Sam asks.

"Manipulating men to do whatever I want," she says. "You could call it my superpower. I should pitch it to Marvel, right? Put me in a red bodysuit and watch me find the weakness in men."

"I can already see the movie poster," Sam says.

They share a hearty chuckle, and I notice how relaxed he sounds. In fact, I'd say he's more relaxed than he's been in days.

"I can't imagine being with someone who I *couldn't* control," she says. "Men, at least. Women are an entirely different story."

"Are you currently seeing anyone?" he asks.

"A few people," she says. "But most of my time is for Chandler." My hand flies to my mouth to stifle a laugh. *Chandler?* "He's the real reason I wanted to start therapy."

"Tell me about him," Sam says.

She sighs. "I met him at the end of summer, at an opening in New York. The guy I was with is kind of a bore, and I noticed Chandler standing near the bar. He's insanely sexy. You know, in that way older guys are?"

"I'll have to take your word for it," Sam says. "How old is he?"

"Forty-one." She snickers. "Sorry if you're offended by me saying forty-one is old."

"I'm not, but thank you," Sam says.

"Anyway, I went over and talked to him. Asked if he was enjoying the show. And my god, the way he looked at me . . ." She stops there.

"How did he look at you?"

"He drank me up. He was utterly unabashed about it, too." Her voice is distant, and I imagine her on the sofa, languid, her eyes on the backyard. "I still masturbate to the thought of it."

I cringe, wondering what he must make of this girl.

"His wife came over then and introduced herself. She'd curated the show, and we chatted a few minutes. He kept his eyes on me all night, and before I left I wrote my name and number in the guest book near the door."

"And?"

"He texted me within the hour and came over that night." She laughs softly. "Honest to god, best night of my life."

"Do I sense a *but* coming . . ."

"Two days later I showed up for my studio class at the university, and he's the professor. I had no idea, and neither one of us acknowledged it, but at the end of the class he asked me to stay behind."

"Did you?"

"Yes."

"And what did he have to say?"

"Not one word. He locked the door and pushed me to the floor," she says. "It's now a ritual, at the end of every class. There's four other students in that studio class, and I can't even begin to tell you how incredible the tension is between us during that hour." It's silent then, and I picture Sam, in his chair, waiting for her to speak. "Are you appalled, Doctor?"

"Appalled?"

"Yes. An impressionable twenty-four-year-old woman, sleeping with her older, married professor. Certainly breaks a lot of rules."

"What do you think about that aspect of your relationship?"

"I think it's an incredible turn-on," she says. "In fact, nothing turns me on more than crossing a boundary with a man."

"That's something I would like to explore further," Sam says. "But unfortunately, we're nearly out of time." I look at the clock: 2:44. Her appointment must have started at two. I take the notebook I'd hidden in one of Agatha Lawrence's boxes and add her name to the list—"The French Girl"—as Sam shifts in his chair below me. "I'm curious how today felt for you," he says. "You said in your message you've never gone to therapy before. I like to check in and see—"

"It felt great," she says. "You're worth every cent."

"Would you like to make another appointment for later this week?"

"You want me to come twice a week?"

"It's what I suggest for all new patients, at least in the beginning," Sam says. I stop writing. No, he doesn't. "Therapy is most useful to those who commit to it, Charlie." *Charlie*, I jot down in the notebook.

"Can I think about it?" she asks.

"Of course."

They stand, and I hear Sam's office door open. I wait for the outside door to slam shut and her footsteps to pass by the window before sliding the notebook into the box and easing toward the broken window for a peek. She's wearing a hat with a fur rim and a long wool coat. I can't make out her features as she opens the door and gets into the front seat of the green Mini Cooper. I step away from the window and replace the happy-face rug. Pulling my robe more tightly around me, I steal quietly out of the room, back upstairs, uneasy.

He needs to watch out for that one.

chapter
11

SAM RUNS HARD AND fast up the hill, rain-soaked, his lungs burning.

Keep going, he tells himself. *Five more minutes to the top.* It's so quiet, the only sounds are his labored breathing and the soles of his new top-of-the-line running shoes slapping against the cold, wet asphalt, bringing back the memory of the first time he ran this road, the night his dad left. Sam left his mother at the dining room table, the barely touched coconut cake on the table between them. He bolted out of the house, down their cul-de-sac of shitty two-bedroom houses, up into the hills. Albemarle Road. Even the name sounded majestic, and he kept coming back, punishing his body, imagining what it would be like to own one of these big houses, skylights under a canopy of pines, six wooded acres. Rich people lived here. Intact families with two cars and a father who wasn't fucking the girl on page twenty-four of the Talbots catalog.

Annie knows something's up. Of course she does, she's not an idiot. He's been acting weird since he went to the bank four days ago. Called her to cancel their date, made up a story about a patient in crisis, said he needed to make a few phone calls. He then sat in his car for four hours in the high school parking lot, trying to come up with a plan.

Sam hears a car approaching and moves to the side of the road, toward the edge of the shallow ditch. He keeps going, his thighs burning, sprinting the last hundred feet to the top of the hill. He drops down to the ground, panting, his phone heavy in the front pocket of his running jacket.

Do it, Sam. Do what you came up here to do. Call him.

Sam unzips the pocket and pulls out his phone and the slip of paper where he wrote his father's phone number, which he'd spent forty-five minutes digging through old cell phone bills to find. It's going to be fine. He'll tell his father what happened at the bank, and his father will fix everything. He takes a breath, dials.

"Yeah, hello!" Ted Statler chirps on the first ring.

"Hi Dad."

The line goes silent for a moment. "That you, Sammy?"

"It's me, all right," he says through the lump in his throat. "Unless you have another kid I don't know about."

His father laughs. "Well, how about that. How you doing, son?"

"Good. I'm sorry we haven't spoken—" There's commotion on the other end.

"Guess where I am," Ted says.

"I have no idea."

"Peter Angelos's house. You know who that is?"

Sam laughs. "Of course I know who that is. It's the owner of the Baltimore Orioles."

"Right, Sammy! Nice work." Teddy whistles. "He's got a fountain. Anyway, how's things, son? How's New York treating you?"

"I'm not in New York. Moved back home a few months ago."

"To Chestnut Hill?" Teddy laughs, incredulous. "Why would you do that?"

"Mom's sick," Sam says, numb with cold.

There's a burst of laughter in the background. "What'd you say, Sammy?"

"Mom's sick," he repeats, irritated that his father isn't walking out of the room to find some place quieter to talk to his estranged son. "She needed help."

"Sorry to hear that, son."

"And I got married."

"Married! You're kidding." He whoops out a holler. "What's her name? It *is* a her, right? Never can be too sure these days."

Sam forces a laugh, like he's supposed to. "Her name's Annie."

Sam hears muffled voices in the background. "Oh Jesus, Sammy. You're never going to guess who's here."

"Peter Angelos?" Sam offers.

"No." Teddy lowers his voice to a whisper. "Cal Ripken."

Heat floods Sam's face. Cal Ripken, his all-time hero. The man who brought father and son together one hundred and sixty two evenings a year. Hearing his name, Sam is twelve years old again, his mom in the kitchen making homemade spaghetti sauce for Sunday dinner. The house smells like garlic bread, and his father's face is tight with concentration, watching number 8, old Iron Man himself, take the field.

"Should I talk to him?" his dad asks.

"Are you kidding?" Sam stands up and begins pacing back and forth across the street. "Of course you should. It's Cal fucking Ripken."

"Cal fucking Ripken," his dad repeats.

"Who's he with?" Sam asks.

"Can't tell," he says. "He's surrounded."

"I bet he is. How's he look?"

"Good," his dad says. "Still in great shape, too. Oh look. He's with some old broad. That can't be his wife." Teddy chuckles. "You remember the day we watched him break Lou Gehrig's record?"

Sam stops pacing. "Yeah, Dad. I remember." It was the day you met *Phaedra*, stupidest name in history.

"That was a great day, wasn't it, Sammy?"

Sam laughs. "A great day? Are you kidding me?"

"You all right, Sammy?"

"Yeah, I'm fine," he snaps. *Do it Sam, get it over with.* "Listen, Dad. I'm calling about the money you deposited into Mom's account. I went to the bank, and there was some discrepancy—"
There's more commotion and then loud music.

"Things are starting here, Sammy. I have to go. Can I give you a call later?"

"Later? No, Dad, I need—"

"We're getting ready to head off for the winter, down to one of Phaedra's places in the Caribbean. Nice, huh?"

Sam stops in the middle of the street. "We who?"

"Me and the missus," Ted says.

"You and Phaedra are still married?"

"What are you talking about? Of course we are. Better than ever, in fact."

"I thought you got divorced. You said in the letter—"

"Letter? What letter?"

"The letter about the money. On your stationery."

"No idea what stationery you're talking about."

"Dad," Sam says, stern. "The letters you've been sending me. Asking me to call."

"I'm sorry, Sammy, but are you drunk?"

"Drunk? No—"

"Hang on a minute," Teddy says. "Phaedra wants to say hi."

"Sam!" Her voice is breathy, as stupid as her name. "I heard your dad say you got married, which is a real bummer. I opened a bridal veil store. I could have hooked you up. Next time you get married, send her our way."

Ted's back on the line, laughing. "Real good hearing from you, son. You should come down. We got plenty of room. Gotta run. Take care."

The line goes dead in Sam's hand, the realization crystallizing.

His father's not divorced.

Which means there was no settlement.

Which *then* means that—

There is no money.

"She made it all up." Sam says the words out loud.

His mother made it up.

His father didn't write that letter Sam found. And not only that, it appears from what he said that he didn't write *any* of the letters. The stationery. The assurances that his father thought about him, that he loved him, always ending it with an invitation to call, which Sam never did. It was all her—Margaret—the whole time, desperate to make everything okay.

His phone rings in his hand, and he closes his eyes again, allowing himself an absurd moment of hope that it's Ted, calling back, apologizing for being a dick and asking if Sam's got a pen. *Realized I wrote the account number down wrong, Sammy!*

But it's not him, it's an unknown number. *Again.* The dude from the debt collection agency. He says his name is Connor, but there's no way his name is Connor because he lives in India making two dollars a day and Sam can't imagine many boys are called Connor there. He's called twice today already, from the same unknown number.

"Hello, Connor," Sam spits into the phone. "It's nice of you to call again. It's been five hours and I've sort of missed you. Also, I don't know if you know this, but I'm a psychologist and I'd suggest you look hard at some of your life choices because honestly, this job you have—"

"Sam?" It's a woman's voice.

"Yes?"

"It's Sally French, from Rushing Waters."

"Hello, Mrs. French," he says, clearing his throat, embarrassed. "How are you?"

"I'm good, Sam. Thank you." She pauses. "You okay?"

"Yes, I'm fine." *No, I feel like I'm losing control.* "Is everything okay?"

"Yes. Well, no," she says. "James, our head of accounting, was going to call you, but I wanted to do it myself. The check you sent bounced."

"Is that right?" he mutters.

"I'm sure it was a misunderstanding, and we're hoping you can drop another one off tomorrow."

"Yes," he says. "Sure can."

"You're behind, as you know, and—"

"Yes," he says. "I know. I'll take care of it tomorrow."

"Of course," she says. "Thank you, Sam."

"Thank you, Mrs. French."

The wind picks up and he begins to run again, telling himself it's all going to be okay.

chapter
12

I PUT THE BAG of Smartfood in my backpack, on top of my copy of *Infinite Jest*, determined to get to the slow and torturous end of chapter 3. I couldn't resist ordering a used copy from Amazon for four dollars plus shipping. Skinny Jeans won't stop yapping about how creatively inferior the book is making him feel, and rather than yelling at him through the vent to *JUST STOP READING IT*, I'm approaching it the way Dr. Sam Statler would. Empathetically.

Of course, Dr. Statler is showing exactly *none* of that to me. Between his persnickety mood and the box of letters I unearthed in Agatha Lawrence's things, the tension in this house is enough to make me want to call in to my fake volunteer position and ask for extra shifts. The letters were in a sturdy box in the back of a file cabinet drawer. Hundreds of them, in pale yellow envelopes addressed to a person she referred to only as "Beautiful." They're heartbreaking—proclamations of devotion to a forbidden love, not one of the letters sent.

I hunt impatiently for my keys, knowing that if I don't hurry, I'm going to risk crossing paths with Sam. He has this hour free and likes to take himself out to lunch, and I am not in the mood to deal with his bad attitude. I take my jacket from the closet and am opening the front door when I hear a car heading up the hill toward the house. I step back inside. He must have scheduled someone for this hour. Who cares, I think, resolute. I need a break from this house. I'm going out.

I wait until the footsteps pass by and Sam's office door slams shut before stepping onto the porch. I'm wondering if I should try the new sushi place where the Mumble Twins recently celebrated their first anniversary, when I see the car parked next to Sam's. The green Mini Cooper with the white racing stripe.

The French Girl is back, two days after her last appointment.

I turn around and walk back into the house. Consider me called-in-sick.

····

"I'm glad we could make this time work," Sam says when we're all settled in our places: Sam on his overpriced Eames executive office chair, the French Girl on the sofa, me upstairs at the vent.

"Thank you for accommodating me," she says. "Chestnut Hill seems like a place bursting with middle-aged women with things to complain about. I was sure you'd be booked."

Sam chuckles. "My practice here is a few months old," he says, "I'm still building up a steady clientele."

"Where were you before you were here?" she asks.

"New York for the last eighteen years."

"I love New York."

"Have you lived there?"

"Yes. I came here from Paris to study sculpture at NYU."

I suppress an eye roll. The woman's a walking cliché. *I work in the nude, and on the weekends I like to drink whisky on my fire escape and date Ethan Hawke.*

"What drew you to sculpture as a medium?" Sam asks.

"I like manipulating things with my hands," she says. "It's a lifelong passion. Yours is running, correct?"

"Yes," Sam says. "How did you know?"

"I read about you in the newspaper. That little interview you gave. 'Twenty Questions with Sam Statler.'"

"The piece was a little more than I was expecting," Sam says. "Not sure I'd do it again."

"Oh, don't be embarrassed," she says. "You come across quite charming." It's obvious she's flirting, which is annoying, but I agree with her. That piece *was* very endearing.

"Well, thank you, Charlie. That's nice of you to say." A moment of silence passes between them.

"The article said that you were married, but nothing at all about your wife. How long have you been hitched?"

"Can I ask why you'd like to know that?" Sam asks, as I expected he would. It's what he says every time a client asks him something personal, his way of maintaining a boundary and keeping the attention on them.

"I'm telling you the most intimate details of my life, Sam. I think you can manage sharing how long you've been married."

"Fair enough," Sam says. "Fifteen weeks."

"Fifteen *weeks*?" she says. "Are we talking about a marriage or a newborn?"

"My wife and I celebrate each week," he says. "It's a tradition."

"Sounds intense," she says. "And a little needy."

He's quiet for a moment. "Is marriage something you can see for yourself?"

She laughs. "That was a truly expert attempt to turn the

attention back to me, Doctor. Your grad school professors would be proud." She pauses. "No, marriage is not something I can see for myself. Committing to one person forever? Why would anyone want to do that?"

Sam hesitates. "It does have its challenges, I suppose."

Oh, I get it. It's a technique. He's trying to show he relates to her, on a personal level, to build her trust and encourage her to commit to the work. Smart.

"How long did it take you to know your wife was the one?" the French Girl asks.

"I proposed after six months," he says.

She scoffs. "That was ballsy."

"Why, thank you."

"So it happened for you, then. The when-you-know, you-know."

"Yes." He pauses and I realize I'm holding my breath. "I suppose."

"Oh?" she murmurs. "You sound unsure."

"You said it yourself—committing to one person has its challenges."

"What are the challenges of your marriage?" she asks.

A series of loud knocks obscures his response. At first I think it's someone downstairs in his waiting room, pounding on his door, but then a doorbell rings, and I realize it's not coming from downstairs but from up here. Someone's at the front door.

Annoyed, I slide the rug over the vent and steal out of the room.

"Well, hello, neighbor!" It's her, the Pigeon, standing on the porch. I wipe my palms on my jeans and open the door. "Did you hear?" she says. "We're expecting a storm."

Of course I've heard. I'm not Amish, I watch the news. It's the type of weather event local meteorologists like Irv Weinstein live for, and he's been yelling about it at six p.m. for the last two evenings. Franklin Sheehy, Chestnut Hill's trusty and long-employed police chief, was on the news this morning, explaining the importance of staying off the road and stocking up on groceries and bottled water. Storm Gilda, they're calling it, and only an idiot wouldn't have printed a list of emergency supplies to have on hand in a Category 2 storm expected to create a lot of mayhem and difficult travel conditions. "A storm in the middle of *October*," the Pigeon says. "That's unheard of."

"Climate change," I say, impatient.

"Exactly. I've been thinking about organizing a march. You know what Drew said when I told him that? 'If there's one thing that's going to stop climate change, it's a march of ten stay-at-home moms in Chestnut Hill, New York.' Idiot. Anyway—" She smiles and holds up a Pyrex dish, like we're on an episode of *Desperate Housewives*. "I made too much veggie chili and couldn't bear to throw it out. You like chili?"

"Are there people who don't?" I ask, taking it from her. "That was nice, thank you."

"You're welcome. And cool eyeglasses," she says. "Where'd you get those?"

I touch them—the bright blue frames I dug out of one of Agatha Lawrence's boxes, a perfect match to my prescription. *They belonged to the woman who died here, and I liked them.* "The city," I say. "Way back when."

"They look great," she says, and then gestures at the two rocking chairs on the porch. "You should bring this all inside. Winds are going to be bad."

"Good idea. I'll ask Sam to do it when he's finished." I hold up the tray. "Thanks again."

I go inside and place the dish in the refrigerator. Before heading down the hall to the vent, I pause, and then change my mind and turn toward the stairs. I think I've had all I can take of that French girl for one day.

chapter

13

SAM LIES ON THE bed, his laptop growing warm on his stomach, and rewinds the video again. "Bottom of the fifth, and you know what *that* means," a fuzzy version of his dad announces from the screen.

"Why yes I do, Dad," Sam replies, mouthing the rest along with Ted. "It's time for trivia with our friends Keyote and Frank Key." Keyote and Frank Key, the Frederick Keys' two mascots: a coyote that looks like a regular dog and literally a white guy in colonial attire who someone felt was necessary to bring on a few years ago.

"Okay, James from Columbia, are you ready?" Sam's father asks as Sam reaches for the beer resting against Annie's pillow. It's a broadcast of a game on June 12, 2016, available on You-Tube, and Sam has now watched the three minutes and sixteen seconds that his father appears on-screen seventeen times. Annie is visiting his mother at Rushing Waters, and he's on his third beer; his father is standing on a pitcher's mound with an oversize microphone and an arm draped around a pudgy guy in stone-washed jeans.

Most serious announcers probably hate being forced to shill, but Sam can see how much Ted relishes this part of the job—emceeing the trivia game after inning five, introducing

Tonight's Special Guest before the first pitch. Of course he does. Gives ol' Teddy from Freddy the chance to show off his many charms and get a turn in the spotlight, his preferred position in the world. "Get this right, and everyone in section six will go home with a coupon for a large pizza with a topping of their choice from our good friends at Capitol Pizza, where every night is family night. Okay, here we go." Ted lifts the index card. "Where did Frank Key, our good friend and great mascot, get his name?"

That's a cinch. Even if Sam hadn't heard this question seventeen times already, he'd expect people to know it's Francis Scott Key, golden boy of Frederick, Maryland, who wrote "The Star-Spangled Banner." But James from Columbia doesn't know and nobody goes home with a free pizza and Sam closes his laptop, wondering what Annie's going to say when he tells her about the debt.

He's going to do it when she gets home, any minute now. He's been practicing what he's going to say for the last hour. Easy: the truth. His mom made the whole thing up. His father's divorce, the two million dollars, the letters on fancy stationery every year, letting Sam know he was loved . . . and oh yeah, guess what, there's no money! He read the letter again, which he'd filed away in the drawer where he kept all of his "father's" letters, understanding the depth of his mother's delusion. *I don't think there's been a day since I left that I haven't thought about you, Maggie. I'll always regret what I did.*

Sam will argue that he's having a hard time deciding who's more pathetic: Margaret, for pining away for the asshole for twenty-four years, or Sam for falling for it. He'll explain the holes in his thinking, how he should have taken Annie's advice and waited for the money to come before financing a shiny new Lexus RX 350 with leather interior and automatic ignition. If he had, maybe he would have realized how unlikely it was that the father who thought to call his son twice a year at most and each time only to talk about himself—"Can you *believe* it, Sam, you're talking to a guy with a goddamn wine cellar!"—suddenly gave the family he abandoned $2 million because he cared about their *happiness.*

Additionally, Sam will point out, it *also* probably would have been a good idea to consider the possibility that the letter wasn't written by his father but by a woman with a rating of 2 on the Clinical Dementia Rating scale, the stage marked by a disorientation with respect to time and place, a lack of judgment, and a propensity for alternative realities such as, for example, that the selfish prick she married regretted ruining her life.

Sam heads to the kitchen for another beer. He's going to tell Annie as soon as she gets here, and she's going to understand. Who knows? Maybe she *won't* walk straight out the door and return to New York. Maybe she'll forgive him. Hell, maybe she'll even feel sorry for him. "I think you're an idiot for spending money you didn't have," she'll say. "But I get it. You wanted to believe the money was real because it meant getting the one thing you'd been searching for your whole life. Proof your dad loved you."

"Yes, that's right," he'll reply, relieved. "Classic case of wishful thinking, or, more technically, decision-making based on what is pleasing to imagine as opposed to what is rational." It's so obvious, Sam will have no choice but to smack himself in the head. "You'd think, given my training, I would have been smarter about the whole thing."

He takes the last beer from the refrigerator and hears a car pulling into the driveway. Annie's home. He twists off the beer cap and takes a long pull. I can do this, he thinks, as his phone beeps on the counter.

Hello Dr. S. It's me. Charlie. Your favorite new patient. What are you doing?

Charlie. He considers telling her the truth: *Well, Charlie, I'm waiting for my wife to walk in so I can tell her I'm in a shitload of debt. What are you doing?*

Hi Charlie, he writes instead. Is everything okay?

Yes. I want to thank you for the session yesterday. I have a whole new lease on life.

I'm glad.

It's true what the women of Chestnut Hill are writing about you on Yelp. You're very skilled.

Annie's engine quiets in the driveway. Thanks, he writes. That's nice to hear. Would you like to set up a time to meet again?

Yes, I would. Tomorrow.

He glances out the window. The light is on in Annie's car. I have some time in the morning, he writes.

I mean tomorrow night.

Annie's car door slams. Tomorrow night? He hears Annie's footsteps on the path outside as the porch light clicks on. "Hey handsome," she says, stepping inside and bringing in a rush of cold air. He puts his phone in his pocket as she drops her bag on the counter. "How we doing?"

"We're doing fine."

She kisses him hello. "You okay?"

"I'm fine."

"I stopped for takeout," she says, reaching into her bag. "Thin mints and red wine. You hungry?"

He hesitates, considering his options. He can sit down with

his wife and tell her the truth, ruining his night, if not his en-tire life, or he can escape to the back room and talk to Charlie.

"I have some work to finish," he says, draining the beer. "Might jump in the shower and then tackle that."

"Okay," Annie says. "But don't expect any leftovers." He kisses her forehead on the way down the hall to the bedroom, and into the master bath. He closes the door and pulls out his phone as a new message arrives.

Yes, Dr. Statler, tomorrow night.

I don't understand, he writes.

Of course you do, Sam. Would you like me to beg?

He waits, riveted, as she types.

Because I will if you want me to.

He leans against the sink, the adrenaline rushing. *Game on.*

chapter
14

"**WELCOME TO LOWE'S. CAN** I help you?"

The man is wearing a blue vest with ASK ME ANYTHING printed across his chest, and I consider asking him why Sam is being so distant and cold, but instead I ask him where I can find a four-pack of Everlite door silencers.

I don't get it. I've been trying my best to be understanding and patient, going back and forth between giving Sam space and trying to help him, but neither seems to be working. He's still walking around with a long face.

But it's okay, because I'm going to make everything better. This evening, during a special happy hour, I'm going to confront him gently, ask him to talk. He *has* to be open to it—he has, after all, made an entire career of encouraging people to spend time in "the muck," as I've heard him call it downstairs, and what better way for us to enter the muck than over a cocktail I designed myself? Spent two hours this morning experimenting with different concoctions from the liquor bottles I discovered in Agatha Lawrence's pantry, settling on a spiced pear martini, going out of my way to poach three pears in star anise and half a bottle of brandy. (I've decided to name it the Gilda, after the impending storm.)

"Here you go," the guy in the blue smock says when we reach

aisle 9J. He hands me the door silencers and I drop them in my cart, on top of the plant food and extra batteries. I smile and make my way toward the kitchen appliances, liking the energy of this place. Only in America can you buy a twelve-pack of Everlite door silencers for $4.99 and a Craftsman Dual Hydrostatic zero-turn lawn mower for $2900. I stop to examine the machine. I should buy it. It's something I've always wanted, ever since I first saw my neighbor across the street in Wayne, Indiana, Craig Parker, driving his lawn mower around his front yard.

Mr. Parker was a lawyer, and Mrs. Parker volunteered in the cafeteria every Monday, selling milk and ice cream sandwiches for a quarter each, passing out gum to all of Jenny's friends. That was their daughter—*Jenny,* a name I can't say without whining. She was a cheerleader, one year ahead of me in school, and I'd stand in the window and watch her and her family sometimes. In the summer, Mr. Parker would drive his lawn mower up and down, making straight lines in the grass, while Mrs. Parker and Jenny wore matching hats and pulled weeds from the garden on the side of their house. They'd finish and disappear inside, where I imagined Jenny went to the refrigerator for a cold can of grape soda. (I know for a fact she drank grape soda. Six times I was inside their house, and each time I checked.) Theirs was the nicest and biggest house on the block, extravagant compared to the two-bedroom ranch my dad did not pay $42,000 for just to see my goddamn shoes in the middle of the living room floor.

But even so, that's no reason to buy this Craftsman Dual Hydrostatic lawn mower, and I pass by the display, heading toward the checkout. Unloading my cart, I watch the girl behind the register, hardly any enthusiasm at all for her job. She's a local, I can tell by her skin, seeing the pretty girl she'd be if she'd been born somewhere with better schools and cleaner water.

"That'll be thirty-two dollars and six cents," she says when she's finished.

"And this," I say, snatching a bag of candy bars from a metal rack near the front of the belt. "Why not, right? I'm celebrating."

She obviously doesn't believe she's being paid to ask customers what it is they're celebrating, but the fact of the matter is that Josh Lyman and Donna Moss finally kissed. *West Wing*, season 7, episode 13. I've been too mad at Sam to tell him I've made it to season 7, but I have, and I know that Donna left the Bartlet White House to work on a campaign, and she and Josh were both so happy with some new poll numbers that they made out inside Josh's hotel room. It was tender but also exceedingly hot, the way everyone knew it was going to be, and if that isn't a reason to splurge for a Kit Kat, I don't know what is.

The rain has started and the wind is picking up when I exit the store and rush toward my car. I take the roads carefully, heading along the railroad tracks and turning right onto Cherry Lane. The Pigeon's house is lit up, and I slow down as I pass, imagining her inside, counting her bottles of wine, making sure she's got enough to get her through the expected school closings.

I go over the bridge and pull into my driveway. Skinny Jeans's shiny white Audi is parked next to Sam's car, and I dash up the driveway, the wind blowing leaves across the path. Leaving my boots outside and my jacket in the foyer, I hurry to the kitchen, contemplating the idea of going to the vent for a quick update on how young Mr. Jeans has been feeling creatively. I decide against it, however, choosing instead to open the fridge and pour myself a Gilda, from the pitcher I mixed this morning—*liquid courage,* as my mom used to call the two glasses of red wine she drank each evening before my dad got home. I take a long sip and head upstairs to get ready.

It's important I'm at my best.

chapter
15

THE DOOR SLAMS BEHIND Christopher as Sam watches the sky darken and the storm roll in. Gilda, they're calling it: heavy rains and winds as high as eighty miles per hour, a travel warning in effect. He checks the time: 5:03 p.m. The wind whips the windows as, from the bottom drawer of his desk, he takes the bottle of Johnnie Walker Blue that Annie gave him the day he officially opened for business. There's a little left, and he empties what remains into a glass and takes his phone from his pocket.

He opens a new message. Hi Charlie. I've been thinking about your invitation, he types.

Typing bubbles appear immediately. And?

And I'll be there, he replies.

What about this storm? It looks bad out there.

I'll be fine. He throws back the whisky. What's the address?

He takes his raincoat from the closet as she types, leaving the umbrella on its hook, not wanting to draw any extra attention to himself as he sneaks out. He steps into the foyer and closes the outside door slowly behind him, praying he can get out unseen. He lifts his collar and hurries along the path, toward the driveway. As soon as he gets to the porch steps, he hears the front door of the house open, the tinkle of ice against glass, the greeting that's starting to grate on him.

"Hey there, heartbreaker."

Damn it, he thinks. I'm trapped.

chapter
16

SOMETHING IS WRONG.

My mouth is sour and my head is pounding, like it's been cracked open with a hammer. I squint at the clock—9:03 a.m.—and reach for what's left in the water glass on the bedside table. Near the door, I notice mud prints on the wood floors, and then the empty pitcher on its side, near the closet door. I bolt upright and pull back the covers as it comes back to me suddenly. Last night. The storm. Happy hour.

I squeeze my eyes shut, remembering it. I was waiting for Sam on the porch with the drinks and a bowl of Chex Mix (in all my excitement about the cocktail, I'd completely overlooked the snacks). The rain was coming down in sheets by then, the wind whipping the branches. I'd brought two blankets to drape over the rocking chairs, thinking it would be nice to watch the storm and hash it out.

And he ignored me. Like I wasn't even there, standing in the cold, two cocktail glasses in my hands. I was dumbstruck as I watched him sprint toward that ridiculous car, as if he were afraid of being seen. He got in, drenched, and pulled quickly out of the driveway, his taillights fading in the fog before he reached the bridge.

My head throbs as I ease myself out of the bed, nauseous, a vague memory of downing both of the Gildas rather quickly. And then I must have gone to the kitchen for the pitcher and brought it up here, drinking the whole thing and passing out. I take Agatha Lawrence's robe from the hook behind the door and keep a hand on the wall for balance as I hunt for Advil in the bathroom medicine cabinet and swallow four with a palmful of water. I stare at myself in the mirror—noticing the new strands of gray—wishing I could call Linda and tell her what happened last night, how badly Sam hurt my feelings. But of course I can't. We haven't spoken since I left the city, and I can't pick up the phone and start complaining about a man she's never met. She'll tell me what I already know to be true: it was an asinine decision to uproot my life and move here, believing I could start over and actually be happy. I hardly need her to tell me what a fool I've been.

I walk to the window on shaky legs. Thick branches litter the front yard and the sign—DR. SAM STATLER, PSYCHOLOGIST— that I installed before Sam opened his practice downstairs is on its side in the street. And then I notice something else. Sam's car isn't here.

I feel a chill run through me as I hurry out of the room, down the stairs, through the kitchen. When I open the door to Agatha Lawrence's study, I'm hit with a blast of cold air. The floor is wet, and shards of glass litter the floor. The window blew out in the storm. I rush to the corner and push aside the happy-face rug, and before I even put my ear to the vent, I can sense the emptiness downstairs.

I stand and run for the hallway, barely making it to the toilet in time to empty last night's pitcher of pear martinis into the bowl, sure beyond doubt that something is terribly wrong.

. . . .

A few hours later, I'm sitting in Sam's office chair, staring at the clock on the floor near the sofa and listening to Sam's buzzer sound for the third time. The Mumble Twins are outside, here for their twelve o'clock appointment. They wait another ninety-six seconds before giving up, and I picture them under an umbrella, traipsing back to their car, every right to be annoyed that Sam didn't call them to cancel.

The wind blows hard against the floor-to-ceiling window offering a view of the back lawn, and the woods beyond. I hear the car engine disappear down the hill, picturing the first time I walked through those woods, the week I moved in to the Lawrence House. The sun was shining, and I drifted alone among the trees, using a garden machete I'd picked up at Hoyt's Hardware to clear my way, looking back at the grandeur of the house, unable to believe something so nice could be mine.

Another wave of nausea rises, and I close my eyes, feeling the weight of the credit card bills in my hands. Nine in all, totaling more than $120,000, hidden down here, in Sam's desk drawer, stuck between the pages of the Stephen King novel he was reading on the porch a few weeks ago.

He lied. When we met, he told me he was financially secure—that he'd never had trouble paying his bills or covering his rent. And now I don't know what to believe.

Of course, who am I to cast stones? It's not like I can claim to have been honest with him one hundred percent of the time. In fact, the proof of my lies is upstairs, in the purple binder in my library, where I keep my lists, including my most shameful one.

Things I've Lied to Sam About: In Order of Significance

1. Our meeting was not a chance encounter. I knew exactly who he was, the day that fate brought us together. I'd read every paper he'd written, watched the lectures he gave on the intersections of mental health and childhood trauma. I was so taken by him that I—

The phone rings in my lap, startling me, and I check the caller ID. It's a number I don't recognize—some telemarketer or survey taker, probably. Someone who's not going to understand that I'm not in the mood to talk.

"Yes, hello," I say, curt.

"Oh good, you're there." It's a woman's voice, relieved. "I'm sorry to bother you, but is Sam there?"

"Sam?" I grip the phone and sit up straight. "Who is this?"

"It's Annie," the woman says. "Sam's wife."

PART II

chapter
17

"ANNIE." I STAND UP, the stack of bills and the book thudding to the floor. It's *her*, his wife. "Is everything okay?"

"No," she says. "Sam didn't come home last night, and I'm worried. I found your number on the lease you and he signed. Was he downstairs in his office this morning?"

"No . . ." I stammer. "I haven't seen him since yesterday, when he left for the day."

"Did you speak to him?"

"No." *I tried, Annie, but he walked by me, without one word, like I'm worth nothing to him.* "I saw him from my window. Running to his car. He didn't have an umbrella."

"I need you to do me a favor and let me in to his office," she says. "I can be there in fifteen minutes."

"His office?" I turn and look around the room. "I'm sorry, Annie. But I can't do that."

"Why not?" she asks, brusque.

"I'm not allowed downstairs," I say. "You'll see the restricted access clause right there in the lease he and I signed. I can only enter his office with his explicit permission."

"I understand," she says. "You can give me the key, and—"

"I don't have a key."

She's silent a moment. "Are you serious?" she says. "You're Sam's landlord, and you don't have a key to his office?"

"Your husband insisted on it," I say, my voice steady. "He's very conscientious about protecting his patients' privacy."

She swears under her breath. "I honestly don't know what to do."

"Have you tried calling him?"

"Yeah, I thought of that," she says, impatiently. "He's not answering my calls or my texts. He never does that."

"Well, I'm sure there must be some explanation."

"This is my cell, but can I also give you my home number?" she asks. "In case he shows up?"

"Yes, of course. Let me find something to write with." I scan the room, spotting the Stephen King novel on the floor. I pick it up and find a pen in Sam's desk drawer. "Go ahead," I say, opening the front cover and writing down the number she recites. "I'll be sure to call you the minute he shows up. And don't worry, Mrs. Statler. I'm sure everything will be okay."

"Thank you," she says. "And it's Potter."

"I'm sorry?"

"It's Annie Potter. We have different last names."

"Potter. Got it," I say, printing the name under her number. "Good night now."

The phone goes dead in my hand, and I stoop down to collect Sam's bills, slide them into the book, and head toward the door. Inside my foyer, I hide the extra key the locksmith was kind enough to make for me, remove my latex gloves, and head toward the computer in the library, buzzing with excitement. Of course. *Potter*, not Statler. That's why I could never find you in a Google search, Annie.

....

Sitting at the desk in the library, I sharpen my pencil and scan my list.

Things I'm Learning about Sam's Wife: A List

1. Annie Marie Potter is a forty-one-year-old native of Kennebunkport, Maine.
2. She is, as my father would say, the ambitious type:
   i.   A PhD with distinction in comparative literature from Cornell University.
   ii. A teaching position at Columbia University, in the Department of Gender Studies, which is apparently something they made up in the 1970s.
   iii. Since this past September, she has held a visiting fellowship at a small, private university in Chestnut Hill, New York, where, as far as I can tell, she teaches just one class: *It's All in Her Head: Women and Madness in Literature. From the mad heroines of classic Victorian literature to the rise of the unreliable female narrator, the psychological vulnerability of women has long been a captivating subject. Tuesday and Thursday. 10:00 a.m. Higgins Hall auditorium.*
3. She's not as pretty as I was expecting. I know there's probably a whole host of classes in Annie's gender studies department devoted to why it's wrong for me to comment on her physical appearance, but it's true. She wisely seems to have eschewed all social media, but I found a photo of her on the university website, which I've been studying for the

past hour. Attractive, I suppose, but not the model type I was expecting.

4. I *never* would have spoken to either her or Sam in high school, each for different reasons. Him because he would have thought he was too good for me; her because confident girls scared me.

I knew, in theory, that she existed. For one thing, she was mentioned (in passing) in the interview Sam did with the local paper, and then he brought her up a few times himself, like the day he responded to the flyer I'd stuck under his windshield. He came right over to look at the space, spent an hour walking back and forth, listening to my ideas to spruce the place up. *You could position your office back here. Knock out this wall, replace it with glass.* "My wife Annie is better at envisioning these things," he said, excited. "But I think you're right. This could be great."

Silly me. I should have pegged Sam as a man who'd choose the type of woman who keeps her maiden name. Dr. Annie Marie Potter. Not Ann or Anne or Anna but *Annie*. (Not exactly the name a parent would give an infant daughter for whom they had high hopes. Girls named Annie dream of growing up to be airline stewardesses or home decorators showing up to color-coordinate your sweaters, not someone who is going to one day—May 6, 2008, to be exact—publish a well-reviewed article in *Feminist Theory*, some journal I've never heard of.)

I figured she and I would run into each other one day, bump carts in the organic meats department at Farrell's, where couples like Sam and Annie went to nourish their grass-fed beef habit. Not that she'd care, but I'd love the chance to tell her about myself.

1. I'm fifty-one and single.
2. I was, for twenty-five years, a certified home health aide with Home Health Angels, named employee of the month three times.
3. I took good care of her husband since he moved in downstairs, three months ago. I gave him everything he asked for, in fact—nontoxic paint, heated floors—you'd think he would have appreciated me more.

Who knows, maybe Annie and I will still meet. Maybe she'll stop by tomorrow to commiserate about Sam's disappearance, and I'll tell her how sorry I am to hear that she lost both her parents when she was eighteen.

Their names were Archie and Abigail Potter, and their double obituary appeared in the *York County Coast Star* out of Kennebunkport, Maine, June 12, 1997. *Devoted husband Archie and loving wife and mother Abigail were killed in a helicopter crash over the Hudson River on the afternoon of their twentieth wedding anniversary, survived by an eighteen-year-old daughter.*

What a story. Archie had a lifelong fear of flying, which Abigail was determined to help him confront. She booked a surprise thirty-minute private helicopter ride from a launch in New York City, only for the engine to fail, killing both in a fiery crash into the river.

The clock on the desk chimes—one p.m. already. Where has the day gone? I remove my glasses and rub my eyes, my hangover easing into a dull headache. I turn off the computer monitor and leave the library, sliding the pocket doors closed behind me. Upstairs in my bedroom, I pause at the window and take the binoculars from their hook to check in on the Pigeon. Her car's in the driveway, and I picture her inside, drinking coffee from an oversize mug emblazoned with the phrase *THIS IS REALLY WINE*. I replace the binoculars and turn away as a car appears on the hill. It passes her house, crosses the bridge, and turns into my driveway. I close the curtains and go to the closet to change out of my robe.

The police are here.

．．．．

I open the front door as a man steps from the driver's seat of the police cruiser.

"Good afternoon," he calls as he approaches the porch. "Hoping to speak to the owner of the Lawrence House."

"That's me," I say.

"Franklin Sheehy." He flashes his badge. "Chief of police."

"I know," I say. "I saw you on television, warning everyone about the storm."

"Would have been nice if more of them had listened," he says as a young man approaches from behind. He's tall and baby-faced, no older than twenty-five. "This is officer John Gently. We're sorry to disturb you, but—"

"Is this about Dr. Statler?" I say.

"You've heard?"

"Yes, his wife called earlier today. She sounded worried."

A cold wind lifts the collar of Sheehy's nylon police jacket. "Mind if we come inside?"

"Not if you don't mind removing your shoes," I say. "I just mopped the floors."

"Sure thing." Sheehy steps into the foyer and pauses to remove a pair of black boots, exactly the sensible footwear you'd expect a police chief to wear. "Just you here?"

"Just me," I say.

He walks into the living room and looks around. "Big place for one person."

"Seven years in the city," I say. "I was craving some space."

"New York?"

"No, Albany. I think New York is vile."

"Got a nephew at SUNY Albany. Nice place."

"So, about Dr. Statler," I nudge, reminding him we're here to talk about Sam, not trade TripAdvisor reviews on major US cities. "Is there reason to worry?"

"His wife thinks so," Sheehy says, bringing his focus to me. "She was expecting him home last night, and he never appeared. Understandably upset." He reaches inside his coat and pulls out a notebook and a pair of tortoiseshell reading glasses, not the style I would have chosen for him. "I've been told he's been renting an office from you, downstairs."

"Yes," I say.

"For how long?"

"Three months," I say. "Moved in July first, to be exact."

Three thirty in the afternoon, to be even more exact. I remember it perfectly, watching from an upstairs window as he pulled in to the driveway, parking that nice new Lexus behind my car. He hustled six boxes from the trunk to his office and knocked on my door before he left. "That's a nice touch," he said, gesturing to the sign I had installed at the end of the driveway. DR. SAM STATLER, PSYCHOLOGIST. "I appreciate it."

"Welcome to the Lawrence House," I said. "I hope you'll like it here." He then told me he had arranged to have an extra lock installed on his office door, but had to catch a train to New York; would I mind letting in the locksmith? His name was Gary Unger from Gary Unger Locksmiths, Sam said, adding how he wished he'd been part of the focus group Gary Unger must have hired to come up with the perfect name for his business. I laughed and told Sam I'd be happy to let him in. In fact, I was always happy to help.

"And how well do you know him?" Sheehy asks, jarring me back to the room.

"As well as any landlord knows a tenant," I say. "We say hi when we cross paths."

"Was he a good tenant?"

"Very good."

"Pay the rent on time?"

"He didn't pay rent."

He and the boy cop snap their heads at me. "Nothing?" Sheehy asks. "That's awfully generous of you."

"Well, before you go out of your way to recommend me for sainthood, we had an arrangement. Sam agreed to help me around the house. Small things. Changing lightbulbs. Taking out the trash. As you said, this house is a lot for one person."

"Especially old ones like this. Always something." Sheehy shakes his head like he has some experience with this. "What about strange characters? You seen any of them hanging around downstairs?"

John Gently smirks. "Aren't they all a little nuts? I got a sister who goes to therapy. Two hundred dollars she pays to complain about her husband for forty-five minutes. Rich people sure are good at coming up with ways to spend all that money."

I force my face into a neutral expression. If this young man only knew the number of people Sam has helped—the things he's done for me, just by *osmosis*—he would know Sam is worth every penny. "No, no strange characters," I say, addressing

Franklin Sheehy. "Of course, a therapist always has to be careful about issues around transference."

"Excuse me?" he says, peering at me from under the frames of his glasses.

"It's not uncommon for patients to idealize their therapist," I explain. "Develop an unhealthy need to be close to them." *Like, for instance, the French Girl with a history of inappropriate relationships, who, if I were you, I'd look into.*

"He talk to you about his patients?" the kid asks, trying to insert himself.

I laugh. "Of course not. That would be a clear violation of HIPAA. But anyone with half a brain can imagine that that type of work is as difficult as it is rewarding."

"Uh-huh," Sheehy says, looking bored. "And the night of the storm. His wife told us you reported seeing Dr. Statler leave his office?"

"Yes, that's right. Around five," I say. "I'm kicking myself for not telling Sam about the travel advisory you'd put into place. I doubt he has time to check the weather report when he's down there helping people all day. I could have—"

"Oh I wouldn't beat myself up if I were you," Sheehy says, peering down at his notebook again. "You know how some people are. Can't tell them anything."

"Do you think he had an accident?"

"Not ruling anything out," Sheehy says. "Got an eye out for his car." He closes the book. "Shame we can't get inside his office for a look around. No key, I hear?"

"Privacy issues," I say, shaking my head. "Sam was a real stickler."

"That's what you like to hear," Sheehy says. "A person who still values privacy."

"Yes, indeed," I say. "I'm sorry I'm not much help."

Sheehy sticks his glasses in his front pocket and stands up. "You'll call us if anything . . ." he says as I lead them through the foyer.

"Of course. Good luck," I call after them as they head back to the car under a cold rain. "I hope you find him."

chapter
18

ANNIE STANDS AT THE window and dials the number again. "St. Luke's emergency room, can I help you?" It's the same woman who answered a few hours ago.

"Yes, hi, this is Annie Potter," she says. "I called earlier, inquiring if there have been any reports of an accident since last night. My husband didn't come home—"

"His name again?"

"Sam Statler."

Annie hears the woman typing. "Give me one second." The line fills with a Richard Marx song. This is the third call she's placed since eight last night, and not once before was she put on hold. Maybe this means they found his name in the register and—

"Sorry about that," the woman says, returning to the line. "Had to sneeze. And no, no accident victims brought in tonight."

Annie exhales. "Thanks," she says, hanging up. She slides the phone into the back pocket of her jeans, and remains at the window, willing his stupid car to appear in the driveway. She imagines him parking under the pine tree, in his usual spot, and running toward the house, a pepperoni pizza in his hands. "Waited nearly fifteen hours for this thing," he'd say, shaking the rain from his hair. "The service at that place is *terrible.*"

She paces the room, ending up in the kitchen. Sam's hoodie is where he left it yesterday, draped over a stool at the island, and she slips into it, opening the refrigerator and staring blankly inside. Her phone rings in her pocket, and she scrambles for it, her heart sinking when she sees the number. It's not him. It's Maddie, her cousin, calling from France.

"Hear anything?" Maddie asks when Annie answers.

"Nothing." Annie called Maddie last night, telling her they were having a bad storm and Sam was two hours late coming home. The town had issued a travel warning, the chief of police advising people to stay off the roads. Annie's calls were going right to his voice mail, and she'd decided to brave the roads and drive to the Lawrence House, praying he had decided to stay at the office to wait out the storm. The rain battered her windshield so hard she could barely see. Downtown was dark and deserted, large branches strewn across the street. Her phone vibrated on the passenger seat as she drove over the bridge on Cherry Lane toward the Lawrence House: an emergency alert from the National Weather Service. Flash flood warning in effect. Avoid high water areas. Check local media.

The Lawrence House was dark, and Sam's car wasn't in the driveway. Annie got drenched as she raced down the path to Sam's office, where she cupped her face to the glass. The waiting room was dark, the door to his office closed.

"Did you call the police?" Maddie asks.

"Yes, last night. An officer took my statement, said they'd keep an eye out for his car."

"That's good, right?" Maddie says.

"None of this is good."

Maddie sighs heavily. "How are you holding up?"

"I'm terrified," Annie says.

"You want me to come over?" Maddie asks.

"Of course I want you to come over," Annie says. "But you live in France." Maddie, her cousin, is the closest person to her, the daughter of her mother's twin sister, Therese. It was at their house Annie spent holidays after her parents died, with the aunt and uncle who opened their home to her as if she were their daughter.

"I know," says Maddie. "But they have airplanes now. I can be there tomorrow."

"I'm fine." She tells Maddie she'll call if she hears anything and then heads down the hall to the bedroom. She stops at the French doors that open onto the stone patio and sees they've lost one of the young oaks they planted a few weeks after moving in. Sam will be back to clean up the yard, she thinks. He'll be out there tomorrow, piling branches into his wheel-barrow for firewood.

She sits on his side of the bed and rests her face in her hands. Something's been off with him. For a few weeks now he's been distracted and distant, sleeping poorly at night. She asked him the other day, over breakfast, if he wanted to talk about what was on his mind, and he grumbled something vague—the new practice, his mother—making it clear that he didn't. She left it alone, figured he'd tell her when he was ready.

She lies back and closes her eyes, and she's on the cusp of sleep when she hears a car in the driveway. She scrambles out of bed and looks out the window. It's the police.

"Franklin Sheehy," the man says when she opens the door. "Chief of police."

"Did you hear something" she asks, terrified.

"No, ma'am. Checking in." A kid with a baby face appears behind him. "This is John Gently." Annie recognizes his name; he's the officer who took her statement last night. "Got a few minutes?"

"Yes, come in." She ushers them inside, into the living room.

"We just came from the Lawrence House," Franklin Sheehy says. "Both the owner and the neighbor across the street saw your husband leave the office around five p.m. I'm assuming you've heard nothing from him?"

"No, nothing," she says, as the cops sit on the couch opposite her. "I've been calling his phone, but it's dead."

"How do you know it's dead?" Sheehy asks.

"It goes right to voice mail."

"What I mean is, how do you know he didn't intentionally turn it off?"

She frowns. "Because why would he do that?"

Sheehy ignores the question and takes a notebook and reading glasses from the inside pocket of his jacket. "I know you went through things with Officer Gently, but mind if I get some additional background?"

"Of course," she says.

"Any problems we should know about?" Sheehy asks. "Gambling, drinking?"

"No, nothing like that."

"How's his mood been?"

She hesitates. "Fine," she says. "Mostly. He's been a little distracted."

"He talk to you about it?"

"No," she says. "But we're going through a big transition. Moving here, taking care of Sam's mother. It's a lot."

Sheehy shakes his head and tsks. "Heard about Margaret.

Real shame. She never was the same after Ted left for that girl." He clasps his hands. "I hate to ask, but any chance your husband might have a little something on the side himself?"

"No," Annie says. "Nothing on the side."

"How do you know?"

The two men are watching her. "Because I know my husband, and he wouldn't do that."

John Gently laughs loudly. "Sorry," he says, clapping a hand to his mouth and glancing at Sheehy, embarrassed. "It's just . . . Stats and I went to the same high school, years apart. The guy's a legend."

Annie gives the kid a cursory glance. "Yes, well, that was twenty years ago. Sam's evolved." She turns back to Sheehy. "Were you able to get into my husband's office?"

"No, unfortunately. You were right. Landlord doesn't have a key."

"I know," she says, confused. "But can't you get in some other way?"

"No, ma'am," Sheehy says. "The evidence required to enter someone's office needs to be arguable, which I'm afraid is not the case here."

"Arguable?" Annie says. "What does that mean?"

"Gently?"

"It means," he says, sitting up straighter, "that if Chief Sheehy were to take a letter requesting a search warrant to the district attorney and ask her to show up in Judge Allison's courtroom when all the chief has is a guy who didn't come home from work, nobody's going to be happy."

"Bingo," Sheehy says.

"Didn't come home from work?" Annie says. "I hope you're not suggesting there's any chance that Sam . . . left?" She's doing her best to stay composed. "He drove home in a terrible storm. He was probably in an accident."

Sheehy and Gently exchange a look, and then Sheehy nods and returns the notebook to his pocket. "We've got an eye out for his car, as do the state police. If he was in an accident, we'll find him and get him help. In the meantime, Mrs. Statler, the best thing you can do is get some rest."

She forces a smile and stands up. "Thank you. I'll give that a try."

She leads them to the door, remaining at the window until the headlights of their car disappear down the driveway. Taking her phone from her pocket, she checks again—no missed calls—and opens a new text message. Hello dear husband, she types, swallowing the fear. I really hate this. Can you please come home now?

chapter
19

I LOG IN, STRETCH my neck, and begin my review.

MISERY, BY STEPHEN KING.
My head is still spinning.

I stumbled across a friend's copy, and while I planned to skim the first few pages, I read the whole thing in one sitting. I've noticed some reviewers are using words like *deranged* and *lunatic* to refer to Annie Wilkes, but I find that both wholly unfitting and highly insensitive. It's clear to me that our protagonist's suffering is the result of deep psychological wounds inflicted in childhood. As an adult, she is coping the best she can, using a variety of defense mechanisms—fixation, denial, regression—not to mention (unsuccessfully) trying to repress the anger she feels as a childless, middle-aged woman. Does she always make the best choices? Of course not. But it's not evil that drives her, it's anguish.

(Those interested in this topic should check out the lecture "Misery and Womanhood," by Dr. Anne [sic] Potter, a former Columbia professor and Guggenheim fellow, available on YouTube.)

Ending was rushed. Four stars.

I post the review and push away from the computer, exhausted. I came across Annie's lecture yesterday evening, after dinner. They'd spelled her name wrong in the description, which is why I missed it in my initial search. "Misery and Womanhood." After seeing the title, I was looking forward to hearing her address the innumerable reasons why so many women are unhappy, but then I watched it and realized that she meant the horror novel by Stephen King, the same book Sam had been reading (how sweet). Forty-two minutes of Dr. Potter exploring Annie Wilkes's psyche and contemplating her role as both mother and seductress—which I watched six times in a row—and my curiosity was piqued. Before I knew it, I was turning the last page at two o'clock in the morning.

Heading through the kitchen, I open the door to Agatha Lawrence's study, taking in the clean scent of the room. I did it—I got this place in order finally. I couldn't fall asleep after finishing the book and decided to make myself useful. At first I was simply going to put away Agatha's papers and get rid of the boxes—be done with her for good—but before I knew it, I was sixteen miles away at two in the morning, standing in line at the twenty-four-hour Home Depot with an aching back and the supplies to fix the window myself.

You'd think I would have stopped there and gone to bed, but instead I transformed the study into a guest room with freshly laundered curtains and a single bed I dragged down from upstairs. The result is *cozy chic,* with a tranquil palette and the warm light of a stained-glass desk lamp I discovered in a closet.

I give the room one last look, pleased, and return to the kitchen with the mop. Wringing it out at the sink, I see today's issue of the *Daily Freeman* on the table where I'd left it, the article about Sam on the front page. I was surprised when I opened the door this morning and saw his soggy and wrinkled face smiling up at me from my welcome mat. I shouldn't have been. Of course the story is going to be of interest: local resident and beloved therapist goes missing the night of the storm. It doesn't hurt that he's good-looking, and the fact that he and his new wife are relative newlyweds certainly ups the intrigue. Enough, at least, for an editor at the *Daily Freeman* to assign the story to young and intrepid Harriet Eager, with a journalism degree and a last name that fits, tasked with reporting the bad news that Sam hasn't been seen in two days.

> Dr. Sam Statler was reported missing two nights ago by his wife when he did not return home from work. Anyone with information regarding the whereabouts of Dr. Statler should contact reporter Harriet Eager at tips@DailyFreeman.com.

He looks exceptionally handsome in the photograph they printed alongside Harriet's story, in a smart blue suit with a tie that brings out his eyes. I imagine it was Annie who took it, sitting on the front porch of their house at 119 Albemarle Road. Four bedrooms on six acres with a newly renovated chef's kitchen and a first-floor master, cost them $835,000. I found the real estate listing—photos and all—after Harriet's editor proved himself eager to print Sam's home address, where his new wife Annie is living alone now, no man around to protect her.

I take the scissors from the drawer and take a seat at the kitchen table, wondering what Dr. Annie Marie Potter would think if she knew about the overdue credit card bills her missing husband appears to have been hiding from her. Why else would he keep them stashed in his office, inside the pages of a novel, if not to keep them from her? I've been going through the line items, and I'm dumbfounded at what he was willing to spend on things.

Truth be told, I'm more than a little hurt that Sam didn't tell me about his situation. That's absurd, I know. Being trapped under $120,000 of debt is far too unhappy a topic for happy hour, but I could have helped him process what got him into this situation and devise a plan to tackle it. (On the other hand, I also have to admit to feeling a *smidge* better about things. Sam's coldness these last few weeks wasn't because of anything I did. He was worried about the debt!)

I've just finished cutting out the article when a flash of color passes by the window. I rise from my chair for a look. It's the Pigeon. I consider slipping into the bathroom and waiting for her to leave, but it's too late. She's waving at me through the window. I put the scissors away, walk calmly to the door, and fix on a smile.

"Did you see the article?" she squawks the second I open the door. "About Sam?"

"I was just reading it."

"I'm a wreck." She squeezes her eyes shut and then does the last thing I would expect: she reaches out for a hug.

The last time someone touched me: A list
March 4, seven months ago, the day I left Albany.

Xiu, the oldest of the four girls whose parents owned Happy Chinese on the first floor of my building. I watched her and her sisters grow up in that restaurant, working behind the counter, taking turns accepting the two-dollar tip they knew was coming when they handed me the plastic bag of food—chicken-fried rice on Mondays, barbecue spare ribs on Fridays, every week for six years.

Xiu was sitting on the floor in the foyer near the mailboxes, chewing the end of her ponytail and reading *The Diary of a Wimpy Kid.* She asked me where I was going with such a big suitcase, and when I told her I was moving and wouldn't be back, she stood up and hugged me goodbye. I couldn't believe it, a gesture so sweet it brought tears to my eyes that persisted an hour into the Greyhound journey toward Chestnut Hill, New York. (*Coach* seats on Greyhound. I'd just deposited a check in my name for more money than I could have ever *dreamed* of and yet there I was, in seat 12C, staring down six more inches of leg room and a reclining seat three rows in front of me, just $29 more.)

"Saw the police stopped by your place, too," the Pigeon says, finally letting go. She lowers her voice, as if she's afraid the dog might hear. "What'd *you* tell them?"

"Oh, you know. That I saw Sam leave for the day, dashing to his car, probably hoping to beat the storm."

"I saw him drive by, too. He was *crazy* for driving in those winds. A friend of mine got a tree through her roof, and most of the town lost power."

"I heard." I was up early, with local meteorologist Irv Weinstein, who could hardly contain himself on the 6:00 a.m. news (*Hundreds of downed trees! Electricity out in the eastern part of the county!*).

"Poor Annie," Sidney says.

"She must be worried sick," I agree.

"I saw them together, a few weeks ago, at a thing. They

seemed happy. Still can't believe someone pinned that guy down." She pauses. "Sam and I dated, you know."

"No, Sam didn't mention it."

She laughs. "Why would he? It was a long time ago. And brief. Anyway"—she takes a folded piece of paper from her back pocket—"I came to tell you there's going to be a search. Some guys from our class are organizing it. Everyone's meeting at the bowling alley in an hour."

I take the flyer. "'Community search for Sam Statler,'" I read.

"Well, for his car, I suppose. Chances are he was in an accident, right?"

"Or a fugue state." I googled it last night: *Why do men disappear without a trace*. "There was a guy from Delaware who went out for doughnuts," I tell the Pigeon. "Found him two weeks later, trying to get a face tattoo in San Diego. Had no idea how he got there. Anyway"—I hold up the flyer and take a step further inside—"Thank you for letting me know."

I close the door and stay in the foyer, listening to her retreat down the driveway. When she reaches the hedges, I turn the lock and read the flyer again. "Meet at Lucky Strikes at 10 a.m.! Dress warm!"

In the kitchen, I take my clipping of Harriet Eager's article and go to the library, where I slide open the pocket doors and remove the purple binder from the shelf. At Agatha Lawrence's desk, I carefully punch three holes into the flyer and the article and then snap open the metal rings, putting them in place at the back of the binder. I close the rings and page forward through the contents, past Sam's credit card bills, which I added this morning, to the very first entry in Sam's binder. The interview he gave.

I'll never forget the day I came upon it and first learned about Sam. I'd been living in Chestnut Hill for three months—alone, in this big house, filled with a dead woman's memories. I called a contractor to come fix a leak in the living room ceiling, and came downstairs as he finished to find the wood floors covered with duplicate copies of the *Daily Freeman*, Sam's face peeking out every few feet. I picked up a copy and read the interview. Local boy, he was moving home to take care of his mother, the former secretary at the high school. His answers were charming and funny and I went straight to Google, staying up into the night, reading about his work, and I knew right away that he was someone I wanted to know.

I close the binder, return it to the shelf among the others, and go hunt for my boots. The search for Sam starts soon. I should go.

chapter
20

ANNIE SITS BEHIND THE wheel, Sam's dirty T-shirt in her hands. She presses it to her face, breathing in the lingering scent of his sweat, imagining him coming home from the gym earlier in the week in this shirt. Four women pass in front of Annie's car, wearing matching purple St. Ignatius Catholic Church raincoats. They open the door to the bowling alley and disappear inside. Lucky Strikes, the unofficial headquarters for the Search for Sam! event advertised on flyers some classmates from Sam's high school photocopied and hung around town this morning, exclamation points in no short supply. "Meet at Lucky Strikes at 10 a.m.! Dress warm!" Annie's been sitting in her car for twelve minutes now, watching cars pull up and people jog through the rain toward the entrance in waterproof boots and hoods pulled up under a misty rain.

She imagines Sam in the passenger seat beside her, the two of them just another couple here to join the search, happy for something exciting to do on a Friday morning.

Look at what you've done, she whispers. *Moving home and bringing the town together like this. You should run for mayor when you reappear.*

Good idea, he replies. *Will you host the Greet and Meet?* She can feel his hand reaching across the seat to take hers. *You have to go inside.*

I don't want to.

Why not?

I don't know, she whispers.

Of course you do, dummy. He threads his fingers through hers. *It's because you're deathly afraid that at some point today someone inside that bowling alley is going to come across my car, and discover my remains, and you can't bring yourself to face it.*

Her phone rings on the passenger seat, startling her. It's Gail Withers, the branch manager at the closest Chase Bank, twenty-nine miles away.

"Ms. Withers," Annie says, snatching the phone. "Thank you for calling me back."

"You left quite a few voice mails this morning," Gail says. "How can I help?"

"My husband has a checking account with your bank, and I'm trying to find out the last time his ATM card was used."

"Are you listed on the account?"

"No."

"I see."

"I've spent a lot of time on the phone, calling different 1–800 numbers, trying to get some answers."

"And what were they able to provide you with?"

"Jack shit." Annie presses the ache that is building behind her eyes again. "Which is why I tracked you down. I thought talking to someone more local, that maybe . . ."

"I'm sorry, Ms. Potter, but the bank doesn't share information with unauthorized users. It's for our customers' protection."

"I'm not asking the *bank* to do this, Gail. I'm asking you."

She hesitates. "I'm sorry, Annie. I wouldn't be able to do that even if I wanted to."

Annie takes a breath, resisting the urge to scream. "I haven't spoken to my husband in two days," she mutters. "I don't know what to do."

"I'm sorry," Gail says again, sounding genuinely pained. "I saw the article this morning. I know how difficult this is."

Annie wants to laugh. *Is that right, Gail? So your husband also vanished into thin air, and to avoid the image of him dying a slow death under the world's most douche-y car, your brain is keeping busy running in circles, trying to find out if his bank card was used?* "Thank you, Gail." She ends the call, opens the car door, and walks briskly toward the bowling alley, ready to get this over with. Inside, she's hit by the scent of french fries and lane grease. A woman approaches with a clipboard and pen. She's in her sixties, with hair the color of Concord grape jelly.

"Name, please?"

"I'm not staying," Annie says. "Just dropping something off."

A man rushes by with two fresh boxes of doughnuts, which he sets on a nearby table under a sign taped to the wall: WITH GOOD THOUGHTS FROM EILEEN'S BAKERY IN CENTERVIEW PLAZA. "Get one before they're gone, Mrs. Escobido," he says as he passes.

She shakes her head. "Day fourteen on this new diet, and the only thing I've lost is two weeks of happiness." Annie walks past her. People are milling about, pouring coffee from pots set on the bar, Bon Jovi on low. An assembly line of women stand at the bar tables, spreading peanut butter onto stacks of white bread. One of them waves, sad-faced, and it takes Annie a minute to place her. Sidney Pigeon, the woman who lives across the street from the Lawrence House. Another ex-girlfriend making googly eyes at Sam from across the room. It was a political fundraiser, and Annie remembers getting in the car that night, pretending to be Sidney Pigeon, class of 1998. When they got home, she led Sam into the bedroom, tipsily describing the things she'd been fantasizing about doing with him during PTA meetings for the last fifteen years.

Annie nods and turns around to scan for a grown man who goes by the name of Crush. Crush Andersen, all-star linebacker for the Fighting Cornjerkers. ("I don't even want to know," Annie said when Sam first mentioned the name of his high school football team.) Annie met Crush at Mulligan's, the local haunt, soon after they moved to Chestnut Hill. They were ten minutes into a plate of nachos and frozen margaritas when six guys with the same haircut walked in. There were slaps on the back and a quick round of intros—Crush, Tucky, Half-a-Deck, the entire cast of *Happy Days*, super-stoked to hear their old buddy Stats moved home.

One of the guys on the police force had told Crush about the APB issued for a Dr. Sam Statler, and Crush wasted no time coming to the rescue. Flyers. A Facebook page. Securing the use of the bowling alley at no charge, as long as everyone's out by five p.m. when Family Fun Night starts. Two women in orange parkas approach the doughnut table. "Barbara said someone from the television station is going to be here," one says, fingering the crullers. "You think it's going to be one of those national programs?"

"Don't be silly," says the other. "He's not JonBenét."

"Annie, sweetheart, you made it!" Crush is coming toward

her, arms outstretched. "How you doing?" he asks, giving her a bear hug she would have preferred to evade.

"Shitty," she says, holding up Sam's T-shirt. "I brought this for you. You said you wanted stinky, so . . ."

He takes it, sniffs. "Whew," he says, drawing back. "Zander will *love* this." He means the retired search-and-rescue dog someone has offered to bring.

"You've gone all out," Annie says. Sam's voice pops into her head again. *What did you expect?* he scoffs. *I told you Crush was voted Most Likely To Spearhead the Search for Sam Statler When He Disappears in Twenty Years.*

"Stats would do the same for me," Crush says. *No, I wouldn't,* Sam replies. "You sticking around?"

"No," Annie says. "Not really my thing. But you'll call me if anything . . ."

"Don't worry, sweetheart. I'll keep you posted every step of the way." She thanks him and heads back toward the exit, back to her car. With a sick feeling in her stomach, she drives faster than she should down Route 9, turning left up the mountain. She slows around the turns approaching their driveway, straining for a view over the guardrail and down the ridge, trying not to imagine the worst. *The wind was stronger than he was expecting, he took the turn too fast . . .*

The sky has turned a dark gray when she arrives home. In the living room, she turns on the light, seeing the mess. Piles of papers on the floor, books scattered about, the contents of the kitchen junk drawer strewn across the coffee table. She drops her coat on the sofa and walks into the kitchen, lacking the energy to deal with the chaos she created last night while looking for the spare key to Sam's office. She knows he had one made. She can see it clearly: Sam flashing a heavy gold key hooked onto an orange plastic keychain reading

GARY UNGER

GARY UNGER LOCKSMITHS

It was their two-week anniversary, and Sam had arrived ten minutes late at the Parlor, complaining how he'd had a hard time extricating himself from a conversation with the lonely, eccentric owner of the Lawrence House, from whom he'd just started renting.

"Spare to my office," Sam said. "In case of emergency."

"Like what?" she said. "You're trapped under a particularly big ego and can't get up?"

But then he didn't tell her where he put the key, and she was up until three in the morning, tearing apart the house, wondering what kind of idiot makes a key specifically designed for an emergency and then tells *nobody* where it is. It's pointless. She knows that. The police told her that Sam's landlord saw him leave, and if he'd gone back to the office, his car would have been there. But she's too restless to do nothing.

In the kitchen she opens and then closes the refrigerator door, unsure of the last time she ate. Agitated and restless, she goes to the bedroom and considers picking up the notes she'd started for her next class, but she's too distracted, imagining everyone at Lucky Strikes receiving their assignments and heading out with their soggy maps to search for any signs of Sam.

She climbs into bed, the letters she found last night still strewn across his pillow. They were in a box on a shelf in the closet, a short stack from Sam's dad, typed on expensive-looking letterhead. She'd fallen asleep reading through them, each one the same basic message: *Hi Sammy! I'm thinking about you all the time, son. Call any time you need! Love you, son!*

She pulls up the blankets, remembering the pained look on Sam's face when he told her the story about his father—leaving when Sam was fourteen, the unexpected gift of $2 million. She slips her phone from the back pocket of her jeans and opens her voice mail, needing to hear his voice. Her Bluetooth is on, connected to the top-of-the-line sound system Sam insisted on installing. She hits play on a message he'd left a few weeks ago, on his way home from work, and his voice floods the room.

Hello Annie. This is Sam, your husband. She closes her eyes, the pressure building in her chest. *I'm calling you on the telephone, like it's 1988, to tell you I will be stopping at Farrell's in ten minutes and ask if you want anything. Oh—and you still haven't changed your name on your outgoing message to say Mrs. Sam Statler.* His voice gets stern. *I'd like this to be my last reminder. Is that clear?*

She can't help it, she laughs. She's listened to this message a dozen times in the last twenty-four hours, and he makes her laugh every time. But then she stops, and just like that, she's crying and she can't stop. Is this what happens? Things go extremely well for a short time, before tragedy strikes and it all disappears? It's like she's right back there, eighteen years old, waving goodbye to her parents on that pier, the day of the accident. The worst day of her life.

Her phone beeps with a new text message, and she wipes away her tears and reaches for it, seeing it's from Crush.

We're off, Annie. Wish us luck.

chapter
21

"SAM?"

Sam opens his eyes. It's dark, and his head hurts like hell.

"Sam, can you hear me?"

"*Hello*," Sam mumbles. He tries to sit up, but the pain in his skull keeps him bolted to the ground. "Help me—"

"Don't try and move, Sam." It's a man's voice. "Stay right where you are. Here, squeeze my hand if you can." Sam feels a hand in his and squeezes. "Great, Sam. You're going to be okay." There are fingers on his lips, placing pills on his tongue. "I'm giving you something to help with the pain as I get you out of here. Give these things a second to kick in." The man is right, because whatever Sam just swallowed seems to immediately dull the pain. In fact, it's not long before he hardly feels anything at all except a pair of sturdy hands, hoisting him up, dragging him slowly across the sharp gravel. "Hang tight, Sam. You're going to be okay," the man huffs as the terrain changes and the sky opens and before Sam can ask where he is, he closes his eyes and falls back to sleep.

chapter

22

IN THE LIBRARY, I pull my chair up to my computer station and set my tea on a coaster. With a deep breath, I open Amazon, scared to check my rank. My stomach sinks. I've dropped fifteen places in less than a week while Lola Likely from Missouri is number nine, the maniac. It's fine. I'm going to fix it. I'm going to fix everything.

I open my notebook and start at the top of my to-review list: one pair of TrailEnds waterproof hiking boots in ash blue.

> I just finished walking on muddy ground for two hours and suffered minimal seepage. However, I do not for the life of me understand why these things DO NOT HAVE A BELLOWS TONGUE.

I wish I'd taken pictures. *Three* times I had to stop to shake pebbles from my boot, slowing down the eight other people assigned to search the woods on Route 9, an area Sam would have passed on his way home from work the night of the storm. A team of lunch ladies from Brookside High School and I spent the afternoon roaming the woods, looking unsuccessfully for any sign of his car. Everyone seemed reluctant to be outside in the rain, and we would have given up an hour earlier if it wasn't for Eleanor Escobido, beloved head cook at Brookside High for thirty-five years. (I recognized her face as the one smiling from the back page of the yearbook every year, waving goodbye through the cafeteria door.) It was cold and dreary in the woods, and Mrs. E did her best to keep everyone's spirits up by sharing stories about Sam, the good-looking boy everyone seemed to like, his mother devastated after that no-good husband left for an underpants model.

I wanted to interrupt and tell stories of my own, of course. How Sam rented the downstairs office in my house, and how much I enjoyed listening to his sessions. And also how lonesome I feel, knowing I can no longer walk down the hall and hear his voice dispensing expert advice in that gentle tone of his. Of course, that hasn't stopped me from placing my ear to the cold metal vent twice in the last hour, wishing things were different.

I'm starting the review of the six-pack of Dab-A-Do! bingo daubers that arrived the other day ("Color is vibrant, exactly as pictured") when I detect the faint sound of a car driving up the hill. I pause my typing to listen. I'd guess it's the Pigeon returning home from a day of shopping with the #girlsquad she's always tagging on Instagram, but I saw her hopping on the exercise bike in her bedroom ten minutes ago. I click off the monitor, put on my robe, and go downstairs. The dark gray fog outside is pierced by two beams of light as a car crests the hill and approaches the bridge. I move away. The car turns into my driveway, and the engine quiets. I hold my breath, expecting to hear footsteps thudding up the porch steps, but whoever it is jogs by the porch, down the path toward Sam's office door. I pull back the curtains, and see the car—a green Mini Cooper with a white racing stripe—parked in my driveway.

The French Girl is here.

I move away from the window and go to the closet for my

coat, resigned to be the one to have to tell her: Dr. Statler has been missing for forty-eight hours and is not available to indulge her insecurities for the next forty-five minutes. I open the front door and step onto the porch in my slippers. Perhaps I should offer *my* services, volunteer to be the one to tell her the hard, cold truth: her promiscuity is the result of low self-esteem. I happen to have been reading up on the topic since her last appointment, and I've come to understand that her licentious behavior stems from insufficient supervision as a young girl, leading her to use sex for attention, which will ultimately provide her with nothing but empty relationships and increased feelings of low self-worth.

"Hello?" I call into the darkness. "Are you there?" I walk gingerly down the slippery path toward Sam's door. Silence. And then Sam's waiting room light clicks on.

I duck down. *She got inside.* I turn and dash up the stairs into the house. My hands tremble as I lock the front door and race through the kitchen, down the hall to Agatha Lawrence's study, where I drop to my knees in the corner of the room and pull back the smiley-face rug.

I hear the door to his office open, and then the click of the light switch. She's walking around, and—my god—she's opening the desk drawers. I don't know what to do. Call the police? Scream at her to go away? I know. I'll go down there and remind her that this is private property. But as I'm about to stand up, she begins to cry.

"Hi, it's me. I'm at Sam's office." She's quiet. "No, I came alone." She pauses, sniffs. "I found the key in one of his coat pockets." Something is off about her voice, and it takes a moment for me to realize what it is: her French accent is gone. "I just got here."

It hits me then. That voice. I *know* that voice. It's the same voice from that YouTube lecture—"Misery and Woman-hood," which I've now watched at least twenty times. My head swims. The French Girl isn't a French girl at all.

The French Girl is his wife.

chapter
23

"AND?" MADDIE ASKS NERVOUSLY. "How does it look?"

Annie slowly opens another drawer in Sam's desk, seeing a row of pens and the grid notebooks he likes. "Fine," she says. Books in place on his shelves, vacuum lines still in the carpet. "I was here the other day, and it looks the same."

Annie hears Maddie inhaling, and she pictures her cousin standing outside the restaurant she owns in Bordeaux, smoking the one cigarette she allows herself at the end of the night, after the last dinner serving. Maddie and Annie—eleven months apart—were often mistaken for sisters during the summers Annie and her parents spent in France, at the olive farm on which her mother grew up and where her aunt and uncle now live. Maddie and Annie kept a countdown calendar every year, ticking off the days until Annie would arrive and they'd share a room, even though there was space enough for Annie to have her own.

"I don't love you being there by yourself," Maddie says. "Can you go now?"

"Yes," Annie says.

"Promise?"

"Yes." Annie hangs up and scans the room. It's peaceful here. The view of the yard, covered in a carpet of fog. The

Palladian-blue walls that, Sam explained, were meant to evoke serenity. ("I thought that was your job," she told him when he showed her the swatch.) She walks to the table next to his chair, riffling through the papers on top. A copy of an academic article on Anna Freud and defense mechanisms. The latest issue of *In Touch Weekly*, a story of Kris Jenner's secret Mexican wedding on the cover.

She sinks onto the couch and stares at Sam's empty chair across from her, picturing him as he was a few days ago, when she appeared unexpectedly in his waiting room, pretending to be a patient.

She closes her eyes, remembering the look on his face. A woman in a pin-striped suit and red lips had left five minutes earlier, nodding hello to Annie on her way out. "Annie," Sam said, confused, seeing her in one of the white chairs, flipping through a *New Yorker*. "What are you doing here?" He came to embrace her. "I'm expecting a new patient any minute—"

"Annie?" she said in her best French accent. "You must have me confused for another patient, Dr. Statler. My name is Charlie. I emailed to set up an appointment."

"That was you?" Sam paused, and she watched him connect the dots. The email he'd gotten three days earlier from a Google account she'd created for the occasion; twenty-four-year-old Charlie, restless and unsure of her future. He'd written back, suggesting this time, and Annie had been wondering if he'd go along with it. Here, at his office; the most precarious iteration of "the chase" yet. "Yes, of course. *Charlie*," Sam said, as she'd hoped he would. "Forgive the mistake. Please come in. Sit wherever you'd like."

"Anywhere?" she'd said, stepping into his office and removing her jacket. "Even your chair?"

He played his part wonderfully—the principled, curious therapist, asking her questions about her background, speaking in his most professional tone. She savors the thought of it. Sitting on the couch, describing, in explicit detail, the experience of having sex with another man, knowing her perfume would linger, distracting him for the remainder of the day.

She'd planned to bring the game to a close the night of the storm, sending the text from Charlie the evening before, inviting him to her house. That afternoon, she stopped on the way home from teaching to buy two bottles of red wine and the ingredients for Sam's favorite meal: lasagna and a loaf of warm garlic bread. All day, she'd been anticipating opening the front door to him. She planned to pour them wine and light a fire, sit barefoot on the couch. Sam would start, explaining that having feelings for one's therapist was not wholly uncommon. She'd tell him he was smart and then go on to describe the things she's been imagining them doing together. She was starting dinner when his text arrived, right on time at 5:03, after his last patient left.

Hi Charlie. I've been thinking about your invitation.

And?

And I'll be there.

She remembers the minutes passing as she stood at the window, watching for his headlights. *He's making me wait.* That was her thought, initially. He was taking his time, lingering at the office, toying with her. But then it went on too long, and he wasn't answering her calls or texts, and she stopped believing this was part of the chase. Something had happened.

She hears the lightest creak of floorboards above her, bringing her back to Sam's office. Sam's landlord is home upstairs. *Too good to be true.* That's how Sam described finding this space.

He'd taken the train from New York to tour the available office spaces and had called her in the morning, dejected. A few hours later, he called again, giddy. Someone had stuck a flyer under his windshield, advertising an office space for rent. He'd gone to see it: the ground floor of a historic home a few minutes from downtown. It needed some work, Sam explained, but the owner was willing to let Sam design the space himself, create the office of his dreams. "It's fate," he said. "If we were looking for an indication that moving to Chestnut Hill was the right choice, we got it. It's going to be great, Annie. I know it will."

She takes a deep breath and closes the closet door before leaving his office, turning off the light behind her. In the waiting room, she sees that the rain has stopped. She's fishing in her bag for her car key when her phone rings from her back pocket. She scrambles for it, sees Crush's name on the screen.

"Hi," she says into the phone, nervous. "Any news?"

chapter
24

SOMEONE IS TUGGING AT Sam's forehead. "Can you feel this?"

Sam tries to nod, but he can't move his head. "Yes," he manages.

"Good. You're doing great. A few more minutes and we'll have you all stitched up. You hear me, Sam? You're going to be fine."

....

"Sam, sweetheart, hurry up. Your father's waiting."

It's the day of the baseball game and his mother is calling to him from the kitchen, where she's spreading the last of the mayonnaise on two slices of crustless wheat bread while Sam's father waits in the car with the engine running.

"Do you have your bat?" Margaret asks, wiping her hands on a dish towel and coming out into the hall to straighten Sam's cap.

Sam holds up the Easton Black Magic, the best baseball bat on the market, the bat he employed to hit six homers in one game against the Hawthorne Pirates, setting a new record in the under-fifteen division. It's two weeks before his fourteenth birthday, a day he expects will be the all-time greatest day of his life. September 6, 1995. Tickets to see Cal Ripken Jr. at Camden Yards, the day the Iron Man takes the field for his 2,131st consecutive game, breaking Lou Gehrig's record. Margaret is beaming. "Now don't come home until you get that thing signed by the man himself," she says. "Want to go through the plan again?"

"Yes," Sam tells her. "The line forms at the exit near section twelve. Dad and I are going to leave our seats at the top of the ninth inning to get in line." Sam shows her the map of Camden Yards she helped him draw, a thick red Sharpie line indicating the fastest route from their seats in section 72, in left field, to the door at the opposite side of the stadium, where Ripken was rumored to appear immediately after each game, spending exactly ten minutes signing autographs. "They allow one hundred people in. I'll be number one."

"Sam, come on!" Ted yells from the driveway.

"Go on, your dad's waiting for you." Margaret's eyes sparkle as she gives Sam a long hug, telling him to find a pay phone to call her from when they get to Baltimore, and then she hands him the brown paper bag with two ham sandwiches inside. "I put an extra Oreo in there for you," she says.

"I don't want to go," he says.

She cocks her head, confused. "What do you mean, you don't want to go? You've been waiting for this day your whole life."

"I know, but this is where he's going to meet the Talbots model, and then he's going to leave us. Please, don't make me go. Please!"

He opens his eyes.

It's warm and pitch-black, except for a thin strip of light coming from under a door across the room. It smells heavily antiseptic, and his back and head are throbbing.

He's in a hospital. St. Luke's. The hospital where he was born; where a doctor once splinted a broken pinkie finger quick enough to get him back to the field by the sixth inning; where he sat with his mother in a private office on the fifth floor, listening to Dr. Walter Alderman diagnose her with dementia.

"Pre-senile dementia, middle stage, to be more specific," Dr. Alderman is saying as Sam surrenders to the darkness again. "It generally hits people very young."

"Okay, so we got a name for it," Margaret says, straight-backed in her chair, a frozen smile on her face, as if Dr. Alderman has announced she won the blueberry pie contest at the fair again, six years running. "What does it mean?"

"It means you should expect to see more of the behaviors that prompted you to call me," he says. "Confusion. Disinhibition. The binge eating and progressive decline in socially appropriate behaviors." He pauses to look at Sam, the son who rented a car to be there for the appointment and is now sitting stone-faced and silent. "I think we should start planning on you getting some full-time care, Margaret."

Sam takes his mom's hand in the elevator, something he hasn't done since he was little. "Oh, don't worry," she says, patting his arm and fighting back tears. "I'm sure he's exaggerating. I'm not *that* bad."

In the parking lot they walk silently under a cloudless sky toward her blue Corolla, where she stops, unable to remember how to open the car door. She goes to her room when they get home, and he changes into his running clothes. He's out the door, up Leydecker Road to Albemarle, the most punishing route up the mountain. At the top, he screams out the rage, praying to anyone who will listen that he please not lose her too.

He wants to keep screaming, so loudly that Annie will open the door to this hospital room. He can feel her close by. Downstairs, near the Starbucks coffee kiosk, on her fifth cup of coffee, waiting for him to gain consciousness so she can take him home. But when the door opens, it's not Annie, it's the doctor again, checking the wound on his forehead and slipping more pills into his mouth, plunging him back toward a sleep devoid entirely of dreams.

chapter
25

SITTING ALONE AT MY kitchen table, I skim bleary-eyed through the last of the articles I printed from a variety of trusted websites.

In conclusion, most sexual health professionals agree that sexual role-playing, when done appropriately, can help happily married couples further deepen their connection, while being a powerful and enjoyable source of empowerment for both partners. The bored accountant can become a merciless despot. The harried stay-at-home mom can envision herself a seductress. The possibilities are endless.

I set the article aside and take a handful of Smartfood from the bowl next to me. Okay, fine, I get it. Dr. Annie Marie Potter was pretending to be a sultry twenty-four-year-old French girl in order to increase her confidence inside and outside the bedroom, while getting to know Sam in a more intimate manner. The accent. Her age. It was all part of it. This is, apparently, a *thing*, if Dr. Steven Perkins, resident sex expert at AskMen.com, can be trusted. According to his study, nearly

66 percent of all married couples have at some point in their relationship engaged in this type of behavior.

I scrape the last kernels from the bowl and shake my head, convinced I'll never understand the mating rituals of married couples. How could I? My longest romantic relationship was exactly zero days. (Actually, here's something I know: the fact that they chose to do this at his place of *business*, a room I imagine many of his patients consider sacred, is, in my opinion, taking it too far.) I wash the popcorn bowl and begin to water my collection of hanging plants when my alarm dings with a reminder. The news is about to begin.

In the living room, I aim the remote at the television, expecting *Eyewitness News* to open at 11:00 p.m. as it did at 6:00: with local meteorologist Irv Weinstein, standing outside the station, braving the cold. But it's not Irv, it's the blonde with the tight face, wearing a pink polyester dress. The words SEARCH FOR MISSING DOCTOR flash next to her head on the TV screen.

"We begin tonight with an update on Dr. Sam Statler, the local man who was reported missing two days ago. As the police spent the last forty-eight hours trying to piece together what may have happened to the missing psychologist, residents of Chestnut Hill came out in full force to attend a community-wide search this afternoon. For more on this, we'll go to Alex Mulligan, reporting live."

A different woman in a blue rain jacket fills the screen. "That's right, Natalie," she says. "Nearly one hundred volunteers spent this rainy Friday afternoon combing areas like the woods behind Brookside High School"—she jerks a thumb at the copse of trees in shadow behind her—"where Sam Statler was once a star athlete. Unfortunately, not one clue was uncovered to determine what may have happened to him the night of the storm, after he was reported leaving work around five p.m. As everyone knows, there was a travel advisory in effect, and conditions were considered extremely dangerous. I'm here with the man who spearheaded the search." The camera pans back, revealing a smiling Crush Andersen, the beefy former linebacker who was glad-handing everyone at the bowling alley today. "Crush, tell us what you were hoping to find in today's search," the reporter says, tipping the microphone toward him.

"Anything that might help solve this," Crush says. "But mostly his car. We had a great crowd come out today, despite the bad weather, and we were able to cover even more ground than we'd hoped to. If Stats had been in an accident on the way home, we would have found his car."

"Given the lack of clues, what do you think may have happened to your old friend?"

Crush shakes his head, apparently bewildered. "No idea. But we're going to keep the faith that he's okay, and this is all going to turn out fine."

The reporter offers a sympathetic nod before throwing the story back to Natalie at the news desk, who segues into a story about another round of layoffs at a local chicken plant. I click off the television and head upstairs to my room, trusting that Crush is right.

Sam's okay and this is all going to turn out fine.

chapter
26

SAM'S EYES FLUTTER OPEN.

The room is dark and he can't remember the last time he saw light. His body aches and something feels off. It takes him a moment but he gets it, eventually. It's his legs.

He can't move them.

He reaches down, and feels the rough surface of plaster against his fingers. His legs are in casts. Both of them. He tries to lift them, but he can't. Either the casts are too heavy or his legs are too weak. His only option is to go back to sleep and he doesn't know how much time has passed when he's jarred awake by the sound of the door opening, the flash of light from the hallway stinging his eyes. A figure appears next to his bed and he waits for a light to turn on but it doesn't.

"What happened to my legs?" he asks, his throat painfully dry.

"Oh, you're awake." The man's voice is familiar—it's the doctor who was here earlier, stitching up Sam's forehead. "You were in an accident."

"An accident?" Sam says. "How long have I been here?"

"Three days."

Three days. "Where's my wife?" he asks, as the doctor wraps a Velcro band around Sam's bicep.

"You were gotten to just in time," the doctor says, ignoring his question, pumping the band tighter around Sam's arm. "Pulled from the wreckage of that fancy car of yours. You'd think a man of your intelligence would have heeded the police chief's advice and stayed off the roads."

The Velcro rips apart and then a tube of light, like that of a flashlight, appears in the darkness, shining down on a medical chart in the doctor's hands. Sam's eyes adjust enough to make out the details of the room, cast mostly in shadow. He's in a single bed, under a patchwork quilt. There's a closet door and a small window, floral curtains drawn in front of it. Wallpaper—chartreuse yellow shapes feeding on themselves, like some sort of Escher-on-acid creation. Sam squeezes his eyes shut, realizing this isn't a hospital room. It's what looks to be someone's bedroom.

"Where am I?" Sam asks.

"I don't expect you would remember," the doctor says. "The brain's reasoning and cognitive processing centers tend to shut down during traumatic events. A way to help us forget the bad things." The doctor turns to face Sam and Sam sees that what he thought was a flashlight isn't a flashlight but a headlamp secured to the doctor's head. "What am I telling you this for though, right, Dr. Statler? You probably understand that better than anyone."

The doctor is beside him peering down at Sam over a pair of eyeglasses, and Sam can't pull his eyes away from the face, his brain slow to put the pieces into place.

The short hair, graying at the temples. The bright blue eyeglasses hiding the same pair of eyes Sam felt watching from a window upstairs, in the Lawrence House, every day when he arrived for work.

"Albert Bitterman?" Sam says, sure he's imagining it. "My landlord?"

Albert leans closer and smiles. "Hey there, heartbreaker."

"Albert," Sam says again, confused. "Why am I at your house?"

But Albert just shushes into Sam's ear and presses two pills into his mouth. "Go to sleep, Dr. Statler," he says, clicking off the headlamp as Sam floats toward the darkness. "You've been through a lot."

PART III

PART II

chapter
27

"ALBERT BITTERMAN?" THE UPS man shouts from the open door of his truck the next morning.

"Yes, that's me!" I call out, pulling on my jacket as I step onto the porch. He disappears to the back of the truck and then reemerges, pushing a hand trolley loaded with boxes. "You made good time," I say as he approaches. "Saw you on the GPS. A little blue dot leaving the pickup facility just after 8 a.m. Quite a feature on the redesigned website."

The man bangs the hand trolley backward up the steps. "It's creepy, if you ask me," he says and now I wish I'd said it first, because I completely agree. (In fact, if he were to check the recent comments on the UPS Facebook page, he'd see that an anonymous user (me) made the same observation twenty minutes ago: *Am I the only one who sees the danger in allowing any schmo with an internet connection to follow a truck carrying thousands of dollars of top-ranked medical equipment?*)

Rain drips from the brim of his UPS baseball hat as he draws a small machine from his back pocket, and I take stock of the inventory. One metal rolling cart with a retractable arm. One emergency crash cart with an attached trash can and side hooks for both a broom and a mop—one of the few pieces of equipment I've given a five-star rating to as a twenty-five-year employee of Home Health Angels, Inc.

"Looks like it's all here," I say.

"Want me to bring it in?"

"Inside the foyer is fine."

"Suit yourself." He backs the trolley inside and drops the boxes onto the floor. "Cool place," he says, looking into the living room. "Nice and bright."

"Can't take any credit," I say, as he hands me the computer to sign. "It was just as the last owner left it, and I haven't wanted to change a thing."

"Agatha, right? Nice lady."

I pause, the plastic pen hovering over the screen. "You knew her?"

"A little bit. Work a route long enough, you meet everyone at least once." He shoves the computer back into his pocket. "I was sorry to read that she'd died. You know she laid there for five days before she was found by the woman who cleaned her house?"

"It was a man," I say.

"Sorry?"

"The person who found her. It was a man."

"Is that right?" He shrugs. "I heard it was the housekeeper, so I assumed it was a woman. Anyway." He pulls down his hat and tucks into his collar as he steps onto the cold porch. "Have a good one."

I wait for his taillights to recede over the hill before going into the kitchen for the blue Home Health Angels apron I couldn't bear to throw away after losing my job. I tie it around my waist and fill the pocket with my supplies—a tube of Neosporin, a fresh bandage, and a pair of latex gloves. I head down the hall, insert the key quietly into the lock, and flick the light switch when I enter. Sam's stirring in his bed and murmuring his wife's name. I close the door and go to his side, my back straight, my heart full, feeling more useful than I have in a long time.

chapter

28

ANNIE PARKS BETWEEN TWO police cruisers and pulls up her hood, sick to death of the rain. John Gently is behind the desk when she steps into the waiting room.

"Is Chief Sheehy here?"

Gently picks up the phone and presses a button. "You hear from your husband yet?" he asks.

"Not yet."

"Hello, Chief," he says into the phone, adding some heft to his voice. "That doctor's wife is here. She wants to talk to you." He nods twice and hangs up. "Last door on the right."

Franklin Sheehy is sitting behind his desk, his sleeves rolled up, the buttons of his shirt straining against his stomach. "Come right in, Mrs. Statler," he says, waving her inside.

"It's Potter," she corrects him.

"Sorry, I keep forgetting. Want some coffee? It's not the fancy stuff you're probably used to, but it's hot."

"I'd do a line of coffee grounds if you offered," Annie says. "I've hardly slept in three days."

Sheehy presses a button on the desk phone. "Two coffees, Gently," he says. "Milk and sugar on the side." He hangs up. "He hates when I do that."

"I brought you a few more photographs of Sam," Annie

says, digging in her bag for them. She slides them across the desk—three photos, taken the day they were married in their new backyard by a local yoga instructor. Maddie was on Face-Time, serving as Annie's maid of honor from the phone screen, propped on a branch of the tree they stood under. Annie had printed these photos at the CVS and given them to Sam, suggesting he send them to his father. Instead he shoved them into a kitchen drawer and forgot about them.

"I also printed the specs for Sam's car, his exact make and model," she says, fighting the urge to use her nickname for the car: Jasper, the douchiest name she could think of.

She had been upstairs in their apartment, packing for the move to the prairie, when he called and told her to look out the window, like some sort of John Hughes movie. He was parked in front of a fire hydrant, his face lit up. "I bought a Lexus," he said into the phone.

"I see that." A Lexus 350, with leather interior and automatic ignition. He used to *love* doing that: standing in the living room and pressing the button, watching the car light up and the engine start. ("Look at you," Annie said the first time she saw him do this. "Proud as a southern dad at a purity ball.")

The door is nudged open, and John Gently enters, two paper cups of coffee balanced in his left palm, milk and sugar in the right. "Here you go, Chief," he says, extending the cups toward them, spilling a few drops on the desk. He makes a show of pulling the door firmly shut behind him as he leaves.

Annie watches Sheehy comb through the sugar packets until he gets to the Splenda. "Is there any news at all on Sam, or his car?"

"Gently!" Sheehy yells.

The door flies open, as if he'd been standing in the hallway, listening. "Mrs. Statler would like an update on the investigation."

"Yes, sir." John Gently steps into the room. "We sent an APB out on the car three nights ago, immediately after you reported him missing. A silver Lexus 350 with automatic ignition and leather seating. A very nice machine. We also contacted the thruway department and area agencies with license plate readers. If he passed any of those, we can get his route of travel. We are now going through footage from public and private video cameras throughout the area. If his car's out there, we'll find it."

"And if he were in an accident?" Annie asks.

Sheehy shakes his head. "Truth be told, Mrs. Statler, that's unlikely. It's been seventy-two hours, and there's been no report of any accidents. My men have traveled the route from Sam's office to your house a few times now. We would have found his car." He offers a downcast smile, doing his best to appear sympathetic. "I know you're worried, but rest assured we're doing everything we can. We'll call you the minute we hear anything. But the thing you can do, Mrs. Statler, is try to manage those nerves."

"I'll do my best," she says, standing up. "And maybe in return you can try to manage my name. It's Potter."

chapter
29

SAM FEELS THE FAINT flutter of wings against his cheek and opens his eyes. The moths fade to black and it's him again. Albert Bitterman, his landlord, standing at the doorway, a blue apron tied at his waist. "Hey there, heartbreaker," Albert says, pushing a medical cart into the room. "How are you feeling?"

"Confused," Sam says, trying to sit up. "Why am I at your house?" *And why do you have a medical cart?*

"I've told you already," Albert says. "You had an accident." He parks the cart at the foot of Sam's bed and snaps on a pair of blue latex gloves. "A tree came down as you pulled out of the driveway. Lucky for you, I saw the whole thing from my porch. I ran out as quick as I could."

"Why am I not at the hospital—"

"Seems you shattered both of your legs," Albert says, cutting him off. "Don't worry, though. I fixed them all up. And I'm giving you something to manage the pain."

The idea seems strange, and yet oddly familiar—*two broken legs, a steady stream of pills*—but he can't pinpoint why. "Annie," he says. "I need to call Annie, my wife. Can I use your phone?"

But Albert ignores him and takes a bottle of pills from the pocket of his apron.

"No," Sam says. "No more pills. I need to call Annie."

Sam tries to turn his face away, but Albert is gripping Sam's chin and forcing three pills into his mouth, holding Sam's jaw closed with a shaky hand, long enough for the pills to dissolve. The taste is bad, Buckley's Mixture bad, the stuff his mom used to give him when he had a sore throat. "It tastes awful. And it works" is Buckley's actual slogan, printed right there on the box, but even that tastes a million times better than these pills, which work impressively quickly, melting his body, summoning the moths, reducing reality to two facts: his head doesn't hurt anymore, and he is just so very fucked.

chapter
30

"HANG ON, PROFESSOR POTTER," the kid sauntering down the center aisle calls to Annie the following day. "Nice job today," he says, throwing her a smile as she hands him the paper she'd finished grading this morning, barely in time for class, in which he twice put the word "patriarchy" in quotes. "You're almost starting to convince me I should question the assumptions I make when I read. *Almost.*"

"Thanks, Brett," Annie says.

His face reddens. "My name's Jonathan."

I know your name's Jonathan—you're one of the guys who signed up for this class solely because most of the students are women—but Brett is a prick's name, and you seem like a prick. "Sorry," Annie says. "Have a good day."

She collects her notes and waits for the last students to leave before turning off the lights, unsure how she survived that class. Forty-five minutes in front of a packed auditorium of sleep-deprived college kids, exploring how male authors describe female characters in six works of popular fiction, beginning with F. Scott Fitzgerald's *Tender Is the Night.* "'Her body hovered delicately on the last edge of childhood,'" she read out loud from the front of the room, hoping the students didn't notice the way the book trembled in her hand. "'She was almost eighteen, nearly complete, but the dew was still on her.'" She had gone back and forth a hundred times about canceling the class, but decided this morning not to. She's going to lose her mind at home, waiting to hear his key in the lock.

She hurries across the quad to the department building, simple and run-down, nothing like Columbia. But this is what she wanted, what she and Sam both wanted: a simpler life. She'd been carrying a heavy load since getting her degree at Cornell, where she stayed on to teach. She was finishing up her next stint, a two-year gig at Columbia, when she met Sam, contemplating what was next. She'd been offered tenure track at Utah State with little expectation to publish, but she turned it down and accepted a visiting scholar position here, at a tiny liberal arts college in upstate New York, following the first man she ever loved.

There's a small crowd waiting for the elevator, and she decides to take the stairs to her office on the third floor. She's unlocking the door when Elisabeth Mitchell, the dean of the department, steps out of her office three doors down.

"Annie," she says. "What are you doing here?"

"I have office hours," Annie says.

"I know, I mean . . ." Dr. Mitchell hesitates. "I saw the article about Sam."

"Oh, that," Annie says.

"You don't need to be here," Dr. Mitchell says. "You could have—"

"My dad was from a long line of industrious Irish Catholics," Annie says. "I've learned to work through my pain."

"Well, if you need some time . . ."

"Thank you," Annie says, stepping into her office, keeping her door slightly ajar as she checks the clock. One hour. She can do this. She sits at the desk and takes out the sandwich she bought before class, at the café in the student union. A pressed turkey with Swiss cheese and extra jalapeños, the same sandwich she gets before office hours each week. It's a habit of hers, ordering the same thing again and again. It drives Sam crazy. Back in New York, when they first started dating, they'd meet at the same restaurant at least twice a week: Frankies 457, a block away from her apartment. Sam would stare at her, incredulous, as she placed the same order, every time—sausage cavatelli and a green salad.

She can picture the bewildered expression on his face. "You're not going to try *anything* else?"

"I know what I like, and I'm okay asking for it," she told him. "Get used to it."

But today the sight of the sandwich turns her stomach, and she drops it into the trash can and digs for her phone in her bag. She opens FaceTime and calls Maddie, who answers right away. Her brown curls are pulled into a bun, and she's wearing earphones.

"What are you doing?" Annie asks.

"About to go for a jog," Maddie says, and just the sound of her voice calms Annie's nerves.

"You hate jogging."

"I know I do, but everyone at the restaurant's doing some stupid 5K, and— Wait." Maddie stops walking. "What happened? I can tell by your face."

Annie stands and shuts her office door. "Some bills came for Sam," she whispers.

"What do you mean, *bills*?" Maddie asks.

"Credit cards." The first arrived yesterday: Chase Sapphire Preferred, maxed to its credit limit of $75,000. She was stunned, but tried not to read too much into it. The move, the new house—she knew things were adding up. But when she checked the mailbox earlier today, she found another: Capital One, with a $35,000 balance.

"What the hell did he buy?" Maddie asks.

"What *didn't* he buy is more like it." It's ridiculous, what he spent on things. She sat in her car in the faculty parking lot, going through the list. Three hundred for running shoes. Five grand for a rug for his office. Six coffee cups at $34 apiece.

"Did you know he had these cards?" Maddie asks Annie.

"No, but Sam's a forty-year-old man. He's going to have credit cards. We haven't joined our money." She paces the office, eight steps back and forth, then collapses in the chair, hit by a sudden wave of exhaustion. "I guess this explains why he was so distracted."

"Distracted?" Maddie says. "You didn't tell me that."

"We moved to a new town and he's starting a practice while his mother deteriorates," Annie says, defensively. "It would have been weirder if he *wasn't* distracted."

"Annie, do you think—" Maddie stops, her face pinched.

"What?" Annie says.

"I don't know. It's weird he didn't tell you this."

Annie swallows a rising lump in her throat. "I know it is," she manages, hearing steps in the hallway outside. She waits, and they pass by. "I have to go," she says, composing herself. "I'm at work. I'll call you later." She hangs up, opens her door a few inches, and returns to her desk, where she opens one of the books she'd assigned for the next class. It's no use: thirty seconds later she grabs her bag from the floor, reaches inside for the bills, and scans the items again. "Sam, you idiot," she whispers. "Seven hundred dollars on steak knives?"

"Dr. Potter?" A student is standing at the door. Annie hunts for her name. "Sorry, the door was open."

"It's fine, Clara," Annie says. "Come in."

"Are you sure?" She steps inside as Annie slips the bills back into her bag. "Because I got a job offer and could use some advice."

"Of course," Annie says, zipping the bag shut. "Have a seat, let's talk."

chapter
31

THE LIGHT IS ON when Sam wakes up, the room is quiet around him. He holds his breath and listens for Albert Bitterman.

"Albert Bitterman *Jr.*, to be exact. The son my father always wanted." That's what Albert said to Sam, the day they met. He's been combing what's left of his memory for what he knows about this guy and it came back to him earlier—their first meeting. Annie was in New York, finishing the last two weeks of her fellowship, and Sam called her from Chestnut Hill, where he'd spent the morning touring the terrible selection of available offices for rent, resigned to settling on something subpar. And then, like magic, he stopped at the bank and came out to find the flyer on his windshield. "Office space available in historic home, perfect for a quiet professional." He couldn't believe his luck.

Albert was standing on the front porch when Sam pulled into the driveway twenty minutes later, excited to show him the space for rent downstairs. "It's got good bones, but it needs a little work," he said, leading Sam down a path along the front of the house. "You're welcome to design it the way you want it. I wouldn't have the foggiest idea how to do that." He unlocked a door and led Sam inside. The room was large and open, empty other than a stack of boxes along the wall. "All this space, it would be nice to do it right."

Sam looks around, guessing he's in a room on the first floor of Albert's house, the one down a hallway from the kitchen, and just above his office. Albert had given him a tour of his house the day Sam came inside to check a leaky faucet. It was part of their deal, a deal Sam never wanted: free rent in exchange for helping with odd jobs—raking leaves, changing lightbulbs, nothing too strenuous, Albert assured him. Sam tried several times to refuse, telling Albert he'd prefer to pay rent, but Albert insisted, said Sam would be doing him a favor.

Strange. That's the word Annie used when Sam told her about the unbelievable offer: a raw space at the garden level of a Victorian mansion, which he could design himself. "It's not *strange*," Sam said. "It's called being nice. It's what we do in the country. Don't worry, you'll get used to it."

And it *was* nice: Albert told him to spare no expense, and so he didn't. Radiant heat under the floors. Central air. A floor-to-ceiling window offering a calming view of the backyard. The office was perfect, far better than anything he'd ever dreamed. But then Albert was always there, lingering. Drinking his tea on the porch in the morning when Sam arrived. Stepping out to check the mail as Sam was leaving for lunch. Appearing with that goddamn tray of drinks at the end of the day. *Hey there, heartbreaker, how was your day?* Sam felt sorry for the guy. He was lonely up here, with nothing to do all day.

"Hello?" Sam calls out. "Albert? I need to make a phone call."

Silence.

He looks at the door to the hall, gauging the distance. Seven feet, eight at the most. He can manage that. He ran the fastest mile on his cross-country team; surely he has it in him to get himself from this bed to that door, and then out to wherever Albert Bitterman keeps the heavy, black cordless phone someone like him probably has.

Of course Sam can do that.

He takes a deep breath and throws off the blanket, horrified by the sight of his legs. The casts are a disaster, one of his feet twice the size of the other. He puts that concern—along with the question of how, exactly, his landlord has either the supplies or the wherewithal to apply casts to his broken legs—aside for the moment and considers his options for getting out of the bed. Shimmying? Rolling? He chooses a marriage of the two: shimmying to the edge of the mattress and then attempting a gentle roll onto the floor.

"Fuuuuuucccccckkkkkkkk," he moans as quietly as he can as his chest hits the floor hard, his casts close behind. He rests his throbbing forehead against the pine floorboards and breathes through the pain, waiting for the sound of Albert's footsteps racing frantically down the hall.

But it's quiet.

He hoists himself onto his elbows and drags himself toward the door, his legs like boulders attached to his hips. He's sweat-soaked and out of breath when he gets there, but he does it—he reaches the door and grabs for the knob.

No, that can't be right.

It's locked.

He scoots closer and pulls himself up to sit. Gripping the knob with both hands, he rattles the door, praying for this to be a dream. He looks around. The window. He drops to his belly once more and makes his way back across the room. It's all going to be fine. He'll open the curtains, and Sidney Pigeon will be there at the end of the driveway like she always is, with that prizewinning cocker spaniel. She'll come unlock the door, and Sam will say hello and elbow-walk right past her, out the door, over the bridge and straight to the bakery, where the nice old woman who works mornings will give him two Tylenol for his headache and let him use her phone to call Annie.

He reaches the window and catches his breath before hoisting himself back into a seated position and pulling open the curtain. He freezes. The window is boarded over with a sheet of plywood, nailed into the wall on either side of the window, letting in not an ounce of light.

I'm locked in a room with two broken legs. And then it hits him. *Misery.*

The memory is clear. The front porch, the leaves turning gold. Albert came out and asked what he was reading. Sam showed him the cover. *It's totally deranged.*

His skin prickles with heat, and he's quite sure he's going to throw up, but then something else happens. He starts laughing. A giggle at first, and then the dam breaks and he's laughing so hard he can't breathe. Textbook defense mechanism: using laughter as a way to ward off overwhelming anxiety. Of course the whole thing is made even more absurd by that bright yellow smiley-face rug staring at him from the corner of the room.

"Oh yeah, rug?" he says through the laughter. "You think this is funny?" He's still laughing as the panic rises further, the gravity of the situation dawning on him. He stops laughing and cocks his head. He could have sworn he heard the sound of a car engine, but it's quiet. He must have been imagining it. But wait, no, there it is: a car door slamming. Someone is here.

Thank god. He was right. It *is* all going to be fine. Albert's not some crazy, obsessed woman. In fact, at this very moment he's outside, in the driveway, meeting the ambulance that has taken inexplicably long to arrive. He'll show the paramedics the way to this room, offering a perfectly good explanation for why the door is locked and there's plywood covering the window. Annie is probably here, too, yelling at everyone to hurry up, insisting on being the first one inside. They'll all think it's sweet, but the truth is, she's got some things she needs to get off her chest. *Four days, and you couldn't find a phone to call me? Really, dickbrain?*

He waits for the sound of footsteps in the hall, but instead he hears the unmistakable slam of his office door. That fucking door, he thinks, the one that Albert kept promising he'd fix, interrupting his sessions every time someone came or went. Sam's head is pounding, and he's doing his best to make sense of why (1) the paramedics are going to his office, when clearly he's here, in a bedroom upstairs, and (2) how they got in when he has the only key, when the strangest thing happens.

The happy-face rug starts talking to him.

"Do I call you Doctor?" the rug asks. It has a man's voice.

"What?" Sam says.

"Is it Dr. Keyworth?" the rug says.

The voice is familiar. "No," Sam replies. "It's Dr. Statler." The thought occurs to him that maybe he didn't survive the car accident. Maybe, in fact, he's dead and discovering that the afterlife looks exactly like that time he did magic mushrooms in Joey Amblin's backyard the summer of 1999.

"What happened to your hand?" the rug asks.

Sam holds up his hand.

"I cut it putting down a glass." Those words didn't come

from Sam, and he's losing track of who's talking, distracted by the strange familiarity of the rug's voice. And not only that, but in the pauses in the conversation, Sam makes out what he's pretty sure is the sound of someone eating popcorn.

"Who are you?" Sam whispers to the rug, inching closer.

"Dr. Keyworth, I'm the deputy White House chief of staff," the rug says.

"What?" Sam's confused. The voice. Where does he know that voice?

"I oversee eleven hundred White House employees," the rug says. "I answer directly to Leo McGarry and the president of the United States. Do you think you're talking to the paper-boy?"

"The paperboy?" Sam asks the smiley face, lifting the rug and holding it at eye level. Something metal glints on the floor. A vent. He places his ear to it, just in time to catch the unmis-takable whoop of Albert Bitterman's laughter, followed by the sweeping opening notes of the best theme song in television history.

The West Wing.

Albert's downstairs in Sam's office, watching *The West Wing*—"Noël," season 2, episode 10, to be exact—and Sam can hear every word of it through this vent in the floor. It hap-pens again: Sam starts laughing. A big belly laugh this time, as it all comes together: Albert was up here, listening to the ther-apy sessions. Well, by god, of course he was, Sam thinks, tears rolling down his cheeks. He *knew* it; that deeply unconscious sense of Albert above him suddenly becomes conscious—an energy upstairs, moving in and out of this room above him, Albert's rhythm in tune with his.

Sam's laughing so hard that he almost misses the commotion downstairs—Albert's voice through the vent ("My god, Sam, is that you?"), the sound of Sam's office door slamming again. And not only is Sam laughing, he's also taking a great deal of pleasure in beating the absolute crap out of the happy-face rug—a truly flimsy piece of shit—and the rug is in tatters by the time Albert is standing in the doorway, a terrified look in his eyes, a bag of Smartfood popcorn in his hands.

"You were up here listening to me," Sam says.

"What? No—" Albert says.

He stops laughing as the memory of that night returns, clear as day. The storm was building, and Sam closed the door to his office, picturing Annie. She'd be waiting at home for him, stirring something on the stove, wine uncorked on the counter. Albert was on his porch, holding a tray of drinks. Sam pretended not to see him as he ran to his car.

He got into his car and realized he didn't have his keys. He'd left them on the top of his desk.

The memory of what happened next is surprisingly vibrant, even the small details, like running back through the rain to his office, and the band of sweat on Albert's lip when he appeared in the waiting room, rain dripping from his hair, a shovel gripped in his hands. The wild look on Albert's face as he charged toward Sam, the shovel raised over his head.

A wave of fear engulfs Sam. "Please, let me call my wife."

"I'm sorry, Sam, but I can't do that." Albert's expression is vacant and he stands still in the doorway.

"What do you mean? Of course you can," Sam pleads. "Go get your phone."

"No, Sam, I can't."

"Why, Albert?" Sam feels a sob rising in his chest. "Why are you keeping me here?"

"*Keeping* you here?" Albert says, looking as if he'd been slapped. "I'm not *keeping* you here, Sam. I'm taking care of you."

"But I don't want you to take care of me," Sam whispers. "I want to go home."

"Well, then, you should have had that *drink*," Albert spits. "The specialty cocktail I made you. You didn't have to be so rude."

"The . . . *drink*?" Sam stammers. "This is all because of a drink?"

Albert makes a show of taking a deep breath. "No, Sam, this isn't all because of a *drink*. It's because you need help, and I'm the only one who can help you." He walks into the room and picks up the tattered rug before exiting the room and slamming the door behind him. Sam waits until he hears the lock click into place, and then he does something he hasn't done since the day his dad left. He allows himself to cry.

chapter
32

THE PIGEON'S HAVING A party.

I catch glimpses of it from my upstairs window. Six couples, one inconsiderate enough to park on the Pigeon's lawn. Dinner Club, they call it. A bunch of former cheerleaders from Brookside High who take turns hosting every few weeks. Tonight it's the Pigeon's turn, and Drew is making steak. He started the marinade at two o'clock while the Pigeon snapped a photograph to post on Instagram, letting everyone know how #grateful she is to have a hubby that cooks.

The lights are on inside, everyone where they're supposed to be: the men braving the cold rain at the grill out back, the women in the kitchen, sharing guacamole and red wine, probably chitchatting about the article in the paper this morning: "Police at a Loss for Clues in Case of Chestnut Hill Doctor Missing for Four Days."

Young Harriet Eager is starting to make a name for herself, staying on top of the story (not to mention the front page).

Four days into the search for the local psychologist, detectives on the case have exhausted all means to locate Sam Statler. "All that's left at this point is to appeal to the public for any information they can provide," said Chief of Police Franklin Sheehy.

The article was shared dozens of times on Facebook, where some chubby guy named Timmy Hopper had the nerve to make a joke about Sam's reputation back in high school— "Anyone check Sheila Demollino's basement?"—garnering six likes the last time I checked.

A light turns on upstairs at the Pigeon's house. The second-to-last window, the middle boy's room. I check the time. Five forty-six p.m., right on schedule. Fourteen years old and sneaking upstairs every evening, two long streams of smoke out the window, just to get through an evening with his family. The lighter flashes on, illuminating his face, as my oven timer beeps downstairs. I hang the binoculars on their hook and head grudgingly down to the kitchen, hoping Sam will still be asleep when I bring his dinner.

He's asking to go home. I've been avoiding him since yesterday, when I walked in to find him out of bed. I've been puttering around upstairs, mentally compiling my latest list.

Reasons why Sam can't go home: A list
1. Because I *want* to take care of him. It's what you do for the people close to you: you tend to them when they're in need. If anyone is going to understand that, it's the guy who moved home to take care of his mom.
2. Look at all I've done for him. A top-rated mattress, clean sheets daily, fresh flowers to brighten the room, because—
3. If there's one person who understands exactly what a home-bound patient needs to be at their best, it's me, Albert

Bitterman Jr., twenty-five-year employee of Home Health Angels, employee of the month *three* times.

In the kitchen, the Egg Beaters casserole looks done and I scoop a perfect square of it onto a plate, on top of the meat. I set the plate on the cart with a clean set of plastic flatware, and head down the hall. Sam's breathing is raspy when I unlock the door and peek my head inside. Thank god, he's asleep. I take the tray from the cart and quietly set it on the nightstand, then pause at the foot of his bed to admire my work.

Only once have I applied a cast to a broken bone: twenty-five years ago, during the six-week (unpaid) hospital internship required to become a certified Home Health Angel. A doctor allowed me to wrap a hairline fracture in a nine-year-old's wrist. That was nothing compared to what I had here—*two* legs in need of mending, compound fractures in each one, as far as I can tell—and while I'm not typically one to brag, this was a five-star job.

"Something smells good." I freeze. He's awake. "What is it?"

"Steak and eggs," I say, clearing my throat.

"Steak and eggs?" Sam props himself up on his elbows, sleepy-eyed, his hair tousled. "What's the occasion?"

"A little extra protein in the evening is helpful when you're trying to rebuild your strength," I say, heading toward the door. "I hope you like it."

"Albert?" I pause. "You want to hang out for a while?"

I turn back around. "Hang out?"

"I'm going a little stir-crazy," he says. "I could use the company. Unless you're in the middle of something."

"No," I say, clearing my throat again, and smoothing my apron. "I have a few minutes."

"Excellent." Sam winces as he reaches for the tray, and I hurry to help him. "Thanks," he says as I adjust his pillows. "Much better."

There's no place to sit other than his bed, so I stand in the middle of the room as Sam cuts into his meat and takes a bite. "Very good," he says.

"Salisbury steak," I say. "Ground beef, ketchup, and half a can of condensed onion soup."

"Soup. Was wondering what that taste was."

"It's Linda's recipe," I say.

"She a girlfriend?"

I laugh out loud. "Are you crazy? No, she's not a girlfriend. She's quite a few years older and not my type." Sam takes a bite of eggs and watches me. "Linda Pennypiece," I continue. "Great name, right? We worked together, back in Albany." Sam stays quiet, chewing. "Her son Hank used to bring her this meal every Friday." Hank, the meathead. He'd show up in that pickup truck at lunchtime, two thick slices of Salisbury steak and a mound of instant mashed potatoes plastic-wrapped on a Chinet plate. He'd stay to watch her eat and then take the plate home, as if he planned to reuse it.

"Well, tell her she's a good cook," Sam says, taking another bite of steak.

"I can't," I blurt out. "We're no longer on speaking terms." I nearly called her two days ago. It was her birthday, and I saw on the Home Health Angels website that all the girls in the office had a party for her—Madge, Rhonda, Mariposa, posing in birthday hats next to the cake. I considered calling to wish her happy birthday but decided against it, too afraid that ignorant son of hers would get wind of it.

"What happened?" Sam asks.

"People grow apart," I say, waving my hand to dismiss the topic. "Simple fact of life."

"That's the truth," Sam says, taking another bite of eggs. "So, who's your favorite?"

"My favorite?"

"Yeah, of my patients. Who do you like the best?"

"Who do I—"

"Actually, no. Reverse that. What I *really* want to know is who you liked the least."

I'm dumbfounded. "You're not mad at me?"

He shrugs. "I've been giving it some thought, and while I'm not sure my patients would love the idea of you up here, listening to their sessions, the truth is, if I was in your situation, I'd do the same thing."

"You *would*?"

"Name a person who wouldn't. Isn't the desire to see inside people's lives the entire premise of social media?" He takes a bite, chews. "Least favorite."

"Well," I say carefully, "if you'd asked me a few weeks ago, I would have one hundred percent said Skinny Jeans."

Sam looks confused. "Who?"

"Sorry," I say, embarrassed. "I mean Christopher Zucker. I didn't know who David Foster Wallace was, so I looked him up. Literary hero to men? Are you kidding me? He stalked and abused his wife, and what, nobody cares?"

"I know," Sam says. "It's weird."

"I can't tell you how hard it was sometimes, keeping my mouth shut up here."

"I can only imagine," he says. "But then something changed your mind . . ."

"I happened to see him recently, having lunch with his

girlfriend." It wasn't *entirely* coincidental, of course. Rather, I found him under the About Me page on his company's website, which led me to his Instagram account, which then led me to the model girlfriend's, populated almost entirely with photographs she took of herself (I'm aware they're called selfies, a word I refuse to use). It was here that she announced she was meeting Christopher for a date—#datewiththeboy #chestnutcafe—posing in six different outfits, asking everyone to help her decide what to wear. She chose the clingy black jumpsuit, not my first choice.

"He seemed vulnerable," I tell Sam. "Something in his expression when he looked at her. Like he was forcing himself to endure her." I know I should stop, but I can't help myself. "He's been doing this his whole life. Feeling the pressure to date the most beautiful girl in the room. He needs to be told that this is a hopeless endeavor. Did you know that research shows that when two good-looking people get together, they have a high chance of a rocky marriage? Researchers at Harvard did a study on it."

"Is that right?"

"You want to see the study?"

"You have it?"

"Yeah, hang on."

In the library, I locate the purple binder where I've been filing the notes I keep on our patients. I finger through the tabs until I get to Christopher's. "Look," I say, returning to the room and handing Sam the six-page study. "They looked at the top twenty actresses on IMDb and found that a high percentage had unhappy marriages. And those considered to be the best-looking guys in high school had higher rates of divorce than the average guys."

"This is fascinating," he murmurs.

"I knew you'd get it," I say. "I think this all has to do with Christopher's father."

Sam lifts an eyebrow. "How so?"

"Move over," I say, perching at the foot of his bed. He slides his casts to the side, making room for me. "Christopher's father was insecure and vain, which he played out by scrutinizing his son's physicality," I say. "Christopher then grows up and exclusively dates women who are very attractive, but who he finds shallow and uninteresting. Why does he continue to do this? Because they validate the idea that he's physically attractive, and therefore valuable in the eyes of his father."

"Nice work, Albert. That's exactly right."

I open my eyes wide. "It *is*?"

"Yes. You're astute. It's where I was leading Christopher, to that understanding about his father."

"Wow." I'm proud of myself, and confused. "Why didn't you save time and tell him that's what was happening with him?"

"He had to get there himself, and that's delicate," Sam says, handing me the study and returning to his meal. "It takes time. Like a good story."

"Well, you had *me* hooked from the first page," I say. "In fact, I learned a lot from you."

"Oh?"

I cross my legs, nervous. "Yes, about how we're shaped by our childhood. I knew that, I suppose, but the way you talked about it—and not just downstairs, but in the papers you've published, your lectures. Let's just say you've opened my eyes in a new way."

Sam stops chewing and something changes in his expression. "When did you see my lectures?"

My face flames. "I googled you, after you came to see the space," I say, stretching the truth a bit. "Needed to make sure you weren't on the Most Wanted list. I saw the two lectures you gave, on YouTube. I was impressed."

He smiles and finishes his steak. "Well, that's nice of you to say." He sets his napkin next to his empty plate. "And thank you for dinner. It was delicious."

I stand, reluctant to leave, and take the tray from his lap. "You comfortable?" I ask, setting it on the cart. "You like your room?"

"Very much," he says, settling back on his pillows. "Except for that wallpaper. I don't know what kind of drugs the designer was on, but man, that shade of yellow is giving me a headache." I fish the pills from the pocket of my blue apron. Sam's right. The wallpaper is quite dismal. I should have recognized that myself. "And one more thing Albert?" Sam says, as I count out two pills. "I'm sorry for how I acted the other night."

I pause. "You're what?"

"I'm sorry. You've been good to me, and you're right, I was rude to you. I'm working on being a good guy, and I don't always succeed. I'm sorry if I hurt your feelings."

"It's . . . it's okay," I stammer.

"No, it's not. And it's permissible to have feelings about what I did. I can handle it."

I hesitate. "I made a specialty cocktail for you," I say. "It took nearly the whole morning to perfect it."

"And not only did I reject it," Sam says, "I was also rude about it."

"The look on your face," I say. "It was just like my father."

"I'm sorry, Albert. I hope you know that."

"It's fine, Dr. Statler. Thank you for saying so."

"And if it's okay . . ." Sam extends his hand. "I can do it myself."

"Of course," I say, handing Sam the pills. He drops them into his mouth and sinks into the pillows as I push the cart toward the door, feeling something I haven't felt since moving into this house.

Happiness.

chapter
33

ANNIE STARES AT THE timer on the oven display, her chin resting in her hand, counting along with it. *Nineteen. Eighteen. Seventeen.*

She drops the Visa bill on top of the others—four now, the latest one arriving today—and gets the oven mitts. She checks under the foil and then quiets the timer. A honk sounds from the driveway. She snaps the oven door closed and goes to the living room window.

"Evening, Mrs. Statler," Franklin Sheehy calls from the driveway as she steps out onto the porch in her bare feet.

"What happened?" she asks, too anxious to bother correcting him. "Did you find something?"

Sheehy gives a curt shake of his head. "No, ma'am. On my way home, and thought I'd check in and see how you're doing." The motion light on the porch clicks off, casting them in shadow. "I imagine things can feel a little desolate out here."

"That's nice of you," she says, removing the oven mitts. "You want to come in?"

He nods and mounts the stairs. "Nice place you got," he says, stepping into the living room and looking around at the beamed, vaulted ceiling and massive stone fireplace along the far wall. "I bet they don't have houses like this in the city."

"No, they don't," she says, conjuring the last place they lived—a one-bedroom apartment off Washington Square that Sam was provided as a member of the NYU faculty, which he'd invited her to move into three weeks after they met. They'd just finished eating dinner when he left the room, returning with a cheap plastic shopping bag with an "I love NY" logo.

"What is this?" she asked when he set it on the table in front of her.

"If I wanted you to know what it was when I handed it to you, Annie, I wouldn't have wrapped it."

"Not to get technical, but I don't think this is considered wrapping."

"Okay, Martha Stewart. Just open it."

Inside were two hand towels, the fabric so cheap it glowed. "His" was embroidered on the blue one, "Hers" on the pink. "I don't get it," she said.

"They're his-and-hers towels. Like for a bathroom."

"Thank you for that explanation," she said. "I mean, why are you giving me these hideous towels?"

He was starting to blush. "Is it too clever?"

"Is *what* too clever?"

"These *towels*," he said, exasperated. "You know, his-and-hers towels? Like people who live together have in their bathroom?"

"Wait," she said. "Are you asking me to move in with you?"

"Yes," he said. "And so far I appear to be doing a truly bang-up job of it."

She laughed out loud. "That's sweet, Sam," she said, handing back the bag and refilling her wineglass. "But no thank you."

"No *thank* you?" he said. "Why not?"

"I've told you. I prefer my men in small doses."

"I know," he said. "And would you like me to explain why you're like that?"

She set the wine bottle on the table. "Oh, would you? I *love* when guys explain things to me."

He talked for five minutes—detailing how her caution in relationships stemmed from losing her parents in a tragic way at a young age, leading her to see a familial bond as threatening or, worse, dangerous. This, in turn, had led her to construct armor to keep people away: the supremely cool badass not interested enough to commit.

"Nice try, Dr. Phil," she said when he'd finished. "But you're wrong, and we're canceling your show."

"Then what is it?" Sam asked, unconvinced.

She held his gaze and then leaned back in her chair. "Okay, fine, if you want to know. Men are tedious."

He laughed. "Is that right?"

"Don't feel bad. It's a cultural norm. We've been raising our boys to believe they need to repress their emotions. This may have made for easier sons, but it does *not* make for interesting men. Not in the long-term, at least. Six months, tops, that's what I can tolerate."

"Well, I'm different," he said. "I'm *exciting*. Plus, I got a PhD in feelings. You should at least give me a chance."

"Something smells good." Annie startles at the sound of Franklin Sheehy's voice, and realizes she's letting in the cold air.

"Lasagna," she says, closing the front door. "My mom's recipe." The meal she'd intended to make for Sam the night of the storm. The ricotta cheese expired yesterday, but she needed something to do, so she made it, fully aware that she'll likely throw the whole thing in the trash. The radio on Sheehy's hip crackles, and he cocks his head and then lowers the volume.

"Any news?" Annie asks, leading Sheehy into the living room.

"Nothing," he says. "Strangest thing, too."

"What do you mean?"

"Well," Sheehy says. "Unless your husband switched out his license plate—and why would he?—we'd have had a reading on his car by now."

"I don't get it. His car couldn't have vanished."

"No, it could not." Sheehy nods. "You're right about that."

"I need a coffee," she says, drained. "You want one?"

"If it's not too much trouble."

Sheehy follows her into the kitchen, where she pours them each a mug from the carafe sitting on the counter. "Looks like his father," Sheehy says. He's at the refrigerator, leaning down for a better look at the article pinned under a magnet.

"Twenty Questions with Sam Statler," the adorable and ludicrous interview Sam gave the week they moved into the house. The reporter's phone call woke them up from an afternoon nap, and Annie lay with her head on Sam's chest as he stroked her hair and answered the woman's questions, as charming as ever. "The top dessert in Chestnut Hill? I'm pretty sure my mom's blueberry pie is the top dessert in the whole world." "What do you mean you never saw *West Wing*? It's the best show of all time!"

"You know Sam's father?" Annie asks, handing Sheehy a mug. Theodore Statler. The absent larger-than-life man Sam rarely spoke about.

"He taught math to both my girls," Sheehy says. "Before his big adventure down to Baltimore. Got any sugar?"

It's up on a high shelf in the cabinet; when she turns around, Sheehy is standing at the kitchen table, leafing through the pile of bills. "What are you doing?" she says sharply, crossing the room to snatch them.

"Didn't mean to pry," he says.

She shoves the bills into the junk drawer under the coffee-pot, not bothering to hide her irritation.

"Mind if I ask if you knew about those bills?" Sheehy gently takes the canister from her hand.

She hesitates and then sinks onto a stool at the kitchen island, too depleted to put up a fight. "No."

"How much?" Sheehy asks.

"A lot." She watches him pour a slow stream into his mug. "One hundred and twenty thousand dollars, to be exact."

Sheehy releases a slow, sputtering breath. "How do you make sense of this?"

"I don't know," she says. "Isn't that more your area?"

"Sure is," he says, taking a sip of coffee. "But I don't think you're gonna wanna hear what *I* think."

She clenches her jaw. "You think he left."

"What I think is that financial pressure can be hard on people, men especially."

"Are you suggesting he drove off a cliff?"

He shrugs. "Or decided life would be easier elsewhere."

She stands up. "No, Franklin, you're wrong. He texted me before he left the office to say he was on his way home. He wouldn't do that if he was planning on heading *elsewhere*."

"Any chance I can see the text he sent?" Sheehy asks.

Annie takes her phone from the back pocket of her jeans and hands it to him. He retrieves a pair of reading glasses from his shirt pocket and begins to scroll, reading aloud. "'Hello

Dr. S. It's me. Charlie.'" Franklin stops. "I don't get it. Who's Charlie?"

"Me," Annie says, immediately exhausted by the idea of having to explain the text exchange to this idiot. "It's a joke, kind of."

"Oh, gotcha. Good one. 'I broke up with Chandler and would like to see you tomorrow.'" He stops again. "Like from *Friends*? Or is that a joke too?"

"No, they're made-up people. It's something we do."

He returns to the phone. "'I've been thinking about your invitation. I'll be there.' This address you wrote down here. Whose address is that?"

"That's our address."

"Does Dr. Statler not know where you live?"

"Yes, Franklin, Sam knows where we live." She snatches her phone back. "I was pretending to be someone else. A patient named Charlie."

"Let me get this straight," he says, removing his glasses. "You were texting your husband, pretending to be a man named Charlie, and you were asking him to come over?"

"Not a man, a woman," Annie says. "We were role-playing. I was a patient named Charlotte. He was my therapist, feeling trapped in his marriage. He was supposed to be blowing off his wife to come to my place."

"I see." He turns down his mouth and picks up his coffee. "Seems you two got quite a thing going on."

She sighs, drained. "I'm telling you, Franklin. Something happened to Sam. I know him. He didn't leave."

Sheehy holds her gaze, silent for a few moments. "Let me ask you a question," he says. "How long did you know your husband before marrying him?"

"What does that have to do with anything?" she asks. Franklin stays silent, eyebrows raised, waiting. "Eight months," she says.

His jaw drops. "Eight *months*? Why on earth would you marry a man you knew for eight months?"

"Why did I marry Sam?" Annie snaps. "Because he's smart and funny, and unlike most men, he experiences complex emotions. I'm a strong, intelligent woman who's comfortable with my sexuality, and he's the first man who didn't find that threatening. He's also head over heels crazy about me. So crazy, Franklin, that the last thing he would ever do is leave me."

Sheehy nods slowly. "Admire your confidence," he says. "That's a good quality in a woman. And while I'm no relationship expert, even *I* know that might not be enough time to get to know someone. Decide if they got it in them to be faithful."

A piercing scream sounds in Annie's ears, and it takes her a moment to realize it's not in fact coming from her but from the smoke detector in the ceiling. She checks the oven, seeing the smoke billowing from the door. "Shit," she says, snatching the oven mitts and retrieving the smoking lasagna. She drops the pan into the sink and turns on the water.

"Seems you got a lot on your plate right now," Sheehy says. He drains his coffee mug and sets it on the counter. "I gotta say, Mrs. Statler, I admire your faith in your husband. Sure hope this turns out the way you want it to."

chapter

34

SAM DOESN'T KNOW IF he should wake up or stay in the dream, although he can see the advantages to each option. Option one: in the dream, he's with Annie, in Manhattan, on the corner of University Place and Washington Square Park, five days after he'd asked her to marry him on the front porch of the house for sale in Chestnut Hill. She'd finally said yes, in a text, three hours earlier. Okay fine, she wrote on her way into class. I'll move to the country and marry you. He was waiting outside Studebaker Hall an hour later. "Honest to god, you're a walking Nicholas Sparks novel," she said when she saw him. They sat in silence on the subway back to his apartment, arms linked, lost in the idea of what they were about to do. Emerging from the subway, Annie stopped at the table of a man selling hats and chose something with fake fur around the face. "To prepare me for life on the prairie," she told the man, handing him a twenty.

Option two: if he wakes up, he can learn what that noise is. A painfully grating noise that's been assaulting him for the last few hours.

He decides to stay asleep, but then the dream changes, and he's not on the sidewalk with Annie anymore. He's walking down a neon-orange hall at Rushing Waters, heading toward his mother's room. Something tells him not to, but he opens the door anyway. Margaret is alone, sitting in her armchair, waiting for him.

"I don't want to be here," he says.

"Of course you don't, sweetheart," she says, smiling, her voice like it used to be, before the disease. "Only place you want to be is staring at a reflection of yourself." She starts to laugh. "You left your wife."

"No, I didn't," he says.

"Yes, you did, Sam. I knew you would. We *all* knew you would."

"I didn't leave her!" Sam screams.

The scraping stops.

A bright light goes on overhead and Albert appears, hazy, shards of yellow paper stuck to his sweatshirt, a shiny knife in his hand.

"Two more hours, Sam," Albert says, shoveling pills into Sam's mouth. "Go back to sleep."

....

Sam's limbs are immovable, his head aches.

There's a warm light to the room, and he forces himself to stay awake and pay attention. Something has changed.

He's in a different room. He raises himself on his elbows, his hips stiff under the weight of the casts, and takes a better look. He's in the same single bed. The same floral curtains are drawn in front of what he assumes is the same boarded-up window. In the corner of the room, that's the same closet door.

It's the yellow wallpaper. It's been torn from the walls.

He flops back on the mattress, elated. "It's working," he

whispers. The plan is working. Do what Paul Sheldon did, in *Misery*: befriend the motherfucker.

Two days now, Sam's been buttering him up, trying—in the lucid moments between the pills Albert forces upon him every few hours—to earn his trust so he can figure out what the fuck he wants. *He wants to kill you.* Sam squeezes his eyes shut, sending the thought back into his subconscious. *No. If that's what he wanted, he would have done it already.*

He wants to be close to you.

His skin crawls, imagining Albert up here, listening. It makes sense now, at least, how Albert always seemed to know when Sam finished work. Even on the days when Sam tried to slip out, making sure the door didn't slam behind him, Albert would be there, smiling from the porch, holding two glasses in his hands.

Sam's been racking his brain for any details Albert's shared about himself. He tended to zone out as Albert nervously rambled; what he mainly remembers is that Albert knows a surprising number of useless facts about the family who built his house, and that he volunteered at the Chestnut Hill Historical Society as a tour guide.

The cut on Sam's head is throbbing, and his legs are itching inside his casts. He wants to go out to dinner with Annie and have a hot shower. He wants to understand what this guy wants, so he can give it to him and get out of here.

Oh, I get it. Annie's voice pops into his head as he hears the rattle of Albert's cart down the hall. *You're going to charm him and then screw him, the way you did with all those unsuspecting girls in high school. Good thinking, Sam, use your superpower.*

"Whatever it takes to see you again," he whispers as the key enters the lock and the door opens. "Good morning, Albert," Sam says, fixing on a smile. "How nice to see you."

chapter
35

"OH FUDGE, YOU'RE AWAKE," I say to Sam, disappointed. "I wanted to see your reaction." I push the cart into the room and set the brake. "Well?"

"You took the wallpaper down," he says. He's sitting up in bed, color back in his cheeks.

"As best I could." I smooth my palm along a gluey patch. "What do you think?"

"I think it looks great," Sam says. "The room has a much calmer feel now."

"Oh, good. That's what I was hoping you'd say. Studies show that homebound patients heal faster in a pleasing environment, and you were right, that wallpaper was a little much."

"How'd you do it?" Sam says, downing the cup of water I've poured for him.

"A box of four-inch putty knives, scalding hot water, and some good old-fashioned elbow grease. Gave you something to sleep through it—I wanted it to be a surprise. And that's not all," I say. "Close your eyes."

I return to the hall for the chair and push it into the room. "Okay, open."

"No way." He looks genuinely stunned. "Is that my Eames chair from downstairs?"

"Well, not your *exact* Eames chair," I say, wheeling it toward him. *That one needed to stay downstairs in case your wife decides to come back and snoop around.* "A brand-new one. I had it shipped overnight."

"Wow, Albert," he says. "Why'd you do that?"

"Because you need to get out of that bed or you'll develop decubitus ulcers, and I couldn't think of a more comfortable option." I caress the soft leather, remembering the first time I sat in this chair. I watched from the window upstairs as two men carried a large box down the steps and into his office. I couldn't resist. Later that night I used the extra key I'd asked Gary Unger from Gary Unger Locksmiths to make and I spent a half hour in the silence of the room, cradled in the most comfortable chair in the world. Italian leather, hand-crafted chrome frame, and locking wheels.

I park it next to his bed now. "You want me to . . ."

"Get me out of this bed and into this chair? Yes indeed," he says. I fold back the sheets. "Scoot to the edge," I instruct, hooking one arm under his casts, the other at his midlumbar, and then use my knees to lift.

"Well done," Sam says after I set him gently into his chair.

"A lifetime of moving people in and out of beds," I say, pausing to stretch my back before retrieving the ottoman I took from the living room. I drag it inside and hoist his legs on top, one at a time. I then return to the hall for the table, also like the one he kept in his office, and set it next to the chair, then arrange his things on top: the yellow Kleenex box next to an academic paper on Anna Freud and the October issue of *In Touch*, with a cover story on Kris Jenner's secret Mexican wedding. The final touch is the small clock, placed on the floor across the room from him.

"Just as I'd left it," Sam says.

"That's right." I step back, spread my palms. "How does it feel?"

"Like I'm back at work," he says, gripping the armrests. "In other words: like heaven."

"I'm glad," I say, barely able to contain my excitement. "Now let's take a look at those stitches." I snap on a pair of latex gloves and pull back the bandage on his forehead. "This contusion is healing nicely," I say.

"You seem to know a lot about medicine," Sam says.

"Twenty-five years in the health-care field," I say, taking a folded sweatshirt from the bottom of the cart, LOYOLA GREYHOUNDS printed across the front. "Put this on. It's chilly in here."

"Were you a doctor?" Sam asks, slipping it over his head.

I laugh loudly. "From your mouth to my estranged father's ears," I say. "No, home health aide, recently retired. 'Home Health Angels, helping people age in place while providing peace of mind to the whole family.'"

"What kind of things did the job entail?" Sam asks.

"Whatever the client needed," I say, taking a tube of ointment and a fresh bandage from my apron pocket. "Bathing and meal prep. Companionship." I dab ointment onto Sam's cut. "Wound care."

"I bet you were good at it."

I pause mid-dab. "What makes you say that?"

"You have a calming presence," Sam says.

"Well, I'm not one to brag, but I *was* employee of the month three times," I say, my cheeks burning. I finish with the bandage and return to the cart.

"Mind if I ask what happened between you and your father?" Sam asks. I fidget with the plastic container of cotton swabs and keep my back to him. "You said you and he are estranged. I'm curious why."

I hesitate. "It's a long story."

"I have some time." His tone is gentle. "Would you like to sit down?"

I turn toward him. "Why?"

"I imagine it'll be more comfortable."

I scan the room, hesitant. "On the bed, or should I get a chair?"

"Whichever you'd prefer," he says.

"The bed is fine, I suppose." I sit squarely in the middle and press down on the mattress with both hands. "Nice and firm."

Sam nods. "It's comfortable." He stays silent and tents his fingers in front of his mouth.

"I haven't spoken to my father in more than thirty years," I say.

"Why's that?"

"He's ashamed of me."

"What makes you say that?"

"It was obvious," I say. "We were different."

"In what ways?"

"He's a real man, and I'm a sissy."

"Wow," Sam says. "Is that what he called you?"

I swipe dust from my pant leg. "He wasn't wrong to do so," I say. "I wasn't like other boys. Always hated sports and couldn't fight to save my life."

"I see."

"I'm not his," I say before I can stop myself.

"What do you mean by that?" Sam asks.

"I mean Albert Sr. is not, in fact, my biological father." I've never said this out loud before, and the words tumble out. "I had a hard time at school. I could usually hold it together, but sometimes, when I got home, it felt like too much and I had to let it out. My mother would sit with me on the couch until I stopped crying. My father came home early one day. There was a fire where he worked, and they closed the plant." I can see him standing in the doorway. That look on his face. *What's sissy boy crying about this time?*

"And?" Sam asks.

"He was furious," I say, my chest tight. "Looked me right in the eye and said 'I thank god every day that kid's not mine.'"

"How old were you?" Sam asks.

"Eight." My heart is beating so loud I'm afraid Sam can hear it from his chair.

"Did you know what that meant?"

"Not right away, but sooner or later I put together that my mom had an affair." I force a laugh. "I felt relieved for him, to be honest. At least he didn't have to blame himself for having such a weak son." I take a deep breath to compose myself. "My mother died when I was fourteen, and then it was the two of us."

"Oh, Albert." Sam looks genuinely pained. "I'm sorry to hear that."

"Breast cancer," I say. I can picture her, biting the ridges off a Pop-Tart one by one, asking if I wanted to stay home from school and be with her. I said yes, every time, not because I didn't like school but because she needed me so much I was sure she'd die if I went. We'd hide upstairs, listening to the bus pass by the house, and then she'd make us scrambled eggs and turn on the soaps.

"How did your father deal with her death?" Sam asks me.

"He was angry," I say. "One thing Albert Bitterman Sr. never saw for himself was life as a single parent. I did what I could to please him, but nothing did. Over time, we figured out how to just stay out of each other's way, and I left home as soon as I could. We haven't spoken since."

Sam allows a few moments of silence. "Fourteen is a hard age to lose one's mother," he says eventually. "How did you cope at the time?"

"I pretended I was part of the family across the street." I laugh. "Crazy, right? The Parkers."

Mrs. Parker started dinner at four thirty while Jenny watched television in the living room, a bowl of ice cream on her lap, nobody worried she'd spoil her dinner. On the weekends Jenny had sleepovers, all the popular girls crowded on the living room floor, staying up late with popcorn and grape sodas. She knew who I was. I lived across the street, and not once did she consider me worthy of a hello. The only time she ever spoke to me was when Mrs. Parker dragged her over to deliver a pan of lasagna and say how sorry they were to hear my mom had died.

"After my mom died, I decided Mr. Parker was going to admit that he and my mom had an affair and come claim me," I tell Sam. "I went into their house a few times."

"So you got to know them?" Sam asks.

"No. I went when they weren't home. I knew from watching that Mrs. Parker hid a key under a flowerpot on the side porch. I'd go Sunday mornings, when they were at church." I look down at my feet, unsure why I'm telling him all this, prepared for him to echo the words I grew used to hearing back then: *You're a freak.* But his tone is gentler than ever when he speaks.

"What was it like being inside their house?"

Cinnamon air freshener and clean laundry. Grape soda in

the fridge. "It was thrilling," I say. "I wouldn't stay long. I just wanted to see what it was like. But then one of the girls got sick at church, and they came home early." I was in Jenny Parker's bedroom when I heard the front door open. "Mrs. Parker found me hiding in her daughter's closet. It was terrible." I bite down on my lower lip, willing myself not to cry.

"That sounds traumatic," Sam says.

"I know," I say. "Mrs. Parker was terrified every time—"

"No, you've misunderstood me," Sam cuts in. "I mean traumatic for you. What you did was perfectly natural. But I can't imagine anyone understood that."

"It was?"

"Absolutely. You were grieving, and trying to find an anchor in your mother's absence."

"They made it seem like I was doing something perverted, but I wasn't," I say. "I swear to god. Mr. Parker kept me barricaded in the bedroom until the police came, and then my father was called." I close my eyes, hearing the front door slam behind us after my father dragged me home, the absolute terror as he charged at me, calling me those names. I stand up. "Can I go now?"

Sam looks stricken. "You want to leave?"

"Yes, can I?"

"Of course."

"I'm tired," I say. "I think I need to lie down."

Sam smiles. "Of course, Albert. I think that's a good idea." His posture relaxes, and he pats the arms of his chair. "And I think *I* need to sit up. Thanks again for the chair."

I nod, and lift the foot brake on the cart. "You're welcome," I say. I step into the hall and go upstairs and shut the door, praying he won't hear me cry.

chapter
36

SOMEONE IN THE KITCHEN drops a tray, startling Annie, the sole occupant of the dining room at Rushing Waters. The residents are off to Applebee's in the strip mall for their weekly outing, but the nurses told Annie that Margaret has been having trouble sleeping—they found her roaming the halls at three in the morning, two nights in a row. Annie returns to the email she's writing to Margaret's doctor, urging him to prescribe something new to help Margaret sleep; whatever the white pills are that she's taking have stopped working.

Annie sees Josephine, one of the women who works the reception desk, pushing a cart into the dining hall. "That's a nice touch," Annie says, as Josephine places vases of fresh carnations on each table.

"Trying to spruce this place up," Josephine says, dropping a copy of the local newspaper on the table in front of Annie. "Free newspapers now, too." They both see what's on the front page at the same time: a photograph of Sam under a bold headline: LOCAL THERAPIST REPORTED MISSING LAST WEEK FOUND TO BE IN SIGNIFICANT DEBT.

Annie picks up the newspaper and scans the article.

It turns out that Dr. Sam Statler, a therapist known for help-ing people with their problems, may have been concealing a few of his own including multiple credit cards, maxed to the limit. According to Chief of Police Franklin Sheehy, this discovery is leading investigators to consider the idea that the missing Chestnut Hill man's disappearance may not, in fact, have been accidental. The debt was a surprise to Statler's wife, who teaches literature at the university.

"Oh my god," Annie whispers. "That asshole called a re-porter."

"I'm sorry, Annie," Josephine says as one of the women from the kitchen appears with a plate of fettuccine Alfredo wrapped in plastic.

Annie can't pull her eyes away from what she's reading, shocked Sheehy didn't take it a step further and tell the reporter about the text exchange he read on Annie's phone. *According to Chief of Police Franklin Sheehy, Mr. and Mrs. Statler also enjoyed a perverted sexual ritual in which Mrs. Statler pretends to be a patient named Charlie.*

She stuffs the newspaper in her bag, takes the food, and exits the dining hall. Margaret is watching television in her arm-chair, a blank look on her face, when Annie enters.

"Here you go," Annie says, trying to sound cheerful. "Lunch." She puts the tray on the metal cart next to Margaret's bed and unrolls the silverware from the napkin. "And remember, Sam's away for a little while. I'll be coming on his days. I have to go to class. You need anything else?"

Margaret stares silently at her plate of food and then begins to eat. Annie kisses her cheek and steps into the hall as a woman with a walker is about to knock.

"Here, give this to Margaret," the woman says, handing Annie a purple bingo dauber. "Her son left it behind last night."

"Her son?" Annie says, taking it from her.

"Yes. They were at my table, and he gave me this. It's no good. Leaks everywhere."

"Are you sure?"

"Yes, I'm sure." She holds up her right hand; blotches of purple dot her wrist. "Can't get this stuff off."

"No, I mean about her son being here."

"Oh. Yeah, he was here. He comes every week for bingo." She shoots Annie a look. "I'm one of the few people here who's still with it. Trust me, it was her son."

"Thank you," Annie says. The woman turns and shuffles down the hall into her room. Annie heads to the lobby, dropping the dauber into a trash can she passes. There's no one at the desk, and Annie pauses to scan the guest register, trailing her finger down the list of signatures, searching for Sam's name. She shakes away the thought. Of course he wasn't here yesterday, you idiot, she thinks. That woman is demented. She exits through the sliding doors, but when she gets to the parking lot, she turns around and hurries back inside, unable to stop herself. The door to Sally French's office is slightly ajar. She knocks and peeks her head in. It's empty.

"She's getting lunch in the dining room," a young woman says as she passes. "She'll be right back. You can take a seat and wait if you want."

"Thanks," Annie says. The young woman enters the staff room, and Annie finds her phone in her bag.

"This is Annie Potter," she says when John Gently answers. "Is Chief Sheehy there?"

She hears a clicking noise, and then Sheehy comes on the line. "Good morning, Mrs. Statler."

"It's Potter, and why the hell did you go to the newspaper about Sam's debt?"

"I'm sorry?"

She lowers her voice. "Don't play dumb, Franklin. Why on earth would you call a reporter and tell her—"

"First of all," Sheehy says, cutting her off, "I didn't *tell* her about the debt. She knew about it already."

"What do you mean, she knew about it?" Annie asks.

"I mean she knew about it. 'Hello Chief, this is blah dee blah,'" he says, apparently imitating the reporter. "'We received a tip that Sam Statler was in significant debt at the time of his disappearance. What do you have to say?'" She can hear the springs of Sheehy's chair squeaking under him. "What do you want me to do? Unlike some people in this country, I still believe in a free press."

"A *tip*?" Annie says. "Two people know about the debt, Franklin. You and my cousin. And it wasn't my cousin."

"And it wasn't me, Mrs. Statler."

"It's *Potter*," she says. The door to the outside slides open, and a couple in their seventies enter. "I think I understand what's behind the debt."

"Oh? Please, go on."

"Sam has some money coming from his father," she says. "It's a gift."

"Can you be more specific?" Sheehy asks.

Annie turns her back and speaks softly. "Two million dollars."

Sheehy whistles softly. "Guess Ted did even better than I

thought, chasing that girl. Funny you didn't mention this to me earlier."

"It didn't seem relevant," Annie says, watching the couple sign the guest register before disappearing down the hall. "The money's been fraught for him."

"Makes sense," Sheehy says. "Getting two million dollars can be hard on people."

Annie bites back her annoyance. "Sam's been auditioning for his father's love his whole life," she continues. "Getting the money felt like he'd earned that love. But it also felt cheap, like he'd allowed his father to buy him. So he spent it as quick as he could on some incredibly *stupid* shit." She's studied the bills, shocked at what he paid for things. The top-of-the-line lawn mower and professional surround sound installed in the house. $5,000 *chair* for his office. "He got carried away, and before he knew it, he was in over his head. He kept telling himself everything will be *fine*—it's a thing he does—because the debt was temporary. As soon as his dad's money comes, he'd pay it all off."

"I see," Franklin Sheehy says. "And let me guess. There's a twist."

"The money hasn't come yet, and it's taking longer than Sam expected."

"And why's that?"

"His mother has to sign papers over to him, but her health hasn't been good, and the money is delayed." It became clear to her yesterday, as she paced the house, nursing her third cup of coffee. His mother hasn't signed the papers yet, and the debt's been adding up, stressing him out. That's why he'd been in such a bad mood the last few weeks, too anxious to sleep.

"Sounds innocent enough," Sheehy says. "But then why not tell you about it?"

"He was ashamed, and scared I might leave him." She takes a breath. "I'm telling you, Franklin, you can't allow this to side-track the investigation. Something has happened to Sam. I'm sure of it."

Sheehy is quiet on the other end of the line and then sighs. "Two million dollars sure would be a nice amount to start over with. You sure he didn't get it?"

"*Yes*, Franklin. I'm sure. He would have told me."

"Listen, Annie. Like I told that reporter, we're doing everything we can with the information we have."

She's done wasting time. "Well, thank you for all your hard work. Have a nice day, Officer Sheehy."

"It's Chief Sheehy."

"Oh, that's right," she says. "I keep forgetting." She ends the call, her hands shaking.

"Annie?" She turns around. It's Sally French. "Josephine said you wanted to speak to me."

"Yes." Annie manages a weak smile. "A resident told me that Sam was here yesterday. I know she's probably confused, but I need to at least ask if anyone saw him."

Sally hesitates, and there's something about the look on her face that makes Annie uneasy.

"What?" she says.

"I haven't seen Sam here in several weeks, Annie."

"What do you mean? He comes every other day. We take turns."

The door opens again, and a woman enters, clutching the hand of a little girl, her face painted like a cat, a red helium balloon gripped in her fist. Sally nods. "Let's ask Josephine. She'd be the one to know."

Annie follows Sally to the front desk.

"A resident said Sam was here and took Margaret to bingo," Annie says to Josephine. "Any chance . . ." She allows the sentence to trail off.

"No, sorry." Josephine flashes a tight smile. "A volunteer has been taking Margaret to bingo. The resident was probably confused."

"When did you last see him?" Annie asks.

"It's been a while," Josephine says. "Two months, maybe?"

"You're sure?" Annie's voice is quavering. *Because that would mean he's been lying to me.*

"Yes." Josephine's expression is pained. "I'm here every day, and pretty much see everyone."

"Okay," Annie says, as the little girl with the cat face abruptly lets go of her balloon. "Thank you." She heads toward the doors, watching the balloon float slowly toward the ceiling, where it settles against a light fixture. She hears a loud pop, followed by the young girl's shrieks, ushering her into the cold, gray afternoon, transformed just like that into the most cliché character of them all: the guileless wife.

chapter
37

SAM STARES AT THE notes he jotted down in one of the grid-lined notebooks Albert brought up from his office yesterday.

Client initials: KJ

Marital status: Newlywed

Presenting problem: Got married in a secret ceremony in Mexico and is feeling conflicted. Also devoid of a conscience, grandiose sense of self-importance, and exploits others without guilt or shame.

Treatment plan:

Sam pauses to think about it.

Annulment, followed by round-the-clock therapy in an inpatient environment and a lifetime ban on interacting with impressionable young women.

Pretty good, Sam thinks, dropping the pen on top of the copy of *In Touch* magazine with Kris Jenner on the cover. Kris Jenner: his imaginary patient Nancy Neumann (Tuesday, 10 a.m.) had accidentally brought the magazine in from the

waiting room and left it on the side table in his office. It included a famous actress's weight-loss program and a two-page
interview with the cover girl, which he is bored enough to
have read four times in the last six hours. He grips the arms of
the chair and begins a set of tricep dips, telling himself that'll
be him one day, on the cover of all the magazines.

Therapist Held Captive by Landlord Speaks!

Dr. Sam Statler, pictured here, at home with his wife Annie and two perfectly good legs, escaped after murdering
his deranged landlord, Albert Bitterman, in a tremen-
dously violent manner. He says the experience only made
him a better man.

The ladies of *The View* will dig up a photo of Albert as a kid
and beg to know more about him. Sam will use a professional
tone, and explain that according to his assessment, Albert Bitterman is, as they'd say in the business, batshit crazy.

A picture is emerging. Emotionally stunted by his mother's death at a young age, Albert was left in the care of an
abusive and distant father, whose ideas of masculinity were
at odds with his son's sensitive nature. As an adult, he was
deathly afraid of rejection, making it difficult to form attachments, leading to a lonely and isolated existence and an ob-
session with his tenant, whom he would eventually attack
with a shovel and then keep him captive in his house. The
ladies will all want to know the same thing—why was Albert
Bitterman, a single fifty-one-year-old man, living alone in a
five-bedroom mansion in the first place? But Sam will only
shrug, explaining that this was one topic Albert wouldn't

touch. Twice now Sam has broached the subject, asking what brought him to Chestnut Hill, sending Albert abruptly out of the room both times.

He starts another series of reps, imagining the live studio audience cheering his bravery for surviving an entire week without Annie. One week, that's how long Sam's been in this room. He's been keeping track on the hand-drawn October calendar Annie made, which he found folded inside the academic paper Albert also brought up from downstairs. Pink- and blue-shaded boxes, "Visits to Yo Mama!" written across the top in Annie's perfect handwriting. Each morning Sam makes a light mark, keeping track of another day.

Annie's one of the smartest people Sam has ever met, which means that it's only a matter of time before she knocks on the door of Sam's (lonely and apparently deranged) landlord to ask if he's seen Sam. Or maybe she won't even have to knock. Maybe she'll drive by and see Sam's car in the driveway— because where else would it be? She'll do the smart thing and call the police, who will confirm that it's Sam's car, and then open the door and ask if he'd like to go home.

Then again, maybe she's not looking. Maybe, instead, she's discovered the variety of ways he's been lying to her. Chances are she's going to open the credit card bills that are likely arriving in their mailbox, addressed to her missing husband. He hates himself for chickening out and not telling her the truth like he'd planned. The events of that evening have been on repeat in his head—the speech he'd rehearsed all day, preparing to spill everything. The made-up money. The credit card debt. The fact he hasn't visited his mother. And then the invitation from "Charlie" arrived, which Annie had obviously sent from their driveway, inviting him to trade in all his worries for an evening of incredible sex. How could he say no?

His triceps are stinging as he slides his casts to the edge of the ottoman and then onto the floor. Using his hands, he pulls himself around the room, from one stupid end to the other, dragging his useless legs behind him. He passes the door to the hallway (locked!), the wall with the window (boarded up!), pausing after the tenth lap to catch his breath. When he rotates the chair and begins to move again, he notices a flash of silver on the floor underneath the nightstand. The toilet flushes upstairs, and he checks the clock on the floor: 8:46 p.m. Albert will be down any minute to put him into bed. Quietly, Sam scoots himself forward to the nightstand. He reaches down.

A four-inch putty knife. The sharp metal edge is sticky with wallpaper paste; the sturdy wooden handle is emblazoned with the logo of the hardware store on Main Street. HOYTS HARD-WARE: OPEN EVERY DAY 'TIL 6!

He hears Albert's tread on the stairs, and slips the putty knife under his hip, then scoots his chair back in place next to the table. He gets his legs onto the ottoman just as the door opens. Albert enters backward, pulling the cart behind him.

"Good evening, Doctor," Albert says, pressing the brake on the cart. "You're looking robust."

Sam smiles. "Feeling great," he says.

"That's what I like to hear. Time to get you into bed." Albert approaches him, arms outstretched.

"Would you mind . . ." Sam gestures toward the bottom of the cart.

Albert stops abruptly. "Already? You went an hour ago." He shakes his head as he gets the bedpan. "I knew I shouldn't have given you that extra glass of milk so late in the day." He places the bedpan on Sam's lap. "I'll wait outside."

Albert closes the door behind him, and Sam waits a moment before easing the putty knife from under his hip and sliding it down the front of his sweatpants. His hands are shaking as he picks up the bedpan and waits.

"All good?" Albert says, opening the door an inch.

"False alarm, I'm afraid," Sam says.

"Probably stage fright," Albert says, entering. "I'll leave it here on your table."

Albert pushes Sam's chair close to the bed, hoists him up, setting him gently onto the mattress. "Either I'm getting weaker or you're gaining some weight," Albert says, standing up and massaging his lower back.

"It's all the good food," Sam says.

Albert laughs and pats Sam's arm. "You keep it up, you'll be able to get up and walk right out of here in no time at all."

As Albert grips the handle of the cart and heads toward the door Sam chuckles, feeling the hard edge of the putty knife against his thigh. "Won't that be something?"

chapter
38

1. *Thistle*, I scrawl.
2. *Lavender*.
3. *Oil of—*

A THICK BLACK BOX appears on the screen, covering the rest of the list.

Natural Remedies to Get Rid of Moths is available to subscribers only. To keep reading, log in or sign up.

I close the website and shake my head. The Pigeon was right: consumerism *is* destroying our culture. She wrote that on Facebook yesterday, posted it under a photograph of a large pile of plastic floating somewhere in the Pacific. Only someone without a soul could see that and not respond with a frowny emoji. (I recently read online about a growing movement of people who believe emojis were created to stifle humans' ability to express emotion, which is certainly something to consider.)

I return to the search bar and am typing in *What is thistle?* when the alarm on my watch beeps. I drop my pen and reach for my blue apron. Back to work.

. . . .

"Come in," Sam calls when I knock.

His face brightens when I walk in. "Good morning, Albert," he says, and then sees what's in my hand. "Is that a coffee in my *favorite* mug?"

"Yes it is." A Le Creuset mug, identical to the ones next to the Nespresso machine downstairs in his office, which cost an astounding $34 apiece. (I'm loath to say it, but it's exactly these kind of exorbitant purchases that explain why Sam's photo was on the front page of the paper yesterday next to a story about his "financial troubles," but I certainly don't have the heart to tell him that.)

I push the cart closer to his bed and step on the brake. "Guess who slept with a call girl?"

Sam struggles to swallow a mouthful of coffee. "Wait, *what?*"

Seeing the look on his face, I burst into laughter. "No, not *me*," I say. "Sam Seaborne, deputy White House communications director in the Bartlet White House. Rob Lowe's character." I empty the pitcher of warm water into the basin and reach for a washcloth. "I'm watching *West Wing.*"

"Is that right?" Sam says. "That's my favorite show."

"No kidding?" I feign shock. "Mine too." (This is not a lie. I finished the series last night, and I'm so hooked that as soon as the last episode ended, I went back to the beginning to watch it all again.)

"In fact, I'm kind of a *West Wing* fanatic," Sam says, animated. "The woman's name is Laurie, and she's played by the actress Lisa Edelstein. She's a law student, trying to pay her way through law school. Sam Seaborne didn't know she was a prostitute when he slept with her."

"At least not on a conscious level," I say under my breath as I dunk the washcloth into the water.

"Sorry?" Sam says. "What did you say?"

"Sam Seaborne hasn't had a stable relationship in his life. And okay, fine, while he says he wasn't aware of her profession, it's clear that deep down, on some level, he knew she was unavailable. That's why he was attracted to her."

"Huh," Sam says. "Interesting."

"And you want to know why he's like this?" I continue, wringing out the washcloth. "Because of his father's affair. When Sam Seaborne found out that his father had been having an affair, for *twenty-eight years*, while married to his mother, it deeply shook his idea of what he can and cannot depend on. And don't even get me started on Josh Lyman." I approach Sam's bed. "What?" I say, noticing the look on his face.

He shrugs. "I don't know. It's just . . ." He takes a deep breath. "I can relate to what you're saying."

"You can?" I ask, tilting his chin toward the ceiling. "How?"

"My dad left my mother for another woman," he says. "Moved out on my fourteenth birthday, to be exact." I gently clean around his stitches. "Learning that your dad is unfaithful can mess with your mind, and like Sam Seaborne, I used girls to make that pain go away." Sam grimaces. "It's shameful how good I was at manipulating girls."

I step back. "I never understood guys like you," I say. "No offense, but it always seemed like the bigger the jerk a boy was, the more girls who wanted to date him. How on earth did you do it?"

Sam looks me in the eye. "You want in on the secret to seducing a girl?"

"Are you serious?" I ask.

"Sit down," Sam says, nodding at his chair.

I slowly make my way across the room.

"Taking advantage of a girl is a delicate dance," Sam says when I'm seated. "But it comes down to one thing in particular." He pauses.

"What?"

"Finding their weakness and exploiting it. You have to make them think you care about them. Convince them you've never felt this way before. But the quickest way to get her?" He leans forward and lowers his voice. "Tears."

"*Tears?*"

"Yeah, a past regret. A dead dog. A dad who walks out on your fourteenth birthday. Throw some fake tears into that mix, and you're going to have a naked girl underneath you in ten minutes flat."

"That's repulsive," I say.

"I know it is. Now, I mean. I didn't see it that way when I was younger."

I hesitate. "Can I offer a theory?"

Sam nods.

"You used girls to feel validated," I suggest. "A series of stand-ins for what you ultimately wanted: your father's love."

He holds my gaze. "Huh," he says. "Maybe you're right. Maybe I blamed myself for my father leaving, and sleeping with a new girl was the only thing that made me feel worthwhile. I was always on the hunt for the next." He closes his eyes, wincing. "I hurt quite a few people."

"In some ways, you were doing what was expected of you," I say. "Being a boy."

He nods. "It hasn't always been easy, being a guy." He laughs. "I can imagine my wife's face, if she could hear us. Two white guys bellyaching about our lot in life. That would *not* go over well."

"I hope you still don't believe it's your fault your father left," I say.

"I don't, actually. Not anymore. All thanks to Clarissa Boyne."

"Was she a girlfriend?" I ask, settling back into Sam's chair.

"That was the plan," Sam says. "Ithaca College, psych major, class-A tits. I signed up for a class she was taking, Abnormal Psychology, thinking it'd be the fastest way into her pants. But then I got distracted by what the professor was saying." He's looking past me, pensive. "Third week of class, Dr. Robert Carlisle stood at the front of the room and read a list of symptoms. 'An inflated sense of one's own importance. A need for excessive attention and admiration. Complete lack of empathy.'"

"Narcissist personality disorder," I interject.

"That's exactly right," Sam says. "Narcissistic personality disorder. We read a few case studies, each one a perfect description of Theodore Statler. I started to read everything I could about it, coming to the conclusion I'd been searching for since my fourteenth birthday: my dad didn't leave because there was something wrong with me, but because there's something wrong with him."

"That sounds like a transformative moment."

"Very much so," Sam says. "It sparked a serious interest in psychology while forcing me to examine who I had become as a man. I've been working hard on being a good guy, but the truth of the matter is, I've never stopped being afraid that I'm going to turn out like him." Something is changing in his face. My god. He's starting to cry. "Now that I've found Annie, I don't ever want to lose her."

"You shouldn't worry about turning out like your father,"

I say, fidgeting in my chair. "You're a good man. Smart. Generous. Brave."

He laughs. "Brave? I'm the biggest coward there is."

"Sam," I say gently. "That's ludicrous."

"No, Albert, it's not. You want to know how brave I am?" He holds up a finger. "One: I haven't visited my mother in months. Two: I've kept things from my wife." He looks away. "I didn't get Cal Ripken Jr. to sign my bat."

"What?" I say, lost.

"I was thirteen." Sam closes his eyes, tears spilling onto his cheeks. "My mother surprised my father and me with tickets to see Ripken play at Camden Yards. Best moment of my life, opening that envelope." He wipes his eyes with the sleeves of the MIT sweatshirt I loaned him this morning. "I'd read that at the end of the game, Ripken would stand in a certain area and sign one hundred autographs. I couldn't sleep for weeks, thinking what it was going to feel like to meet him."

I take the Kleenex box from the table and extend it to him.

"My mom and I devised a foolproof plan," Sam continues, pulling a tissue. "My dad and I would leave our seats at the top of the ninth. Get there in time, but not so early that we'd miss a lot of the game." He falls silent.

I clear my throat. "And?"

"And then this girl shows up in the seat in front of us, and I knew right away I was fucked. 'His weakness,' that's how he'd describe a pretty woman any time the two of us were together." He swallows back more tears. "Top of the ninth rolls around, and my dad's got his fingers hooked around her belt loop, whispering something in her ear. I couldn't pull him away. He told me to go by myself, and I couldn't."

"Why not?" I ask, gently.

"I was afraid of what would happen if I left the two of them alone. I was afraid he'd cheat on my mom if I wasn't there to watch him." He starts to cry again. "And so I stayed. Missed the one chance I'd ever have to meet my hero." He blows his nose. "I don't know what's worse. That my dad cheated anyway, or the sight of my mom standing in the living room window when we pulled into the driveway the next morning. 'So?' she asked, all excited. 'Did you get his autograph?'"

"What did you tell her?"

"Nothing," Sam says. "I just held up my bat and showed her the black scrawl of Cal Ripken's autograph, which I drew myself in the car ten minutes before we got home."

"Oh, Sam," I say. "You're such a good man."

He smiles. "And you're a good clinician."

"What?"

"You have a mind for this work," he says, blowing his nose. "I've never shared any of this before. It feels good to talk to you."

"That's like Van Gogh telling a street painter he has talent," I say, blushing.

Sam laughs and then presses the heels of his hands to his eyes. "Good lord. I need a nap."

"Of course," I say, standing up and returning to the cart. "You should rest."

"Thank you, Albert," Sam says as I hand him the pills. "And you know what? I've been thinking about something." He hesitates. "You want to have that drink?"

"Drink?" I ask.

"Yeah, the one I turned down the night of the storm. I don't know about you, but I sure could use a stiff cocktail."

"Sure," I say, exhilarated. "When?"

Sam shrugs. "I'll have to check my calendar, but I'm pretty sure I'm free tonight. Six p.m. work?"

"Six p.m.," I repeat, as I watch him toss the pills into his mouth. "I'd like that very much."

chapter
39

SAM CHECKS THE CLOCK on the table beside him—three minutes to six—and then taps the waistband of his sweatpants one more time, making sure the pills are still there. Six of them, which he'd spit out after Albert left the room over the past two days, hiding them in his pillowcase. It hasn't been easy. The pills put him to sleep almost immediately, and given all his options, sleep consistently ranks high on the list, but it's all been worth it for this moment.

He closes his eyes and imagines it again: slyly dropping the pills into Albert's drink. Two sips, and Albert's speech will slur. Three, confusion and drowsiness will set in. By the fourth he'll be unconscious, at which point Sam will strangle him and then, for good measure, stab him with the putty knife tucked under his thigh. His beloved four-inch putty knife, which he's kept hidden under the mattress, carefully smoothing away every remnant of wallpaper paste, polishing it until it glows. He envisions it piercing the soft spot on Albert's temple, again and again, watching that sad, deranged brain unspool all over whatever dumb college sweatshirt Albert will be wearing tonight.

Sam closes his eyes and sighs. Freud was right. Aggression really is as satisfying as sex.

The clock strikes six, and Sam hears the key in the lock.

"Hey there, heartbreaker," Albert says, sticking his head into the room. "You ready?"

Sam smiles. "Sure am."

Albert steps inside, leaves the door open, and parks the cart near the wall. It's set with two glasses and something hidden under a yellow dish towel. "I have a surprise for you," Albert says, excited. He pulls the towel off the bottle with a flourish.

"Johnnie Walker Blue." Sam is stunned. "How did you know—"

"That this is your go-to drink on special occasions? You said so, in the interview with the newspaper. Question number twelve."

"Didn't know you saw that," Sam says, surprised.

"My mother instilled me with an appreciation for local journalism," he says, turning his back to Sam. "I read the paper religiously and remember you mentioned this drink."

"Lucky for me," Sam says. And he means it, too. Not only is it the world's finest scotch, it's also going to deal quite a blow when mixed with a gazillion milligrams of whatever the hell these pills are.

"You sure do have expensive taste," Albert says.

Sam nods and keeps his eyes on the bottle in Albert's hand.

"May I do the honors?" Sam asks. "Nothing like the first whiff of Johnnie Walker Blue."

Albert hands Sam the bottle, and he pauses to stroke the smooth glass, appreciating its weight. "This was my mom's drink," Sam says, turning the cap and leaning in for the scent. "Kept a bottle in the cabinet. After my dad left, she poured herself a glass every year on her wedding anniversary."

"That's sad."

"Sure is." Sam takes the glass tumbler Albert hands him. "Most bartenders believe a pour is one and a half ounces," he says, watching the whisky stream slowly into the glass. "But I find that amount is inadequate, especially for a first drink."

"Not too much," Albert says, holding up his hands. "I've never had scotch before."

Sam pours a drink for himself and then sets the bottle on the bedside table as Albert sits in Sam's chair. "To a return to happy hour," Sam says, raising his glass.

"That's exactly what I was going to say," Albert says, red-faced. "To happy hour."

Sam raises his glass to his lips and then lowers it quickly. "Wait. Stop. This isn't right."

"What's wrong?"

"The ice cube."

"What ice cube?"

"For the drinks. It's key," Sam says. "A slight chill enhances the flavor."

"You know so much about everything," Albert says. "Hang on." He sets his glass on the bedside table and walks out of the room.

Game time.

Sam pulls out the square of paper towel holding the pills and gently unfolds it. Beads of sweat sprout on his forehead as he crushes two pills over Albert's glass.

"How many?" Albert calls from the kitchen.

"One ice cube for each of us," Sam says, watching the powder dissolve in the copper liquid, leaving a chalky film that rises to the top of the glass. "Medium ones." Sam drops the last four pills in and swirls the glass, his hand trembling so badly he fears he's going to drop it. He replaces the glass on the table and picks up his own just as Albert walks into the room, an ice cube in each palm.

"Perfect," Sam says, the sweat pooling on his lower back, as Albert drips a cube into his glass. "Thank you."

Albert sits down. "One more time," he says. "Cheers."

Sam watches as Albert takes the tiniest sip. "Good lord. It tastes like lighter fluid."

"Whisky is an acquired taste," Sam says. "But trust me, it's worth it." He lifts his glass, allowing himself one swallow. The whisky warms him immediately, and he has to hold himself back from drinking it all in one satisfying gulp. There will be plenty of time to sip whisky at home, with Annie, and he needs a clear head.

Albert brings the glass to his lips again, barely wetting them. "Yum," he says, grimacing. "So—" He takes a deep breath, eyes wide. "What do you want to talk about?"

"What do you mean, what do I want to talk about?" Sam says, his gaze on Albert's drink. "We're two dudes having a drink at the end of the day. I want to talk about either girls or sports."

"Oh!" Albert laughs, blushes. "Well I don't have much to say about either one of those things."

"Course you do." *Take a drink, Albert.* "Who was your first crush?"

Albert winces. "Kathleen Callahan," he says right away. "We worked together at the 7-Eleven." He shifts the glass to his other thigh. "She was intimidating. Girls like her never paid attention to me."

"What'd she look like?" *Take a fucking drink, Al.*

"Brown curly hair. Eyeglasses."

"You two talk?" Sam asks.

"A couple times. She let me listen to some songs on her head-phones. The music she liked was *loud*."

"Metal chicks are the best," Sam says. He takes another sip, hoping Albert will follow suit, but he just recrosses his legs.

"And then my dad showed up to buy cigarettes." Albert grimaces. "I hated the way he looked at her. Brought her up at the dinner table that night; told me I should ask her out. His exact words: 'What about it, Al? You man enough to get some of that?'"

"Your dad sounds like a serious prick," Sam says, unable to help himself.

"It gets worse," Albert says. "He came back a few days later and told Kathleen I had a thing for her. Said that I'd been jerk-ing off to her, if the state of my bedsheets meant anything."

"God, Al," Sam says. "That's awful." *Tragic really, like every story you have, so please, brother, take a drink and end this thing.* "What did you do?"

"I waited for my dad to drive away, and then I left. Never went back to the job. Everyone heard about it at school. It was mortifying."

Albert's expression is pained, and Sam can't help but feel for the guy. "I'm sorry, Albert," he says.

Albert shrugs. "I googled her recently. She married a Mor-mon."

"You want my professional opinion?" Sam asks. "How to make yourself feel better about the whole thing?"

Albert looks up, hopeful. Sam lifts his glass and points to the whisky. "A whole bunch of this stuff. It's exactly those types of experiences this is manufactured to forget."

Albert laughs. "Well, then, in that case . . ." He raises his glass again. "To Kathleen Callahan, and her seven children."

"Go ahead," Sam says. "A good long sip. Get the full experience."

Albert touches his lips to the glass and then abruptly stands up. "Who am I kidding? You shouldn't be wasting this stuff on me." He empties his glass into Sam's. "Just the smell of it turns my stomach."

Sam feels the air leave his lungs, the rise of bile in his gut, as he stares at the poisoned contents of Albert's glass mixing with his own.

"Go ahead," Albert says. "Don't deprive yourself on my account."

Sam holds up the glass and takes a good look at it. Do it, he thinks. Drink the whole thing. It's time to face the facts. He's got no usable legs, no key to that door, and a very slim chance he'll ever see Annie again.

He places the glass on the bedside table. A slim chance is still better than none.

"Funny thing," Sam says, "but I think I've lost my taste for it."

Albert rolls his eyes. "Well I guess that's one hundred and sixteen dollars down the drain." He takes Sam's glass, sets it with his on top of the cart, and then returns to Sam's chair. "Where were we?" he says, crossing his legs and clasping one knee. "Oh right. First crush. Your turn."

chapter
40

ANNIE SITS AT THE kitchen island, her chin in her hand, picturing Sam beside her.

So let me get this straight, he says in his most professional tone. *You're aware that I hid a shitload of credit card debt from you, and I lied about visiting my mother, and yet you're still waiting up at two o'clock in the morning, wondering if I'm coming home?*

Not only that, Annie admits. *But before opening my eyes in the morning, I pretend you're behind me, your arms wrapped around me, still the man I thought I knew. I have to say, Sam, this denial thing is pretty great. I can see why you like it so much.*

The kettle whistles behind her and she stands up, makes a cup of tea, and returns to the home office she and Sam shared. Sam insisted on having everything custom-built: one side for her files, one side for his. She's been going through his side for the last hour, page by boring page, amazed by the things he saved. A receipt for a computer he bought in 2001. The user manual for a vacuum cleaner, filed away in its own file labeled VACUUM CLEANER USER MANUAL. Tax returns for the last twenty years, on which he listed every single item he donated to Goodwill, trying so hard to be the good guy who plays by the rules, nothing at all like his dad.

She returns to the open drawer and continues, still not sure what, exactly, she's looking for, coming across two expired passports, one with a stamp from a trip to Honduras he apparently took in high school, a trip he never mentioned. Maybe *this* is what she's looking for. Confirmation that Franklin Sheehy is right, that she never knew Sam Statler at all.

Mom, Medical

She spots the folder at the back, the words in thick Sharpie letters. Inside is a stack of Margaret's medical records. The early symptoms. *Deteriorating personal hygiene. Difficulty planning the day's schedule. Frequent mood swings.* The official diagnosis last March. *Disease progressing quicker than expected; having hard time managing daily tasks.*

Patient has stopped speaking. Mutism may be the result of progressing disease.

He can't deal with it. That's why he hasn't been visiting his mother: a perfectly innocent explanation. He isn't a pathological liar, he's a scaredy cat, unable to bear seeing his mother in the state she's been in—silent, expressionless—and too ashamed to tell Annie the truth. So he hid it from her, probably hating himself for being such a coward.

You're doing it again, Sam's voice chides from inside her head. *You're believing in me when I've given you every reason not to.*

She pages through the rest of the papers in the file—insurance letters, six issues of the facility's monthly newsletter, printed entirely in Comic Sans. She's about to return the folder to the drawer when she sees an envelope tucked into the back, addressed to Sam. She pulls out a letter. Three pages from the attorney at Rushing Waters, "Living Will and Durable Power of Attorney for Margaret Statler" printed along the top.

I hereby designate Sam Statler of Chestnut Hill, New York, my attorney-in-fact, in my stead and for my benefit. As my attorney-in-fact, Sam Statler shall exercise power as fiduciary, including the power to receive and deposit funds in any financial institute, to withdraw funds by check or otherwise pay for goods and services. If necessary—

Alarmed, she flips to the last page, seeing Margaret's signature at the bottom, next to a notarized stamp, dated two weeks ago. *Signed, executed, and immediately in effect.*

No, she thinks, her skin suddenly clammy.

His mother signed the papers. He got $2 million of his father's money. And then he left. She laughs and then drops the folder and reaches into her back pocket for her phone. The call goes straight to voice mail.

"Hello, dear husband," she says, her voice breaking with anger. "You're probably occupied at the moment, toying with whatever unknowing victim you've seduced this time, but I wanted to call and congratulate you. You did it, Sam, the one thing you tried *so* hard to avoid. You ended up *just* like your father."

chapter
41

FUCK.

Sam stares at the patches of torn wallpaper clinging to the wall.

Fuck fuck fuckfuckfuckfuck.

He's losing his mind.

He can't lie here anymore under the weight of these casts, confined to what he's been told is the number-one-ranked mattress-in-a-box two years in a row. He can't stand how badly his legs itch or one more day of pretending to love frozen crinkle-cut french fries, sweet-talking Albert to save his own life. But he especially hates the sorrow he feels, missing Annie like this.

Well, maybe it's time for Sam Statler to stop whining like a girl and do something about it.

Sam opens his eyes and laughs out loud. Well, look who it is. Teddy from Freddy, talking down to him from a glass booth. "Gee, Dad, what a great idea. I'll just stand up and walk out of here. Why didn't I think of that?" Sam listens. It's quiet. "What am I supposed to do?" he whispers.

What any self-respecting man would do, his father whispers back. *Man up and find a way out of that house.*

Sam takes a deep breath. "Hey!" he shouts at the hallway. "Creepy dude! You home?"

You know he's not home, Teddy says. *You heard him leave in his car a half hour ago.*

Sam stares at the door, his pulse quickening. "Okay, fine, fuck it. Let's do this." He sits up and pulls off the quilt.

Good evening, folks, and welcome to tonight's spectacle, his father sings in his ear. *A chance for Sam Statler to prove he's a man.*

Sam eases to the edge of the mattress and reaches underneath for the putty knife. Sliding it into the back of his waistband, he swings his legs off the bed and rests his plastered feet on the floor. He reaches for the headboard and hoists himself up, his eyes on his chair, six feet away.

Gotta admit it, his dad says. *I'm feeling pretty skeptical he can make it to that chair.*

Sam lets go and takes a step forward. *Unstable gait*, his father says. Sam takes another step. *Forward propulsion is compromised. Annnnd . . . he's down.*

Sam hits the ground hard. Pushing the pain aside, he hoists himself onto his elbows, dragging himself toward the chair. *Okay*, Teddy murmurs. *He did it. He got there.* Sam pulls himself onto the chair and propels himself toward the door. Winded, he removes the putty knife from his waistband, a girl's name springing suddenly to mind. Rebecca Kirkpatrick, summer before sophomore year. She was two years older, and her family had a cabin on Lake Poetry, forty minutes north. Twice they skipped school and drove there in her yellow Jeep, where Sam would use the credit card Rebecca's father gave her to pick the lock on the back door to the cabin.

He slides the blade of the putty knife between the door frame and the lock, recalling how it worked. Rebecca sat on the grass, rolling a joint, as Sam concentrated on using the tip of the credit card to catch the edge of the lock and push it aside, opening the door to all the wonderful things that awaited inside that room—

Well, by golly, would you look at that? Teddy from Freddy purrs as the lock clicks open. *He did it. Ol' Stats actually opened the door.*

"I did it!" Sam breathes, elated, imagining the roar of the crowd. "I fucking did it." He tucks the putty knife back into his waistband and throws open the door to a hallway, giddy. It smells overwhelmingly of the pine-scented chemical shit Albert mops his room with three times a week. Sam propels his chair down the hall, which opens into a kitchen with apple-green walls, the back wall covered in the cascading leaves of at least a dozen hanging plants. He considers stopping to search the drawers for a knife but keeps going into the living room, where a large picture window offers a view of the sky he hasn't seen in eight days. It's raining. He's imagining the feel of the rain against his dry skin when he arrives at the front door, and reaches for the knob.

Strike one, Teddy says quietly to the hushed crowd.

Sam rattles the doorknob. Nonononono.

The guy locked him in. Teddy tsks. *That's some bad luck.*

Sam moves quickly to the table in the foyer and opens the slim drawer. He slides his hand to the back, extracting a single key on a bright orange keychain labeled "Gary Unger, Gary Unger Locksmiths." Sam returns to the door and jams the key into the lock. It doesn't fit, and Sam knows exactly why. It's not the key to this door. It's the key to Sam's office, the same square key Sam has on his keychain. The key Albert is not supposed to have.

"No big deal," he tells the crowd, tossing the key on the floor and grabbing once more for the putty knife, his hand shaking. He did it once, he'll do it again. He can taste the salty tang of the sweat on his lip as he jimmies the putty knife between the door and the frame, sliding it up and then down—

Snap.

Strike two, Sam's dad whispers.

Sam holds up the wooden handle of the putty knife; the metal blade is stuck in the door. "No," he whispers, reaching for the blade. "Come back." He bangs the door, attempting to free the metal edge. It's no use.

Looks like it's time for plan B, Teddy says.

The window. Sam slides into the living room and uses the arm of the sofa to pull himself close to the window, getting a glimpse of Sidney Pigeon's house through the hedges at the edge of Albert's property. There's smoke coming from the chimney. Someone's home.

Time's running out.

"Shut up, Dad," Sam whispers, focusing on his options. *I can break the window and scream for help. Someone at Sidney's house will hear me.*

Is that a joke? Ted murmurs. *No way anyone will hear him, all the way up here.*

I can break the glass and jump out the window.

But then what? his father scoffs. *Find himself with two broken legs and covered in glass shards and caught in a rosebush? That's what I call a lose-lose-lose situation.*

Sam scans the room, noticing the details. Bright-blue walls, crowded with large abstract paintings. A soft white rug. Floral couches. Admittedly not the design aesthetic Sam expected. *What's Statler doing?* Teddy from Freddy whispers. *He's got five minutes to save his life, and he's sitting there thinking about paint colors.* Sam keeps going, through a series of rooms—a formal dining room with mauve walls and a large chandelier. Another sitting room, two plush chairs in front of a fireplace. Along the far wall he sees a set of pocket doors, and makes his way over to open them. It's a library. Quite a magnificent one at that. Floor-to-ceiling mahogany shelves, a ladder on a rail. It smells like a real library, one of his favorite places that his mom took him to as a kid, and he moves slowly toward the shelves and pulls out a book. *A Tree Grows in Brooklyn*, first edition.

He puts the book back, searching for a sign of a telephone, and spots a row of framed photographs on a nearby shelf. They're all of the same woman. She has bright red hair and a wide smile; this must be VeeVee, the mother Albert has mentioned. Behind the frames sits a row of cheap purple binders, he notices, out of place among the fine books.

Don't do it, his father warns him. Sam can feel the weight of the crowd's eyes on him, urging him to ignore the binders and keep going, but his curiosity wins out. He moves the photographs aside for a better look. The name Henry Rockford is written on the spine of the first binder, and Sam pulls it out. There are pages of photographs in plastic sleeves—two men, one older and one younger, standing side by side, and it takes Sam a second to realize that the younger man is Albert, who looks to be in his twenties in the photographs. Sam flips ahead, finding pages of notes. Medical conditions. A family tree.

Sam closes the binder and pulls out another. Lorraine Whittenger. She's got white hair and is confined to a wheelchair, and in these photographs Albert is wearing the same blue apron embroidered with the Home Health Angels logo that he wears when he comes into Sam's room. Angelo Monticelli,

Edith Voranger—Sam keeps going, putting it together. All of these people were his patients.

Linda Pennypiece

Sam sees the name toward the end of the row. Linda Penny-piece? Albert's "friend" from Albany?

He grabs the binder.

Facts about Linda: A list

1. She loves the Olive Garden
2. *Mary Tyler Moore* and *Frasier* reruns to calm her before bed
3. She turns ninety in March; organize a party!

Linda was a client.

He turns the pages—notes about her stroke, "Linda's Famous Salisbury Steak Recipe"—arriving at a paper with the seal of Albany County, New York, on the top. "Temporary order for protection against stalking, aggravated stalking, or harassment. Linda Pennypiece vs. Albert Bitterman Jr.

"You, Albert Bitterman, the adverse party, are hereby notified that any intentional violation of this order is a criminal violation and can result in your immediate arrest."

A restraining order.

Sam flips the page. "Home Health Angels, Inc. Termination of employment. This letter confirms that your employment is terminated with immediate effect. Any further contact with any clients or staff of Home Health Angels will be reported to law enforcement."

I am not liking where this is going. Teddy from Freddy lowers his voice. *And if I were Sam Statler, I would definitely not look to see whose name is on that last binder—*

DR. SAM STATLER.

Sam's hands tremble as he pulls it off the shelf and opens it to the first page. "Twenty Questions with Sam Statler." He turns the page and sees a copy of the flyer Sam had found under his windshield that day.

OFFICE SPACE FOR RENT IN HISTORIC HOME,
PERFECT FOR A QUIET PROFESSIONAL.
WILLING TO RENOVATE TO SUIT.
CONTACT ALBERT BITTERMAN.

Sam pages forward, through dozens of photographs of himself. The day he moved in downstairs. Arriving for work. Getting into his car at the end of the day. He keeps flipping, through scribbled lists ("Things I've Lied to Sam About"; "Reasons to Remain Happy, Despite Sam's Bad Mood"), the bills he had hidden downstairs in his desk, an Excel spreadsheet Albert made, keeping track of Sam's debt:

- Visa: $36,588
- Chase Sapphire Select: $73,211
- Mortgage: $655,000

Next are pages of notes and observations about people with odd names:

Skinny Jeans
The Mumble Twins
Numb Nancy

Sam scans them quickly. "Numb Nancy has been married for sixteen years. She is the director of development at Meadow

Hills." That's Nancy Neumann. His client. These are *all* his clients. Sam feels the rise of a giggle as it dawns on him— not only was Albert up here listening, he was taking copious notes—and he worries he's going to start laughing and never stop, but then he turns the page.

COMMUNITY SEARCH FOR SAM STATLER!
MEET AT THE BOWLING ALLEY! DRESS WARM!

They're looking for him! Right now, probably. Sam imagines them, out in this rain, searching for his car—wherever the hell *that* thing went! Which means it's only a matter of time before they find him and—

Missing Chestnut Hill Psychologist Discovered to Be in Significant Debt at Time of Disappearance.
Chief of Police Franklin Sheehy says investigators will continue to pursue all credible leads, but in light of the recent discovery of Statler's debt, which is believed to be upward of $100,000, and kept secret from his wife, law enforcement officials are increasingly considering the possibility that his disappearance was not accidental.

No.

He feels sick to his stomach, and yet he turns the page to another sleeve of photographs. It's Margaret, in her room at Rushing Waters, cheek to cheek with Albert.

He's been visiting Sam's mother.

And here we go, folks, Teddy says. *Statler's on the move.* Sam drops the binder and heads through the pocket doors. Back in the living room, he studies the picture window again, wondering if it's worth the risk to throw an end table through the glass and do his best to jump, when something clicks in his head. He turns his chair around and gets himself back to the kitchen, to the wall covered in the cascading leaves of the hanging plants. He yanks a handful of leaves, bringing a plant crashing to the floor. Yes! He was right. There's a sliding glass door behind these plants. He swipes at the leaves, pulling the plants down, one by one, leaving a carpet of dirt on the floor.

Looks like Statler found a way out, his father observes as Sam stares at the sliding glass door that opens onto a small stone patio. He reaches for the lock on the handle. He slides it up. *It works.* A lock in this house that actually unlocks. Sam yanks the door open. He gazes at the backyard, and with one deep breath, he throws himself off his chair, onto his stomach.

Would you believe it? He did it, Ted Statler purrs as Sam crawls out the door into the cold and wet backyard. *Maybe I was wrong. Maybe this kid's not completely useless after all.*

chapter 42

THE CUTE WOMAN BEHIND the bar shoots Annie the perfectly nor-
mal smile of a person pretending not to know she's the one
married to the hot guy who went missing, his face smiling from
the MISSING flyers still hanging on in some places. "What can
I get you?" she asks, setting a menu down in front of Annie.

"A job with a living wage and a restored faith in humanity,"
Annie says.

The woman makes a face. "What do you think this is, the
Netherlands?"

Annie laughs for the first time in eight days. "Gin martini
with five olives." She pushes the menu away. "That counts as
dinner, right?"

Annie watches her mix the drink and she can feel the chill
off the glass when the woman sets it down in front of her.
"Happy anniversary, asshole," Annie whispers, raising the
glass to the empty stool beside her. She takes a long swallow
and considers the idea again: this is part of the chase. He's playing a part, the most fucked-up one yet: the Missing Husband.
She imagines him, his feet up in front of a fire at an Airbnb
in Saugerties, their favorite town in the Catskills, relishing it
all. He's been taking his meals at the diner, sitting in front of
a sausage scramble and bottomless cup of coffee, reading the

articles about his disappearance. He's probably busy planning his return right now, in fact, when he'll burst through the front door disheveled and unshaven, his face artistically streaked with mud for the big reveal. "Honey, guess what? I'm alive!"

He'll take a seat at the kitchen table and spin a story about the fugue state he's been living in for eight days, brought on by a concussion he doesn't remember getting. How he hitched a ride home from New Orleans with a dude in an eighteen-wheeler who chain-smoked the whole way. She'll break down in tears and tell him how much she missed him, and the inevitable sex will be so hot she'll regret not having thought of the scenario herself.

The gin is warming her, and she's aware, of course, that it's far more likely that this was all "the chase," the entire thing, from day one. Sam was the deeply kind and curious man determined to change her idea about love, and she was the schmuck who fell for it. She's got to give him credit: He *really* committed to the role, sweeping her off her feet at a goddamn *Brooks Brothers*. She thought he might be fun for a night, but he surprised her. He was witty and smart, introspective in a way she'd rarely experienced in a man.

It took him only six months to suggest marriage, sitting on the porch of the farmhouse for sale in his sleepy hometown. He had spent his weekend at his mother's house, packing her for the move to Rushing Waters, when he called Annie and told her about the house he'd found for sale. "There's a train leaving in forty-seven minutes," he said. "Get on it and come see it with me."

"I didn't know you were shopping for a house in upstate New York," she said.

"Not *me*," he said. "We. Trust me on this."

He was waiting for her at the train station three hours later in his mom's spotless 1999 Toyota Corolla, with two iced coffees and a very long kiss. They were ten minutes out of town, up in the hills, when he turned at the mailbox for 119 Albemarle Road, down a long driveway to a white four-bedroom farmhouse. It was incredible. Post-and-beam. Six acres.

"I figured it out," Sam said, sitting next to her on the porch after the realtor showed them around. "You can teach at the university, write one of those books you got in your head. I'll open a private practice, make sure my mom's okay. With my dad's money on the way, we can take it easy for a few years. Make a home here. And who knows?" he said, bumping her shoulder. "Maybe someone will finally tell us how children are made."

"Are you crazy?" she said. "I've known you for six months."

"Six months and one day," he corrected her. "You did it, Annie. You tolerated me longer than you thought you could tolerate a man." He wrapped his arms around her and squeezed. "I knew you could." He let go of her then and pulled a thin silver ring from his front pocket. "Want to keep going?"

Her phone rings in front of her on the bar, next to her martini. It's her aunt Therese, Maddie's mother, calling from France.

"Annie," Therese says, and as soon as Annie hears her voice, she starts to cry. Her aunt's voice is identical to her mother's, so much so that Annie can close her eyes and pretend it's her mom on the other end of the phone. "How are you, honey?"

"Terrible," Annie's voice breaks. "I don't understand what's happening. I thought I knew him."

"I know you did, sweetheart. We all did."

Annie stifles a sob. Therese and Maddie were shocked

when Annie and Sam FaceTimed to share the news of their engagement—and then so excited that, with Sam's help, they showed up in New York the next weekend to surprise Annie, celebrating the engagement over a seven-course dinner at a small Italian restaurant in the East Village.

"Annie. I want you to come home." Therese's voice is firm. "Maddie is going to turn the restaurant over to the manager for a few days and come to the house. We'll all be together." *The house*, shorthand for the five-bedroom house on the olive farm where Annie's mother and Therese grew up, and which they inherited together after their parents' death. It was here that Therese, Maddie, and her uncle Nicolas gathered after Annie's parents' funeral, and where Annie spent three months hiding in Maddie's room, before returning to start at Cornell and sell her childhood home.

"I can't come home," Annie says, pressing a bar napkin to her eyes. "I have a job."

"You can take a break," Therese says. "They'll understand."

"I know, but . . ."

"But what?" Therese says.

"But what if he comes home, and I'm not there?" Annie whispers, knowing how ridiculous she sounds. "What if they find—"

"Oh, Annie." Annie hears the pity in her aunt's voice. *Silly girl, he's not coming home. The police are barely even looking for him.* "If that happens, they'll call you immediately, and you'll get on the next plane."

Annie notices a woman at the end of the bar, watching her. She turns away. "I'll think about it," she says. "Thank you, Therese." She drops her phone into her purse and throws back the rest of her drink.

Why wouldn't she go? She's useless here, showing up zombie-like to classes, finding it impossible to focus. In France her uncle Nicolas will cook her favorite meals and make sure there's a good bottle of red wine open on the table at all times; she and Maddie will talk until they fall asleep in the king-size bed upstairs, in the room that was once her parents'.

As she waves at the bartender for the check, someone slides onto the stool next to hers. It's the woman from across the bar. She's younger than Annie thought—early twenties, probably. "Harriet Eager, from the *Daily Freeman*," the woman says, offering her hand. "I'm sorry for what you're going through."

Ignoring her hand, Annie takes a twenty from her wallet. "Well, perhaps you can make yourself feel better by writing another article about my husband's financial troubles." She drops the money on the bar. "For what it's worth," she adds, "I thought the police would use that information to help my husband, not to make him look bad."

"It wasn't the police who told me about the debt," Harriet says as Annie starts toward the door.

Annie turns around. "What do you mean?"

"I mean it wasn't the police."

"Well, then, who was it?"

Harriet shrugs. "A tip. Some reader, emailing to say there was a rumor circulating that your husband was in serious debt. I usually ignore these things, but I decided to call Chief Sheehy. It checked out."

"A *rumor*? There was no rumor. Why would someone do that?"

"CSI," Harriet says right away. "It happens all the time. Amateur detectives, raring to pitch a theory. One guy was particularly persistent in the beginning, saying he had it on good authority that your husband had run off with a patient." She shakes her head. "There are some serious weirdos out there."

Annie's head is pounding. "I have to go." She weaves through a crowd of people waiting near the door to be seated, smack into a man entering the restaurant.

"I'm sorry," he says, taking her elbow to steady her. "How clumsy of me. Are you okay?"

He has graying hair and bright blue eyeglasses, and she doesn't like the feel of his hand on her arm. "Yes," she says, pulling away. "I'm fine."

As she unlocks her car, she hears her phone ringing in her bag.

It's Franklin Sheehy. "Good evening, Ms. Potter." There's a somber edge to his voice. "We need to talk. Any chance you can come down to the station?"

chapter

43

I WATCH ANNIE TALKING on the phone inside her car. Poor girl, alone on her anniversary. She and Sam celebrate every week. I know because I have Sam's appointment book filed away in my library—"Annie, anniversary drinks" jotted down each Tuesday—and I've been imagining how cute they looked, clinking glasses of overpriced alcohol.

"You want a table?" A young woman is eyeing me from behind the podium. She's got tattoos up and down her arms, getting back at her parents, most likely, by defiling her own body.

"No, thank you," I say, watching Annie pull away from the curb. "I just remembered. I have somewhere to be."

My own car is parked illegally in the bank parking lot. I start the engine but don't move.

I feel terrible for her.

I know that I can't, but I wish I could tell her what a mess Sam was at happy hour yesterday. He barely seemed to be listening when I told him about my one experience playing football. It was not easy to talk about. I was seven years old and begged my mother to talk my father out of forcing me to play, but she refused. I stood in a line on the field, someone handed me the football, and the next thing I knew, a boy from my school three times my size threw me to the ground. I couldn't breathe, and was so sure I was dying that when I did finally catch my breath, I burst into tears, right there on Sanders Field, in front of my father and half of the men of Wayne, Indiana. And what did Sam say when I finished telling him? *Nothing.* He just stared at the wall, looking dazed, and then, out of nowhere, he started to talk about Annie, telling me how much he loves her, and how worried he is that she's not okay.

But she looks okay to me. A little too skinny, maybe, and those bags under her eyes suggest she might not be sleeping as well as she should—but she's well enough to get dolled up and take herself out for a drink. That's good news.

I pat the bag holding three cans of condensed onion soup on the passenger seat beside me and put the car into drive. Salisbury steak will cheer Sam up.

The rain winks on and off in my headlights as I follow a truck with a plumbing logo down Main Street and along the train tracks, the guy going so slow I assume he gets paid by the hour. I crack my window an inch, taking in the heady scent of wood smoke and Democrats, and turn on to Cherry Lane. Nearly every light is on at the Pigeon's house; I'm assuming she's lost her interest in climate change, burning all those fossil fuels. I'm approaching the bridge when I spot something in the road and slam on my brakes.

No. Please, my god, no.

I kill my engine, reach for the shopping bag on the passenger seat, and step out of the car into the cold, sharp rain. It's Sam. In the middle of the street, his face streaked with mud, the sleeves of the sweatshirt I lent him—Smith College, one of my favorites—filthy and torn. "No, Albert," he says, and I see that he's crying. "Please. I'm so close."

"Sam?" I tighten my grip on the bag as I walk toward him. "Where are you off to, Sam?"

"Home, Albert," he says, his sobs lost to the drumming of the rain. "Please, I just want to go home."

"Home?" I lift the bag over my head, my head spinning and my vision clouding. "But you are home, Sam." The crack of three cans of condensed onion soup making contact with that strong, perfectly chiseled jaw is louder than I expected. "Come on," I say as he collapses at my feet. "Let's go have some steak."

chapter

44

FRANKLIN SHEEHY IS WAITING for Annie in his cruiser when she arrives at the police station. "Jump in," he says. "Let's take a ride."

She hesitates and then gets in. They stay quiet as Sheehy heads out of town on the desolate road along the railroad tracks. Three silent minutes later, they pull into the parking lot of Stor-Mor Storage. "With all the extra space, you'd think they'd have room for two extra *e*'s," Annie said to Sam on her first visit to town, when they sat in this parking lot in the front seat of his mother's Corolla, making out like schoolkids. Over lunch, she had begged him for a tour of all the places her once-virile young husband convinced the naive teen girls of Chestnut Hill to let him into their pants.

He happily complied, taking her to the abandoned drive-in theater; the strip mall, behind Payless ShoeSource; and then here, to Stor-Mor Storage, where he and Annie fooled around in the front seat and where, earlier this afternoon, the police discovered Sam's nice new Lexus parked inside one of the units, in perfect condition.

"He dropped it off about six p.m. the night he disappeared," Sheehy informs her as they stand in front of unit 12, watching a technician in the front seat dust for prints.

"Why would he do that?" she asks, numb.

"To keep the cops busy looking for something they're not going to find."

"So how did you find it?"

"The place was vandalized recently, and the manager was going through security footage. Saw the car driving in, the night of the storm, and recognized it from the news."

Annie snaps her head at Sheehy. "Is there footage of him?"

Sheehy holds her gaze for a moment. "Come with me."

She follows him toward a building that resembles a wooden shed. Inside is a metal desk with three television monitors and empty Styrofoam coffee cups scattered on top. A cop is sitting in a tattered rolling desk chair in the corner, checking his phone. Seeing Sheehy, he quickly clicks off the screen and drops the phone into his chest pocket. "Chief."

"This is Dr. Statler's wife," Sheehy says. "I want you to show her the footage."

The cop slides to the desk, turns a monitor so it's facing Annie. She sees a frozen image of a blurry car, which starts to move when the cop hits the keyboard. It's Sam's Lexus driving into unit 12. A figure appears on the screen a few moments later. A man. He has his back to the camera as he slides the door shut and then takes an umbrella from under his arm and opens it. His face is obstructed by the umbrella when he turns to the camera, and the cop freezes the video. "This is the best we got," the cop says.

"Can you make it any bigger?" Annie asks. The cop zooms in and then stands up to offer Annie the chair. She sits and leans close to the screen, her heart aching as she recognizes the jacket. A Brooks Brothers' Madison Fit Wool Reserve Blazer in classic navy. The one she picked out for him, the one he kept at his office.

"Can you confirm that's your husband?" Sheehy says. She nods, unable to speak.

Sheehy heaves a heavy sigh. "Sorry, Annie. I know this isn't easy."

The room feels claustrophobic. "Can you take me home?"

"Of course. Let me tell my sergeant."

She stands up and walks outside. Two men in nylon jackets are standing near the gate, lighting their cigarettes from a shared match. "I knew this guy's old man," one says as she passes. "Guess it's true what they say. Like father, like son."

chapter
45

SOMETHING BUZZES IN SAM'S ear, and he opens his eyes.

It's pitch-black and cold.

He's on all fours, in the middle of the street, just over the bridge. He can see Sidney Pigeon's house, a hundred feet away. A light is on upstairs, and a figure is standing at the window. Squinting, Sam makes out bushy brown curls under a baseball hat. The window is open, and he's waving at Sam. "You see me!" Sam yells, waving back, elated. "It's me! Sam Statler!" He starts cackling, waiting for the kid to rush from the window and down the stairs, where he'll spring into Sidney's living room and find an adult to call 911. But the kid isn't doing that. Instead, he keeps waving, and suddenly Sam realizes he's got it wrong. The kid isn't gesturing to him; he doesn't even see him. He is clearing smoke from the joint in his hand and then he's closing the window, turning off the light, and vanishing.

Sam rolls onto his back, tasting the sour tang of blood in his mouth. Headlights are approaching the hill; a car is coming. It's going to be Sidney, on her way back from the gym. She's going to spring from her minivan and ask him what on earth he's doing on the pavement in weather like this . . .

The moths come at him again, and he opens his eyes, the bile rising in his gut, as he remembers the kick to his face and realizes he's not outside. He's back in the house, locked inside the room. He pulls himself up to sit and feels along the wall until he reaches the door. "Come out, come out wherever you are," he croaks. His throat is sore and his mouth is killing him; he reaches up to his cheek and discovers a deep gash. "It's time to change my clothes and give me a shave, Albert. You don't want me to call Home Health Angels and report you for violating the first tenet in the employee fucking handbook— 'When you look good, you feel good!' Do you, you deranged little shit?"

At last his fingers find the light switch. The brightness blinds him momentarily, but then he shakes off the fog, taking in the state of his clothes, the walls around him, the stacks of boxes near his feet.

He was wrong. He's not in the room. He's in the closet.

There's a door within arm's reach, and he leans forward for the knob. It opens, casting light onto the bed with the patchwork quilt, his chair. Sam sits back. This is the closet in his room. He takes a closer look at the boxes, two dozen at least, neatly stacked against the wall, "Agatha Lawrence" written in neat script across each of them.

Agatha Lawrence. The woman who died in this room.

Sam hoists himself up to a sitting position, sending a bolt of pain across his back. He reaches to the top of the stack and pulls down a box. It lands on top of his casts, the contents spilling on to the floor around him. He waits and listens. It's quiet. He picks up a thick black book and turns it over. *Charles Lawrence, 1905–1991*. Inside, there's a black-and-white photograph of a young couple and two boys, posing on the front porch of the Lawrence House.

He staves off a bout of laughter. *Why did he put me in the closet?*

Hmmm, let's see. It's Annie's voice, fighting its way through the ache in his muddled brain. *He put you in a closet with a dead woman's boxes. Maybe because he . . .* She goes quiet, waiting for him to speak. *Come on, you dope. Think.*

"Because he wants me to look inside them?" Sam says.

Annie is silent.

Sam drops the scrapbook and riffles quickly through the rest of the papers strewn across the closet floor—original architectural drawings, newspaper clippings from the 1930s about the founding of Lawrence Chemical, letters written from a naval ship in the Pacific. Box after box, he finds financial papers, bank statements, retirement accounts. A photo falls from one: a teenage girl with bright red hair. She's wearing a cardigan sweater and jeans, a cigarette tipped between her fingers, and Sam recognizes her right away—that flaming red hair—as the woman in the framed photographs on Albert's library shelf. That wasn't Albert's mother, as Sam had guessed. That was this woman, Agatha Lawrence.

He returns to the box from which the photograph fell and finds a smaller rectangular box, holding two neat rows of unsealed yellow envelopes. Sam selects one and removes the letter.

August 23, 1969
Hello beautiful,
I arrived in Princeton this morning and it's as pompous and bourgeois as I imagined. My parents insisted on dropping me off and I could not wait until they left—I'm thrilled at the thought of not having to speak to them for at least three months. Good-bye, family, and good riddance. The campus is crawling with television cameras, determined to

hear what it's like for us, the first women admitted to the
university. The dean had a special reception for all 101 of
us and while we drank wine inside, a crowd of reptilian
men protested, holding signs that read "Bring Back the Old
Princeton." Poor things, not a chance in hell they'll get
laid.

Sam folds the yellowed piece of paper and returns it to its
envelope, then fingers his way to the front of the box and the
first letter. *July 24, 1968. Chicago.*

Hello beautiful . . .

He sinks back against the wall, ignoring the throbbing pain
in his head and the sinking feeling in his stomach, and starts
at the beginning.

chapter
46

I PULL BACK THE curtains with a shaky hand and risk a peek down at the front yard. *Thank god.* The vultures are gone.

Three of them ("journalists"), circling since last night, when the public learned that Sam's car was discovered at the Stor-Mor Storage facility on Route 9. The nerve of them, parking in my driveway, tearing up my lawn with their footprints, pointing their monstrous cameras at my house. "B-roll." That's what I overheard one of them say this morning as I barricaded myself in my bedroom, waiting for them to leave. They did, but not before getting their shot, bantering loudly back and forth the whole time about how the hell this guy's car ended up at a storage unit.

I'll tell you how, vultures: I took the hidden key and went downstairs to Sam's office the morning after the storm, and when I saw him there on the floor and remembered what I'd done—following him down the path, hitting him with the shovel—I panicked. I put on a pair of latex gloves and used the Visa card from his wallet to set up an account online. I locked him in his office and drove to Stor-Mor myself, entering with the PIN number that had been texted to his phone, which I fished out of his jacket pocket. I walked home in the freezing rain, through deserted streets, having no idea what I was going to do.

But then Annie led me to Stephen King, and just like that, I knew *exactly* what I needed to do: nurse Sam back to health myself and make everything right.

It all would have been fine if Sam hadn't decided he was going to pick the lock on the door and go through my personal belongings, including my purple binders, never mind a person's right to privacy.

I know he did it. The evidence was there, in the mess he left me to clean up. Binders ripped at the spine, overturned drawers, the restraining order that Linda's son applied for—all jumbled together in the middle of the floor. If he would have let me, I could have explained.

It's simple. Linda and I were *friends*, and she liked having me around. It was that meathead son of hers, making things out to be something they weren't, suggesting something untoward in our relationship. I knew from day one that he didn't like me—calling me Nurse Nightingale, which I didn't understand until I looked it up. But it didn't matter what he thought, because I wasn't hired to take care of *Hank*. I was hired to take care of his mother from 6 p.m. to 9 a.m. four nights a week. Linda Pennypiece, the kindest person in the world.

She'd had a stroke three months earlier, at the age of eighty-nine. She couldn't speak, but I could see in her eyes how much she enjoyed our time together. On the nights she couldn't sleep, we'd stay up late, watching reruns of *Mary Tyler Moore*. I'd feed her the individual-sized boxes of Kellogg's Corn Flakes the agency gave everyone who worked the overnight shift. She'd stare silently at the television, but I could sense the joy it brought her. Until *Hank* showed up and ruined everything. I swallow back the disgust, remembering the sight of him walking into the kitchen as I stood at the stove in Linda's robe, scrambling eggs. I was fired within the hour.

See, Sam, I'd say. I told you there was a good explanation for that. Just like there's a good explanation for the other big question I imagine is on your mind. How did I come to fill a binder full of facts about you? One word: fate.

The moment fate intervened on our behalf: A one-item list

1. The Bakery, just before lunch, the first Tuesday in April. I was inside the stall at the men's room, wondering if I should complain that the tea I'd just finished wasn't hot enough, and you were at the sink outside, talking on the phone about your fading dream of the perfect office space. I listened to the whole thing—the place you'd come from smelled of marijuana, and the realtor didn't have anything else to show you. You said you were off to visit your mother, and I had no idea until I opened the door that it was *you*—Dr. Sam Statler, the brilliant therapist from the "Twenty Questions" profile I'd come across in the local paper, whose work I'd been obsessively reading. I didn't have anything else to do, and so I decided to follow you in my car, up the mountain to Rushing Waters. I circled the parking lot while you sat in your luxury automobile, and that's when the idea came to me, in a moment of divinity: *I* could give you the perfect office space.

Why would I do that? you ask. Because I'm a nice guy. Because I care about people, Sam, and I appreciated the work you did, helping others understand the trauma of their childhoods.

So much so that I went home and made a flyer. It took me no more than thirty minutes to find your car parked behind the bank, where I stuck the flyer under your windshield. Lo and behold you called just minutes later.

And I did everything you wanted, Sam. Professional lighting. A self-flushing toilet. *Organic* paint. I even did the one thing you couldn't do: I visited your mother. (Anyone with two eyes and a pair of binoculars could see that you stopped going inside soon after you moved to town.) There's a volunteer application available at their website, and bingo! It sounded fun. I know they don't like me there. I see the way people look at me, ignoring the suggestions I leave in the suggestion box, but I don't care, Sam. Because I wasn't taking your mother to bingo twice a week to please them. I was doing it to help *you*.

But I can't tell Sam any of this, because the last time I saw him was yesterday, when I dragged his lifeless body into the closet as the first journalist appeared, afraid he'd wake up and start yelling and someone would hear him. I'm so ridden with guilt over what I did that I still can't bring myself to go down there.

I know, a warm bath will relax me. I search for Agatha Lawrence's bath salts, which I remember seeing in the closet, when I hear a humming noise coming from somewhere in the house. It's not in the bedroom, or the hallway; as I ease down the stairs, the sound grows louder the closer I get to the kitchen. Finally I make my way to the hallway, to Sam's room.

"Good, you're home." Sam's voice from inside is surprisingly firm. "Come in. I need something from you." Hesitant, I return to the kitchen for the key, and return to his door. He's in his chair when I peek my head inside, writing in his notebook. "Come in," he says, waving me forward and then reaching to silence the clock on the table beside him.

"What is it you need?" I ask nervously.

"Your help." I'm filled with shame when he glances up at me and I see the laceration in his lip, the swollen malar bone in his left cheek. "With a patient."

"A patient?" I say, confused. "I don't understand—"

"I'll explain later." He returns to his writing. "This feels somewhat urgent. Here—" He rips the page from his notebook and holds it out to me. "Take a look."

I walk slowly toward him and take the paper from his hand.

"I've given you what I know of the patient's history, a list of presenting problems, and my best guess at a diagnosis. I'd like you to review my work."

"Review your work," I repeat, guarded, sure this is some kind of mean prank. "Why?"

He hesitates a moment and then drops his pen and folds his hands on his lap. "All that listening you did at the vent paid off, Albert. I read through the notes you made on my clients, in that purple binder of yours. I've said it once and I'll say it again. You have a mind for this work."

"I do?"

"Yes. I'm impressed. And while I'll eventually want to discuss some of the other things I found in those binders, I'd first like your help with this." He nods at the paper in my hands. "It's an old case—it's been plaguing me for a while. I could use your help, if you don't mind."

I scan his notes. "I don't mind at all," I mutter. "In fact, I'm honored."

"Good. And I'd like dinner soon, as well. That Salisbury

steak, if you wouldn't mind. And please, Albert, proper silver-ware this time."

"Yes, Sam. Whatever you want."

"Thanks, and I'd prefer you address me properly." He picks up his pen. "It's Dr. Statler."

I nod and turn toward the door, chastened. "Of course. I'll prepare your meal and then get right to work."

chapter
47

"WHY WOULD A GUY text his wife that he's coming home and then stash his car in a storage unit?" Annie says into the phone. She's sitting on the floor of Margaret's room, her back against the wall, drinking from a bottle of Miller High Life. This is what she's been reduced to. Not yet ten a.m., drinking a warm beer she stole from a nursing home dining hall, asking Siri to explain why her husband texted her and then stashed his car at the Sav–Mor Storage facility on route 9, ten minutes from his office.

"I found this on the web for why would a guy text his wife that he's coming home and then stash his car in a storage unit."

Annie scrolls through the results.

How to prepare your car for long-term storage at Edmunds.

What is your ex from hell story (and how not to take the bait when he calls!)?

This last one posted two years ago, on the blog of a woman named Misty.

Annie sips her beer, wondering what Misty might have to say. Maybe it's unanimous. Maybe, like Franklin Sheehy, Misty thinks Sam texted her and then stashed his car because Sam's the type of guy who disappears when the going gets tough, confirming that the apple does not, in fact, fall far from the tree. And maybe Misty will also echo the *other* opinion Franklin Sheehy shared in the newspaper this morning: there's not much more the police can do.

"This shows some planning, and is clearly the work of a cunning mind," said Chief of Police Franklin Sheehy. "Not much left to surmise other than that Sam Statler doesn't want to be found."

She's taking a second pass through the list of results when the phone rings in her hand. It's Dr. Elisabeth Mitchell, her dean.

"I got your message, Annie. Is everything okay?"

"I've been thinking about your offer to take time off," Annie says. "And I'd like to accept it."

Dr. Mitchell is silent a moment. "I'm sorry for what you're going through, Annie. When would you like it to start?"

"Immediately?" Annie suggests. "I've sent a few emails, asking others in the department if they can take over, and I'm hoping—"

"Don't worry about your class," Dr. Mitchell says. "I'll teach it myself. And we can resume your fellowship when you're back."

Annie thanks her and hangs up, knowing it's unlikely she's coming back. For what? A life in Chestnut Hill, alone in that house? Before she can second-guess her decision, she opens her email, pulling up the message that arrived from her aunt and uncle late last night.

We've reserved you a plane ticket to Paris, her uncle wrote. The flight leaves in two days, giving you time to wrap things up. Maddie will pick you up and bring you to the house. The return is open ended. Just say the word, and we'll buy it.

Thank you, Annie types. I'd like to come.

She hits send and polishes off the last of the beer as the door opens. She expects it to be Margaret, returning from getting her hair done by the stylist who comes every week, but it's Josephine, carrying a basket of Margaret's clean laundry. "Annie," she says, seeing Annie on the floor, a beer bottle at her feet. "What are you doing?"

"Living my best life," Annie says.

Josephine chuckles. "Good for you." She flashes the laundry basket. "I was going to put these away, but I can come back."

"I'll do it," Annie says, standing up. "I could use the distraction."

Josephine pauses, giving Annie the look that says *I read the newspaper article about your deadbeat husband disappearing and I'm not sure what to say.* "How are you holding up?" she asks.

"Other than drinking warm beer at ten in the morning, pretty good," Annie says, setting the bottle on the table. "I'm leaving tomorrow, for some time away. I've come to tell Margaret." Annie stacks the laundry on the bed. "I feel a little sick about it, to be honest. She'll have nobody to visit her now."

"She'll be fine, Annie," Josephine says, reaching for the basket. "Everyone here loves her, and that volunteer comes twice a week to take her to bingo. We all call him her boyfriend." She gives Annie's arm a quick squeeze on her way out of the room. "We'll take good care of her, promise."

Five minutes later she's busying herself with straightening the contents of Margaret's bathroom, replaying Josephine's words. Something is nagging at her. She closes the medicine cabinet and leaves the room. The hallway is quiet, and a young woman Annie doesn't recognize is at the front desk. "Can I help you?" she asks cheerfully.

"Yes," Annie says. "Josephine said a volunteer has been visiting my mother-in-law, Margaret Statler. I wasn't aware of that, and I'm curious who it is."

"Sure thing." The girl looks down and taps at the keyboard. "Oh," she says, rolling her eyes. "You mean Albert Bitterman." She leans forward and lowers her voice. "Between you and me, that guy's a pain in the ass."

chapter

48

SAM CUTS INTO THE last piece of tough, tasteless meat, listening to Albert roaming the house. He chews slowly, his bruised jaw throbbing, imagining how it's going to feel to sleep in his own bed again. He can feel it, his first shower, the strong stream of hot water from the Kohler Real Rain showerhead he splurged on, like a man with $2 million on the way. Annie is next to him, lathering Pantene shampoo into her scalp—the same shampoo her mother used, and a scent so distinctively his wife. "Took you long enough to figure out," she says, biffing the suds into his face. "It was obvious the whole time. He didn't want to kill you. He wanted your help."

"Right again, my brainy wife," Sam whispers. He licks the last of the meat from the steak knife and holds it up to the light. "And don't you worry, Albert, because help is on the way."

....

Albert's knock comes at nearly midnight, and Sam is ready. He sits up, sets the alarm for forty-five minutes.

Game on.

Albert's hair is slicked back with gel, a notebook tucked under his arm.

"Did you finish?" Sam asks.

"Yes," Albert says. "I'm sorry to bother you late at night, but you said it was urgent."

"It is." Sam waves him in. "Have a seat. I'm eager to hear what you found." Albert drops the key into the front pocket of his pressed khaki pants and takes a seat on the bed, keeping his gaze on his shoes, a shiny pair of black loafers. Sam stays silent, noting Albert's posture. His hands are gripped in his lap, his jaw is clenched. "Go ahead," Sam says.

"Bottom line," Albert says, "I wholeheartedly agree with the diagnosis you came to regarding this patient. What we're looking at here is a *textbook* case of an adult with an attachment disorder. In fact, I would be a bit more specific and say that he has many of the qualities of an anxious–preoccupied adult."

"Really?" Sam sighs, feigning great relief. "Good. Walk me through it. From the beginning."

"Well." Albert opens his notebook. "As you know, because of an infant's inability to survive on its own, every child is born with a primitive drive to get their needs met by their primary caregivers, usually their parents. This is called attachment theory. Infants who feel safe develop secure attachments. Those who do not, like our patient, develop insecure attachments. As adults they tend to be highly anxious, have a negative self-image, act impulsively, and live with a fear of rejection so severe it can sometimes be debilitating. This can go on to have a significant impact on the relationships they develop as adults."

"In what ways?" Sam asks.

"I made a list." Albert pulls a sheet of paper from his notebook. "Should I read it?"

"Please."

"One: anxious–preoccupied adults behave in ways that seem

desperate and insecure, at times controlling," he reads. "Two: because they lacked security as an infant, they demand constant reassurance that they are special to their partner, in an attempt to allay their anxiety. Three: they believe their partner will 'rescue' or 'complete' them, a wish that is impossible for another person to fulfill." He places the paper in his lap. "As you can see, even as they seek closeness and a sense of safety by clinging to their partner, their desperate actions actually push their partner away." Albert frowns. "It's quite sad, the reasons he's like this."

Sam clears his throat. "Are you talking about his childhood?"

"Yes. His mother died in childbirth, and he was left with an emotionally distant father who rarely showed him attention, let alone affection," Albert says. "Of course he's going to have insecure attachments as an adult."

"That's right." Sam points at Albert and nods. "I forgot that part about his mother. How old was he when she died?"

"Six days old."

"Man, that's rough." He shakes his head. "Remind me again: What was the cause of her death?"

Albert cocks his head, stumped. "Not sure I remember." He licks a finger and flips backward in the notebook. "Here it is. 'Mother, cause of death.' Oh." He frowns. "You left that blank."

"Did I?" Sam says. "Let me see." He opens the drawer of the table next to him and removes the notebook, impressed by the steadiness of his hand. "Place of birth, Chicago," Sam murmurs, reading from his notes. "Oh—" He points at something on the page and makes a show of surprise. "I got it wrong. This patient's mother didn't die in childbirth."

"She didn't?" Albert asks.

"No. She lived until she was sixty-seven. Rather, she was forced to give him up for adoption when he was six days old, to a couple in Wayne, Indiana. Her name was Agatha Lawrence, and she was your biological mother." Sam closes his notebook and looks Albert in the eye. "The patient we're talking about is you, Albert. Or should I call you Beautiful?"

chapter
49

I REEL BACK. "HOW did you—"

"You wanted me to know," Dr. Statler explains, leaning back in his chair.

"No, I—"

"Come on, Albert." He laughs. "It's psych 101 stuff. You put me in a closet with your birth story. It was your unconscious mind at work, seeking my help."

"No it wasn't." I stand up. "I have to go."

"Sit down, Albert. We're going to talk."

I hesitate, and then take my seat again, hands clenched.

"If it's okay, I'd like to ask you some questions." Dr. Statler flips to a clean page and clicks his pen. "When and how did you learn Agatha Lawrence was your biological mother?"

I hesitate, count to ten. *Do it: tell him.* "Last year," I say. "When I received a letter from an attorney in New York." I'm sitting at my kitchen table, eating sparerib tips and white rice from a Styrofoam container. I'm sorting the mail and waiting for *Jeopardy!* to begin when I come across the silky linen stationery with the attorney's logo at the top. "'Dear Mr. Bitterman,'" I say out loud to Sam, reciting the letter. "'Our firm has been retained to locate you, regarding a critical family matter.' They invited me to their office in Manhattan to discuss it in person. Offered to pay my way." He's watching me, intent. "First class on Amtrak."

"What did you think when you read this letter?"

"I thought it was a scam," I say. "One of those Nigerian princes out to get my last thousand dollars. The only family I had left was my father, assuming he's still alive, and if he wanted to contact me, all he had to do was respond to the Christmas card I send him every year." The phone is heavy in my hands, the TV on mute, the faint scent of fried food from Happy Chinese downstairs as I dial the phone number printed on the letterhead. "A woman lawyer answered the phone when I called," I tell Dr. Statler. "I asked her if this was some sort of joke, and she said she'd prefer we speak in person. She sounded serious."

"Did anyone accompany you to New York?"

I laugh. "Yeah, right. Like who? The only friend I had was Linda, and even if her son hadn't applied for that restraining order, the agency would never have given me permission to take her to New York." In Penn Station I made my way through a throng of grouchy people to the top floor, where a man in a wrinkled suit who smelled like cigarettes was holding a sign with my name on it. He led me to a black car, two warm bottles of Poland Spring water stuck into the seat pocket in front of me.

"Their offices were on Park Avenue, and a pretty young woman led me to a conference room." There was a tray of bagels and raw fish, strawberries with their stems already removed. Someone knocked, and then four people in suits marched in, sat in a U shape around me, and showed me photographs of a woman with wild red curls and eyeglasses with bright blue frames. "They told me she had given birth to me fifty-one years ago at a hospital outside Chicago, Illinois."

"I read her account of the pregnancy and birth," Dr. Statler says. "Quite traumatic." My father was some boy she met on a family vacation to the Dominican Republic, whose last name she never asked for. She was seventeen and the top of her class, and her father would not allow it. Arrangements and announcements were made. "Boarding school," they called it. There were five other girls when she arrived. The oldest girl was twenty-two, the youngest fourteen, all equally well connected. She labored alone for nearly ten hours and was allowed to see me a few times a day for the next six days, before the nice couple from Indiana could make preparations to come for me.

"It devastated her," Dr. Statler says. "Having to give you away. But she had no say in the matter." He places the notebook on his lap and folds his hands. "What was it like for you, learning all of this?"

"It finally made sense," I say. "When my father said I wasn't his. I wasn't either of theirs. But I was mostly excited to meet her. Fifty-one years old and a chance to be part of a family."

"And?"

"They told me she'd died." I remember the shock when the woman said this, the way I pinched my palm to stop the tears. "She'd been looking for me her whole life, but she had to die to find me. That's how the attorney explained it to me, at least. It was only after she died that the court would agree to unseal the adoption papers. They had to, in order to let me know that she'd named me the sole heir of the Lawrence family estate."

"Ninety-two million dollars, it says here."

"And the family home in Chestnut Hill, New York," I say. "I'd been out of work for a few months. I didn't know what else to do, and so I moved here, into her house." I squeeze my eyes shut, remembering opening the front door and walking into the house for the first time, everything as she had left it, dust on the furniture and accumulating in the corners.

"She wrote you letters." Dr. Statler pulls something from between the pages of his notebook: one of her pale-yellow envelopes, a letter inside, written in handwriting I've come to adore.

"Two hundred and three of them," I say. "She was determined that I'd know her someday, as well as the family I came from. They were complicated people." I keep my eyes on the ground. "So was she."

An alarm beeps twice. Dr. Statler shifts in his chair. "Looks like we're out of time."

"We are?" I ask.

"Yes, it's time for me to get some sleep."

As he reaches to silence the alarm, I see the time. It's nearly one in the morning. "I'm sorry," I say, mortified that I've kept him up this late. "I lost track of time." I stand and hurry to the door.

"Come back tomorrow morning, Albert," Dr. Statler says as I open the door. "Ten a.m. We'll pick up where we left off. Would you like me to write that down?"

"No," I say. "Ten a.m. I'll remember." I step into the hall. "Good night, Dr. Statler."

He smiles at me, the warmest smile I think I've ever seen. "Good night, beautiful."

chapter
50

FRANKLIN SHEEHY SIGHS DRAMATICALLY on the other end of the phone. "I don't know," he says. "But I'm not convinced that volunteering at an old folks' home qualifies as suspicious, Annie. And if it is, well, you'll have to excuse me, as I need to get down to Catholic Charities to arrest my seventy-nine-year-old mother."

Annie closes her eyes, envisioning pinning him to the wall by his neck. "I'm not suggesting that volunteering, as a concept, is suspicious, Franklin," she says, measured. "But it's not just that."

"What else is it?" he asks.

"The office space," she says. "It was awfully generous, what he did for Sam. Like, to a fault."

"Generous to a fault?" Sheehy says. "You've been in the city too long, Ms. *Potter*. You've forgotten that people are nice."

That's the same thing Sam said, when she first expressed her skepticism about Albert Bitterman and his "generous" offer. Annie was up most of the night, digging out the lease again and combing through her texts with Sam, trying to piece together what she knew about him. Albert Bitterman Jr., new owner of the historic Lawrence House.

Quirky. That's the word Sam used to describe him, guilting

Sam into staying for a drink every once in a while, asking him to help with tasks around the property—taking out the garbage and sweeping the path. Sam felt indebted, couldn't get over his good luck.

"He let Sam design the space himself," Annie says to Franklin. "Sam being Sam, this meant everything cost a fortune. That's quite a few steps up from small-town 'nice.' And now I find out that he's also been visiting Sam's mother?"

Annie got the girl at the desk to show her his file. Albert Bitterman, fifty-one years old, started volunteering at Rushing Waters last month. Assignment: bingo night, every Wednesday and Friday. She asked around. Nobody knew him other than as the volunteer who left a lot of comments in the suggestion box. She googled his name when she got home, finding the author of a children's book and a professor of urban planning, neither of which she guessed was a match.

"What are you suggesting, Annie?" Franklin says. "That your husband's landlord . . . what? Killed him and disposed of his car? Let me guess. You listen to those true-crime podcasts."

She sighs wearily.

"Ms. Potter—" Franklin heaves a sigh of his own. "I didn't want to be the one to have to tell you this, but your husband wasn't the man you thought he was. He hid a hundred grand in debt from you. He wasn't visiting his mother, or paying her bills. And, oh yeah, he got power of attorney over her finances two weeks before he disappeared." Annie's breath catches. "Yeah, that's right. We poked around, talked to people down at Rushing Waters, and we know that part too. You may like to paint us as the bumbling cops who can't tie their own shoes, but we know what we're doing. Bottom line, Annie: he's a pathological liar, and you're the wife, left behind, grasping at straws." She can hear his chair squeaking. "And remember, Annie. You're an attractive woman with a lot of good years ahead of you. Like I tell my daughters, don't waste your time on the wrong guy."

"Thank you, Franklin. That's a good reminder." She hangs up, holds her breath for a long moment, and then the rage rises, too much for her to contain. She screams as loud as she can and throws her phone across the room. It bounces off the sofa cushions and lands on the floor with a crack. She's afraid to look, but she does; the bottom half of her screen is shattered. She drops to the couch, rests her head in her hands, and laughs. "Well, this is a very bad day," she whispers.

Franklin Sheehy is not wrong, you know. It's Sam's voice, from the opposite couch.

"Go fuck yourself," she whispers.

Okay, but it's true that you're grasping at straws.

"You think?" she snaps. "You think that was grasping at straws, Sam? Well, wait until you see *this.*" She takes the phone from the floor and squints through the broken glass, searching Google for a directory of phone numbers at the *Daily Freeman.*

"Harriet Eager," she says, answering on the first ring.

"It's Annie Potter. I need to ask you a question."

"Okay," Harriet says.

"The other day, you said that you'd received a few tips claiming that Sam was having an affair with a patient. Can you tell me who sent them?" Something about hearing this—she hasn't been able to shake it.

"Annie, don't worry about that," Harriet says. "It was some lunatic with nothing else—"

Annie cuts her off. "Do you still have the email?"

"No, sorry. I delete that stuff."

"Okay, thanks," she manages before hanging up. She presses her eyes with the heels of her hands. *That's it. That's all I can do.*

Her phone beeps with a message.

Can't wait. In car yet?

It's Maddie. Annie checks the time. It'll be here in a half hour.

She hits send and stands up. In the kitchen, she finds her passport and ticket on the counter and puts them in her purse.

When her phone rings a moment later, she can't make out the name under the broken glass. She assumes it's Maddie, but it's not. It's Harriet Eager, calling back.

"You got a second?"

"Yes," Annie says, taking a seat at the kitchen table.

"A colleague of mine overhead our conversation," Harriet says. "Turns out she did follow-up on the tip about the alleged patient your husband ran off with. I figured you'd want to know."

"And?"

"And it was definitely false," Harriet says.

"How do you know that?"

"The reporter asked at the university, where this fantasy patient was supposedly a student, and there wasn't anyone who matched her description."

"A student at the university?" Annie feels a twinge of dread. "What was the description?"

"What does it matter?" Harriet says. "It was a bum tip."

"Please, what was the description?"

"Hang on," Harriet sighs. "Let me ask."

chapter
51

I TUG DOWN MY sweatshirt and smooth back my hair. With a deep breath, I open the door.

"Good morning, Albert," Dr. Statler says from his chair, hands folded on his lap.

"Good morning." I cross the room and take a seat on the bed. Dr. Statler observes me in silence. "You're even better than I thought," I say finally.

"Oh?" he asks. "How's that?"

"Leading me to these realizations of myself." I shake my head. "I didn't see myself in those notes, but it makes sense. Insecure attachment, due to losing my mother at birth and being raised by a man like my dad." My palms are clammy.

"What you're going through is a lot to process."

I nod. "Can you imagine what my life could have been like if they'd allowed her to be my mother?" I let myself imagine it last night, lying in the bed she used to sleep in, just as she'd left it. "I wonder if she would have taken me along on her trips. She traveled *everywhere*." In the letters she wrote me, she described the food, the art, the apartments she rented. The affairs. *I hope your parents are kind and your life is full, my beautiful boy.* "She was the most fascinating woman I've ever met. Or *never* met, I should say."

"But you did meet her," Dr. Statler says. "You were together for six days."

"Yes, but I don't remember those days."

"Not consciously, but that experience is still there, inside you. Six days in your mother's arms." Dr. Statler shifts slightly in his chair and then clears his throat. "I want to try something with you. As you may know, Freud believed there was a way patients could get in touch with repressed memories."

"You want me to lie down?"

"Yes," he says. "I think it would be useful. Please, give it a try."

I look at Dr. Statler's bed. "Should I take off my shoes?"

"If you'd like."

I nervously slip off my loafers, set them side by side, and swing my legs onto the bed.

"No, the other way," Dr. Statler corrects me. "So you're facing away from me. The idea is to keep the analyst out of sight, to allow greater freedom of thought." I pivot in the other direction, my head at the foot of the bed, my feet toward the wall. "How do you feel?" he asks.

"Scared," I admit.

"It's okay," Dr. Statler says. "We're doing this together. You're safe. Now close your eyes." I do as he says. "Without thinking, tell me what you feel."

"My body feels heavy," I say. "Like I have a stack of bricks on top of me."

"Where, exactly?"

I touch my chest. "Right here."

"Okay, I want you to stay with that feeling," Dr. Statler gently instructs. "Now, begin to pick up the bricks. Slowly, one by one. Set them aside." I try to do what he says, imagining myself getting closer to my heart. "When you get to the last brick, I want you to lift slowly. Can you tell me what you see underneath?"

"A hospital room?" I whisper. I can make it true if I try. I'm with her, my mother, my chest against hers, my body hardly any bigger than her two hands. Her hair is pulled back off her face. They were right—she's a child still. Far too young to be a mother. And yet it feels natural here, our hearts beating together, a lullaby on her lips.

"Why did she have to leave me?" I whisper.

"She wasn't given a choice."

"Was it me?"

Dr. Statler hesitates. "Was what you?"

"Was it because there's something wrong with me?" The tears sting my eyes. "She could feel it inside me," I say. "The darkness. My anger. That's why she gave me away. I'm sorry. I'm sorry. I know I'm not supposed to cry." I squeeze my eyes shut, trying to hold on to her image in my mind, but my father pushes her aside, a look of disgust on his face at seeing me in tears again. "He wouldn't leave me alone," I say. "He wouldn't let me be who I was. I couldn't feel things."

"But you did feel things, didn't you Albert? Like sadness."

"Yes."

"And when that wasn't allowed?"

A sob escapes. "Rage."

"Yes, that's right. Rage. And you still feel it sometimes, don't you? When you're wronged, the rage comes back easily."

"Yes, Dr. Statler." My voice sounds like a child's.

"Like the night of the storm, and your decision to attack me."

I open my eyes. Dr. Statler has pushed his chair next to the bed. Just inches away, he has a chilling look on his face, and a steak knife in his hand. "No, Dr. Statler. You had an accident—"

"*You* were the accident, Albert." The knife blade glints in his hand as he raises it. "I know what you did. I know you're the reason I haven't seen my wife in thirteen days." Dr. Statler traces the knife along my cheek, catching a tear. "I know you're the person who broke both my legs."

"No," I say. "That's not true—"

"No more lies, Albert." Dr. Statler's voice is stern. "I won't allow it."

"I'm not lying," I whimper. "I didn't break your legs. I put the casts on so you couldn't leave."

Dr. Statler surprises me with a laugh. "Wow, Albert. That is some Annie Wilkes–level crazy."

"No, it's not," I say, offended. "She *chopped off* Paul Sheldon's ankles. I just pretended to hurt yours." I close my eyes again, ashamed. "I'm sorry."

"You're sorry," Dr. Statler says. I feel the knife blade press against my cheek. "That's good to know."

"Are you going to kill me?"

"I certainly could, couldn't I?" He trails the blade along my jaw, to my Adam's apple. "All I'd have to do is apply some pressure right here . . ." I'm too terrified to move. "It wouldn't take more than a minute or so for you to choke on your blood. Nobody would blame me, not after everything you've done to me. Locking me inside this room. Shoveling those pills into my body. But no." He removes the knife from my throat. "I'm not going to kill you. At least not yet."

I open my eyes. "You're not?"

"No. And do you know why?" he asks. "Because you're not evil, Albert. You're wounded. You don't deserve to die. You deserve a chance to get help." He settles back into his chair. "There's one thing we didn't go over yesterday. The prognosis."

"The prognosis?"

"Yes," he says. "In other words, what are the patient's chances of achieving what he wants: a happy life with stable relationships?"

"The prognosis is good," I whisper. "While no treatment is completely foolproof, with a regimen of therapy and medication many anxious-preoccupied adults can maintain healthy connections and live happy lives."

"That's right, Albert," Dr. Statler says. He takes a deep breath. "Now stand up and go get your phone."

"My phone?" I say.

"You do have a phone, I presume?"

"Yes."

"Go get it."

"Why?"

"Because you're going to call nine-one-one and ask them to send two ambulances. One for me, and one for you."

"No, Dr. Statler—"

"You'll be taken to the psychiatric emergency department at St. Luke's," he continues. "Where you'll see Dr. Paola Genovese, the head of the inpatient unit."

"No." I shake my head. "I can't do that."

"Paola will admit you and perform an evaluation. She'll be able to help you. She's one of the best."

"But I—"

"What's the other option?" Dr. Staler interrupts, his voice firm. "You know you can't keep me forever."

"Not forever," I say. "Until you're better."

"Well, guess what? I am."

"You're not—"

"No, I am, Albert. Thanks to you." He pauses. "You've shown me that nothing is more important than being with Annie and making amends for the ways I've screwed up with her." He sits forward and places his hand on my arm. "And now it's your turn to get better."

A strange tingling sensation floods through me. *I can get help.*

"Come on, Albert," Dr. Statler says. "Go get your phone. Let's go together, to the hospital."

I hesitate. "Will you stay with me?"

"Hell, no, I won't stay with you," he says. "I'm going home to my wife, if she'll still have me. But I'll work with your doctors and make sure you get the best help. Now go on, Albert. Go get your phone." He releases his hold on my arm. His other hand still grips the knife. "Trust me."

It's almost as if I can see myself from above as I take the stairs up to my bedroom and remove the black cordless phone from its cradle. Back on the ground floor, I slide open the library doors, inhaling the smell of leather and paper, my mother's scent. I pick up one of her photographs, wiping the dust from her eyes with my thumb. The air is still.

You can do this. It's her voice.

I squeeze my eyes shut. *No, I can't.*

Yes, you can.

My thoughts are racing. *They'll admit you and do some tests. I'll get you the best help.*

I hope your life is full and rich, my beautiful boy.

I set the photograph back in its place and walk through the sitting room, into the living room, resolute, the phone gripped in my hand. I can do this.

I pass the kitchen and am halfway down the hall when I hear Sam's office door slam shut downstairs. My heart stops.

Someone's here.

I wipe my eyes and turn around. I should probably see who it is.

chapter
52

ANNIE STEPS INTO THE waiting room, the faint scent of Pine-Sol in the air. She keeps the lights off and listens. Albert is home, upstairs. His car is in the driveway, and a light was on when she arrived.

He was listening to Sam's sessions. The man with the too-good-to-be-true offer to create Sam's dream office, the same one who has been visiting Sam's mother twice a week, was listening to her husband's therapy sessions. He even went so far as to email a reporter with a description of the patient Sam likely ran off with, a description Harriet Eager shared with Annie.

Twenty-four years old. Sculpture student. Oh, and she's French.

Her phone rings, and she immediately silences the ringer. It's Maddie. Annie answers, hearing music playing in the background.

"Are you in the car?" Maddie asks, cheerful.

"No." Annie swallows. "I'm at Sam's office."

"*What?*" Maddie says. The music goes quiet behind her. "Annie, your plane leaves—"

"The guy Sam rented from was listening to Sam's sessions," Annie whispers. "And he's been visiting Margaret at the nursing home."

Maddie is silent a moment. "How do you know?"

"It's a long story, but trust me," Annie says, opening the door to Sam's office.

"Are you there alone?"

Annie turns on the light. "Yes."

"Annie, please leave right now and call the police."

"I can't." She scans Sam's office. "The police have made up their minds about what happened." She sees it then—the metal grate in the ceiling above the couch. "I'll call you back." Annie hangs up and slides the phone into her coat pocket. She steps slowly toward the couch, her eyes on the ceiling. A vent.

"Dr. Potter, what a nice surprise." She spins around. It's him, Albert Bitterman, standing in the doorway. His eyes are red, as if he's been crying. "What are you doing here?"

"I'm on my way out of town, and I—I wanted to stop here," she stammers.

"You wanted to say goodbye," he says. "I understand. You're in mourning, and you want to feel close to Sam."

"Yes, I suppose you're right."

"Well, I'm sorry, but if you don't mind, I have to ask you to leave. As much as it pains me to say it, I don't think Dr. Statler is coming back, and I consider our lease null and void. In other words, this space is now private property." He turns, gesturing toward the waiting room.

"I need to hear it again."

"I'm sorry?" he says.

She notices the band of sweat on his upper lip as her phone vibrates in her coat pocket. "You were the last person to see my husband, the night he disappeared. I need to hear it again. How he looked. If he seemed—"

"I told you already," Albert cuts in impatiently. "He looked fine. He said good night, and that was it."

"Said good night?" she says. "You said he didn't see you. When we spoke on the phone the next morning, you said you saw him run by the window, outside."

"Did I?" He takes a step closer. "My memory's not quite what it used to be. But please . . ."

He reaches for her arm, and something about the feel of his hand registers as familiar. "It's you," she says, the image flashing in her mind. "The man I bumped into on my way out of the Parlor two days ago. That was you. You were wearing blue eyeglasses then—"

"Annie!"

She freezes at the sound of the voice, coming from the ceiling. She turns toward the vent. "Annie! I'm here, upstairs. Call the police." It's Sam's voice. "Please, he's dangerous."

"Sam!" She's flooded with a momentary rush of relief—*I knew it, I knew he was alive*—before the terror takes hold. She turns and looks at Albert. His eyes are wide and vacant.

"Did Dr. Statler just call me *dangerous*?" he asks, his lips trembling. "It's your fault," he whispers. "You shouldn't have come here. We were in the middle of something."

Terrified, she sprints past him toward the door. He grabs her arm, but she pulls free and runs through the waiting room, out the door. Albert chases her down the path, grabbing her ankle as she bounds up the porch steps. She kicks at him, and her heel makes contact with his chin, sending him to the ground.

She opens the front door of his house and stumbles into the foyer. Her hands are shaking as she turns the dead bolt, locking the door behind her.

"Sam!" she screams, rushing into the living room. "Where are you?"

"I'm here! Annie!"

She follows the sound of his voice. Through a kitchen, down a hallway. There's a door at the end and she throws it open. Sam is inside, lying on the floor, his legs in casts, his cheek bruised and swollen. She clasps her hand to her mouth. "*Sam.*"

"You found me," he says.

There's a noise in the living room—Albert is inside—and she closes the door, blocking it with her body. She snatches her phone from her pocket, her hands trembling as she swipes the cracked screen, trying to wake it up. It takes several tries, but she gets it finally.

"Hurry," Sam whispers, as she hears Albert's footsteps in the hallway. She pulls up the phone app as the door slams open behind her, knocking her so hard she drops the phone. She scrambles for it as Albert Bitterman marches into the room, shouting. She reaches for the phone, Albert still yelling, but it's Sam's voice that stays with her, calling her name, when the shovel in Albert Bitterman's hands makes contact with her skull, smashing everything to pieces.

chapter
53

"NO!" SAM SCREAMS. "ANNIE!" He crawls toward her as Albert leans down and picks up her phone. "Come on, Annie, say something." Albert is standing in the doorway, a gash on his chin, the shovel hanging limply from his hands. "Why, Albert? Why did you do that?"

"You told her to call the police," Albert says, his body trembling, his face ghost-white. "You said I was dangerous."

"Albert—"

"You said you'd get me help, that you'd come with me to the hospital. But you lied to me, Sam. *Again.*"

Albert walks out of the room, and Sam hears him in the kitchen, banging drawers open and shut. "It's okay, sweetheart," Sam says, crawling his way to Annie. "You're going to be fine." He gently pushes back the hair from her face. "We're both going to be fine."

Sam sees it then: a pool of blood spreading from under her head. "Albert, call an ambulance!" he screams. "Call an ambulance. NOW."

The kitchen is silent. Albert reappears in the doorway, his jaw trembling. "I can't do it, Sam."

"That's fine, Albert, I can. Give me her phone," Sam says.

"Come on, man." Tears slide down his cheeks. "Give me Annie's phone so I can get her help."

Albert spots the blood spreading from under Annie's head. "Look what I've done." Covering his face with his hands, he starts to weep.

"Please just give me her phone," Sam pleads. "I'll help you, I promise. We'll go to the hospital," he sobs. "I swear to god. I'll make sure of it."

"I hate to say it, Dr. Statler, but I think you might be suffering from a grandiose sense of self-importance. We both know you don't have the power to keep me from prison." Albert leans his head against the door and closes his eyes. "I'm tired."

"You can sleep," Sam says. "At the hospital."

"I told you, I'm not going to the hospital." He's slurring his words.

"Albert?" Sam says. "Are you okay?"

Albert laughs, and his knees buckle. "You don't have to flatter me anymore, my dear Dr. Statler," he says, sliding down the door. He keeps talking, but Sam can't make out what he's saying, and then he goes quiet, slumping over, his head hitting the floor with an echoing clunk. Something falls from his hand and rolls toward Sam: an empty pill bottle. Sam picks it up and reads the label. "Margaret Statler. Zolpidem, 15mg at bedtime."

His mother's pills.

Albert was drugging him with his mother's pills. It happens again—he starts laughing: a loud, delirious cackle that rises up from inside of him, carrying with it a wave of fear and panic more powerful than anything he's ever known. He drags himself toward Albert and digs in his empty pockets for Annie's phone.

"Yoohoo! Albert?" He stops cold. It's a woman's voice, coming from the kitchen. "Anyone home. The door was open—"

"I'm here!" Sam screams. "I'm back here!"

"Albert, is that you? I saw Annie's car, and I have something for her—" He hears footsteps, and then the door opens. It's Sidney Pigeon. She's wearing workout clothes and is holding a baking dish.

"Oh my god," she gasps, her hand flying to her mouth, the dish falling to the floor, sour cream and refried beans splashing into the air. "*Sam?*"

epilogue

SAM HEARS THE CART rattling down the hallway, outside the room, just as he's falling asleep. He bolts upright and opens his eyes. The footsteps get closer, and he waits, immobilized, for the sound of the key in the lock.

But the sound passes and he exhales, reminding himself he's not at the Lawrence House. He's at Rushing Waters, reclined in his mother's favorite chair, where he must have dozed off after the Wednesday lunch special, fettuccine alfredo. Margaret's asleep in her bed, and he clicks off the television and kicks the footrest into place, checking the time. He has to go meet the movers.

He stretches his legs and stops at Margaret's bed to fix her blankets before sneaking into the hall, closing the door quietly behind him. He signs out at the reception desk, passing a woman on her way in. She pauses and does a double take.

That's right, lady, he thinks. *It's me.*

He guessed correctly: the story is a big deal. Six months since the tabloids got wind of things, and they continue to outdo each other, competing for who can snap the creepiest photo of the Lawrence House, enticing shoppers at the checkout lines with yet another interview with "The Neighbor Who Called 911!"

Sam was impressed with Sidney Pigeon's take-charge attitude about the whole thing. On the phone to 911, summoning the chief of police and an ambulance that apparently took no more than four minutes to arrive. It was the same driver who had come for the body of Agatha Lawrence three years before, this time arriving to cart away her biological son, who'd died in the same room. *Cause of death: overdose of zolpidem, leading to cardiac arrest.* In other words, Albert put himself to sleep and then died of a broken heart.

The Monster of Chestnut Hill. That's what people have come to call Albert, and Sam has to admit it's catchy. But one thing they haven't written about Albert Bitterman is that, like his mother, he was found to be generous at the time of his death. He took care of Sam's debt. The copies of the credit card bills Sam had discovered in the purple binder—Albert wasn't merely filing them away for posterity. He was also paying them down, sending out checks, wiping it all away, as well as making a hefty donation to Rushing Waters that would cover, among other things, Margaret Statler's room and board for the next thirty years.

Sam puts the car into drive and is about to pull out when he sees the green Mini Cooper speeding into the parking lot toward him. The car stops next to his, and Annie rolls down her window.

"What are you doing?" Sam asks. "It's my day to visit."

"I know." She nods at the passenger seat. "Get in."

"Why? I thought you said I had to meet the movers."

"I lied. They're coming tomorrow. Get in."

Sam does as he's told. "Where are we going?" he asks, buckling his seat belt.

"You'll have to wait and see," she says, plugging in her phone and hitting play on a song list marked "*SAM.*" Depeche

Mode's "Just Can't Get Enough" blares as she pulls out of the parking lot. At the bottom of the hill she heads out of town, toward the interstate. He puts it together. It's the chase.

"We robbed a bank," he whispers, venturing a guess, adrenaline rushing. "And we're making a quick getaway."

"Wrong," she says.

They drive another few minutes. "You're an Uber driver, and you're kidnapping me."

She shoots him a look. "Too soon, Sam," she says, turning up the music.

He leans his head back and keeps his eyes on her as she drives. She's prettier than ever with short hair. She required one hundred and six stitches in her scalp, and suffered a serious concussion, but she's recovered. As has he—physically, at least. Albert was telling the truth: Sam's legs weren't broken. It was eventually determined through security footage obtained by the police that Albert took the supplies to cast Sam's legs from the closet at the Rushing Waters Elderly Care Center, where he was a volunteer companion at bingo twice a week. It's how he got the pills, too; swiped them from Margaret's stash, left unattended on a medical cart in her room. Albert replaced them with uncoated ibuprofen, an infraction that cost the head nurse and two staff members their jobs.

That said, it hasn't been easy. While his nightmares are decreasing in frequency, the anxiety remains, and he hasn't returned to seeing patients. His dream office is no longer available, for obvious reasons, and even if that wasn't the case, he's been afraid the dynamic would be too disrupted. Every time he's run into patients, it's been painfully awkward. But he's ready to get back to work—in New York. They're moving back next week. Annie accepted a position at Hunter College, and they're moving into a two-bedroom in Brooklyn, keeping the house for visits back to see Margaret every few weekends.

They drive west for an hour, listening to the playlist Annie made—Wham!, INXS, Jane's Addiction—stopping for cheeseburgers and vanilla milkshakes at McDonald's at the small town of Middleburgh. Annie eventually gets off the interstate and follows the GPS for another thirty miles down a two-lane highway, until they reach a marker announcing "Welcome to Cooperstown, Home of the Baseball Hall of Fame." Annie gets into line behind a long row of cars headed toward the parking lot. A digital sign flashes: "Parking for ticket holders only!"

Sam reads the flags waving from the streetlight posts. "Hall of Fame weekend." He looks at her. "Please god, tell me I'm A-Rod coming to get inducted, and you're JLo."

Annie finds a spot among the Buicks and minivans. "Come on," she says, ignoring him and turning off the car. He meets her at the trunk. She opens it, removes a baseball bat, and reaches for his hand, leading him through the crowd. A young man in a museum uniform hands her a map, which she consults before pulling Sam through the building and into a courtyard, past hundreds of people snaked in different lines. Finally she stops in front of a tent in the back. "Here you go," she says, handing Sam the bat. It's brand-new. "Go get it signed."

Sam sees him then. The man sitting at the table under the tent. The one everyone's waiting to meet. Cal Ripken Jr. Ol' Iron Man himself. Sam looks at Annie for a long moment, and then touches her belly before getting in line.

When it's his turn to be called, he steps forward. "Will you sign it to Quinn?" he asks nervously.

"That you?" Cal Ripken asks, taking the bat.

"No," Sam says. "My kid, due in two months."

Cal Ripken scrawls his name and hands the bat back with a wink. "Good luck. Hope he's a ballplayer."

"Thanks, but it's a she," Sam says. "And she'll be whatever she wants."

....

It's not until they've left the parking lot that he's able to speak. "We're going to be okay?" he asks, his eyes out the window.

"Yes, we are," she says.

"How do you know?"

"Because it's how all good stories work out," she says, reaching for his hand. "With a happy ending."

acknowledgments

This book has been a *process*. A few weeks before turning in a final draft on a similar but very different version, I had an idea to throw the draft away and start over with an entirely different approach. I feared that a call to my agent suggesting this new idea might very well be the end of our relationship— and rightly so, given how much Elisabeth Weed, Literally the World's Best Agent, had invested in the book already. Instead, she heard me out, read a quick outline, and got right on the phone with Jennifer Barth, my brilliant and angelically patient editor at Harper. Jennifer didn't hesitate in giving me her full support and, as is her way, went on to make this book a far better version of anything I could write on my own. I'm eternally grateful to both of these women, two of the very best in the business.

I also want to thank Jonathan Burnham, for his faith and encouragement these past few years, and everyone at Harper—Sarah Ried, Doug Jones, Leah Wasielewski, Katie O'Callaghan, Leslie Cohen, Virginia Stanley, Lydia Weaver, and Suzanne Mitchell; as well as Jenny Meyer, foreign agent extraordinaire, Hallie Schaeffer, and Heidi Gall. Extra special gratitude to Michelle Weiner at CAA.

Thanks also to Jillian Medoff, Liz Kay, Julie Clark, Colleen Oakley, Pam Cope, Madison Duckworth, Stephanie Addikis, Ben Sneed, Carly Beal, Hayley Downs, Kate Lemery, Lisa

Selin Davis, Patrick McNulty, Alex Moggridge, Anne Rosow, Jen Ziegler, Susie Greenebaum, Tara Goodrich, Nancy Rawlinson, Julie Cooper, Whitney Brown, and Sam Miller. And, of course, to Chief of Police L. Edward Moore in Hudson, NY for helping me plot a disappearance.

Thanks to my family— Moira, Mark, Bob, Megan, Patrick, Ryan, Kevin, Abby, Brigid, Mary, Caite, and Madeleine— especially my mother, who allowed me to read her this book over the phone more times than I can say and my father, the reason I am both a writer and a reader. And, most of all, to Noelle, Shea and Mark (and Wish and Millie). There's nobody else with whom I'd rather spend a pandemic.

about the author

AIMEE MOLLOY is the author of the *New York Times* bestseller *The Perfect Mother,* her debut novel. She is also the author of *However Long the Night: Molly Melching's Journey to Help Millions of African Women and Girls Triumph* and the coauthor of several books of nonfiction. She lives in Western Massachusetts with her family.